Mistress

By Leda Swann

Don't miss the next book by your favorite author.
Sign up now for AuthorTracker by visiting
www.AuthorTracker.com.

LEDA SWANN

Mistress

AVON

An Imprint of HarperCollinsPublishers

This book is a work of fiction. The characters, incidents, and dialogue are drawn from the author's imagination and are not to be construed as real. Any resemblance to actual events or persons, living or dead, is entirely coincidental.

HarperCollins books may be purchased for educational, business, or sales promotional use. For information please write: Special Markets Department, HarperCollins Publishers, 10 East 53rd Street, New York, NY 10022.

FIRST EDITION

Designed by Diahann Sturge

Library of Congress Cataloging-in-Publication Data
  Swann, Leda.
    Mistress / Leda Swann. — 1st ed.
       p.   cm.
    ISBN 978-0-06-143122-7
    I. Title.
  PS3619.I548M57 2008
  813'.6—dc22   2007044244

08 09 10 11 12   OV/RRD   10 9 8 7 6 5 4 3 2 1

One

Life usually changes slowly, almost imperceptibly, as one day slides seamlessly into the next. And sometimes life changes in the blink of an eye, with only the turn of a door handle to demarcate the end of one life and the start of another.

Emily Clemens stood motionless in the street, an island of stillness amid the scurrying crowds, and stared at the wooden door in front of her. Clutching her reticule before her like a shield, as if to buffer herself from the change that turning the handle would bring, she twisted the straps around with cold fingers until they dug cruelly into her flesh.

Should she open the door and go inside? Or turn tail and walk away again through the crowds, her dignity intact, back to the school where she worked as an assistant teacher. Her position, though a modest one and very poorly paid, at least provided the basics of life, but there had to be more to life than just a roof over her head and barely enough to eat.

Just a few short months ago, stranded in the workhouse with too little to eat and no prospect of escape, she would have thought her current situation pure heaven. Now that she was managing to survive, her dreams were fast growing wings.

The squalid despair of the workhouse still loomed too close for comfort. Mere survival was not enough for her anymore. She wanted to live. To experience everything the world had to offer.

She nudged at a loose cobblestone with the toe of her boot. Her best pair of boots, they were still new enough to pinch at her toes, and her heels were rubbed into blisters from the long walk through the busy streets.

Turn the door handle, or don't turn. The choice was simple when the problem was broken down to its most basic.

Slowly she turned the handle. It would be a pity if she were to cover her heels in weeping red blisters for nothing. She had come so far already. Just a bit more of a turn was all it would take.

"Keep it moving there." A hoarse voice broke through the general babble of the busy street and into her consciousness. "This ain't a public park, you know."

She whirled around, the handle returning to its original position. The voice belonged to a burly drover brandishing a whip as he maneuvered his cart through the narrow streets.

"Can't a body stop for a moment's rest?" she snapped back at him as she inched closer to the door to ease his passage.

"Not if she's in the middle of the street." He shook the reins, passing her with a few muttered curses. Whether they were aimed at her or at his sorry-looking nag, Emily wouldn't venture to guess.

The crowd had pushed her nearly right against the door. She could no longer make out the lettering over the shop front advertising "Mr. Twyford's Excellent Photographic Equipment and Services—all the way from the Americas." But then, she no longer needed to see it to know what it read. She had studied Mr. Twyford's card for so long she knew every swirl of the lettering by heart.

One of the passersby jostled her in the crowd. She regained her balance with a jerk, and one of her reticule straps snapped in two. She swore under her breath, a word that no lady ought to know, but which she had picked up in the workhouse. If she did not act now, she would regret it for the rest of her days. This choice was not being forced upon her. She *wanted* to change her life. A new path was opening for her, if only she had the strength to follow it.

Before she could change her mind, she once again lifted one gloved hand and without hesitation turned the handle, pushed open the door, and walked inside.

The shop front was small and dark, with little room for anything other than an oak desk and chair and the three large, battered mahogany filing cabinets lining one wall. The piles of books and photographic prints that covered the desk looked in imminent danger of collapse, while several of the filing drawers were half open with their papers spilling out onto the floor.

She paused, wondering if she was at the right place after all.

The whole room was a picture of chaos, not the bustling business she had expected. Had Mr. Twyford's photographic studio moved in the last few days? Or worse, had Mr. Twyford gone back to the Americas to make his fortune there?

Just then she heard a noise from behind one of the side doors, and Mr. Twyford himself entered the cluttered office, wiping his mouth on a red-spotted pocket handkerchief.

His face broke out into a triumphant smile when he caught sight of her. "Ah, Miss Clemens." His nasal twang seemed hideously out of place in this very English room. "I am delighted to see you. I was beginning to wonder whether I would have to hunt you down to bring you here. Indeed, I was thinking it a shame that kidnapping is frowned upon in this otherwise excellent country of yours. And that your Metropolitan Police Force is so efficient."

She inclined her head tightly. Her decision was not a joking matter. "I did not plan to come. But, as you can see, here I am . . ."

Sensing her annoyance, he cut her off without waiting for her to finish. "I was just having some luncheon. Will you come out to the back and eat with me?"

"I . . . I am not hungry. I did not bring any luncheon with me." In such moments as these, her poverty grated fiercely on her.

"No matter." He strode over to the door and flipped a couple of coins to one of the urchins lurking in the street outside. "Fetch me a meat pie and some more coffee from Mrs. Pattinger's stall on the corner. And make it quick."

The grubby child scampered away, the coins clutched in his fist. The door slammed after him, causing Emily to stare once more at the door handle, but this time from the inside. She had made her choice—her fate was set.

In just a moment the boy was back again with his purchases. Mr. Twyford took the food and marched her into an adjoining room. This room contained yet another desk in complete disarray, and a worn armchair and a rickety card table that crowded one corner. He laid out the coffee and pie on the table, which already bore a steaming mug and a plate with another large pie with one bite taken out of it. From the look of things, she'd interrupted him just as he'd started his meal.

He pulled out the only chair and sat her down at the card table, taking an upturned box for himself. "So, Miss Clemens, you want to be my model?"

Emily took a swallow of the coffee. It was hot and surprisingly good. Better than the tepid water and skim milk that they called tea at Mrs. Herrington's School for Fashionable Ladies. "I need the money." It was true enough—the extra coins she brought in would make life easier for her and her sisters. But it was not the thought of a few extra coins that had brought her halfway across London—it was the hope of a new life.

He eyed her serviceable walking dress, her new bonnet. "Excuse me for saying so, but you don't look in dire straits to me."

Angered by his tone, she set down her knife and fork. "Does it matter to you what I need the money for?" Poverty came in many guises and did not always show on the outside.

5

He shrugged. "I like to know what I'm dealing with. It's the American in me."

"That doesn't mean I have to tell you." He had no knowledge of what drove her, and no right to judge her for being prepared to sell what he was so anxious to buy. He would use her to make a living, and in her turn she would use him to make a name for herself. His photos would help her become known all over London to those with the money to buy such luxuries as an expensive and desirable mistress. Her.

A fair enough bargain, in her book.

"Hmm." He looked at her critically as he chewed and swallowed a large mouthful of pie. "Have you done any modeling before?"

She shook her head. "None. But I am prepared to learn."

A frown creased his forehead, knitting his eyebrows together. "I want a professional model, not a lady or an amateur. I want someone who is hungry for success, one who will do whatever it takes to make her mark. I'm an ambitious man, and photography is my profession. I need a model who will turn up on time, regularly, week after week, not someone who will treat it as an amusing pastime, as something to fill in the day if she has nothing better to do."

"I do not want a pastime—I want a new life. Modeling for you will help me to achieve my aim." She did not feel the need to explain to him exactly what the new life she was aiming at was.

Her words must have come out sharper than she intended. He flashed a disarming smile. "Come now, Miss Clemens, I was not trying to offend you, just stating my case. Let's not quarrel over luncheon. The food will grow cold. We can talk business when we have finished eating."

She glared at him. He was the one who had invited her here; he was the one who had offered her work as his model. She had not asked for anything. Now that she had found the courage to take him up on his offer, he could not get cold feet and decide he had no use for her after all. This was her chance to find herself a man to treat her as a pampered mistress, and by heaven, she was going to take it. With her life insulated from petty cares, oh, how she would revel in her freedom.

Still, she followed his example and made quick inroads into her meat pie and coffee. An ex-workhouse brat, even one turned lady again, did not turn down free food when it was offered. Especially not when the pie was hot and tasty and she had walked several miles since a rather meager breakfast.

She finished before he did. Pushing her plate aside, she propped her elbows on the card table and stared at him surreptitiously from under her lashes.

He was just as handsome here in this dingy back room as he had been when she had first seen him in the park last Sunday afternoon. Wild and full of vigor he had seemed then, too large for the small park where he had been selling his wares—tintype photographs for a penny a piece. He'd tried his sales patter on her, clearly thinking her a likely prospect, but she had put him off rather brusquely. She was merely a poorly paid teacher, she told him, with no money for such luxuries as photographs.

He'd stared at her then, seeing her in a new light as a woman rather than as a target for his sales patter and his practiced charm. After introducing himself, he'd handed her his card and asked her to call on him to be his model if she could not afford the fee to have her photos taken for herself. The money, he had promised, would be excellent. Far more than she could earn any other way.

That promise, and the thought of what it might lead to, had lured her here.

In this little back room, he seemed to crackle with suppressed fire. His red-brown hair stood out from his head in corkscrew curls, as if it was simply too full of life to lay down neatly across his brow, and the dark stubble on his cheek and chin showed that it was several days since he had made use of a razor.

His eyes, shaded as they were with sweeping lashes, sparkled green and gold. He was so full of vitality that he made her want to dance around the room and jump about and sing just for the sheer joy of being alive.

He was not, she supposed, classically handsome. For a start, he was taller than was strictly called for, and his arms and legs were long and gangly, as if he had never quite grown into them. His hair was too near auburn and too untamed for beauty, and his nose was too big for his face, not to mention that it had a bump on it where it had clearly been broken and knitted badly. His clothing—baggy dockworker trousers and a loose shirt—was casual almost to the point of being not quite respectable. But the dark hairs on his arms where he had pushed up his shirt sleeves looked soft and inviting, and his mouth could tempt any woman to forget her good upbringing.

Not that he was consciously seductive. Far from it. Though he seemed oblivious to the effect he was having on her, she felt the lure of his energy and of his passion keenly. She wanted to share in his passion, to live her life to the full as he lived his. She wanted to bask in the warmth of his personality, to share in his zest for living.

She wanted to kiss him, to taste his passion and fire.

Enticing. That was the word for him. Just watching him sitting in front of her, simply eating his luncheon, made her mind wander in directions she wasn't sure it ought to be wandering in. She should save such thoughts for the prosperous men who might want to bankroll her.

He took his last mouthful and set down his knife and fork. "Maybe you do need the money," he said, giving a telling look at her already empty plate.

"It's the workhouse brat in me," she replied, her voice savagely sweet, bringing her imagination ruthlessly to heel again. There was danger in thinking such thoughts about a man who was way beneath her notice. He was not even a gentleman. A gentleman would not comment on her table manners. Of course, he was an American, not a gentleman. "If you didn't eat up quickly in the workhouse, someone else would steal your dinner and eat it for you."

His eyes widened. "You've come a long way since your workhouse days."

"It's amazing what changes a woman can make in a year or two if she really wants to."

He leaned on his elbows and stared at her, as she had done to him just moments before. His scrutiny was not as idle as hers had been—she could feel his glance as it traveled over her, taking in everything about her, missing nothing. He was assessing her, sizing her up. "So you are interested in becoming my model?"

She stared straight back at him, not turning her head or flinching as he openly assessed her. "I am."

"I want to take photographs of you." He dropped his gaze to the table, suddenly unable to look her in the eyes. "You know I am a photographer."

His unease sent prickles up and down her spine. "Yes, I do."

"Photographs like this." He turned around and grabbed a stack of small cards from the shelf behind him and thrust them across the table at her. "I want you to model for photographs like this."

Emily spread the cards out across the table. As she had expected they were photographs of attractive, young women. And, also as she had expected, the women were not fully clothed. Not naked, not by any means. There was hardly a square inch of bare flesh showing. Still, they did not have a gown among them. Plenty of undergarments: corsets, stockings, petticoats in profusion, but no gowns.

"They are tamer than I had expected," she remarked, picking up each one and looking at it in turn. Not that their tameness made them any more acceptable. The merest sniff that she had so much as considered posing for such photographs would have her lose her position as assistant teacher faster than she could put her clothes back on. Not that she cared overmuch about that. It was a risk she was only too happy to take in pursuit of her dreams.

Mr. Twyford breathed an audible sigh of relief at her lack of reaction. "You are not shocked? Disgusted?"

She shrugged. "I am not a fool. Photographers do not offer large sums of money to young women to take photographs of them with all their clothes on."

"Yet you came anyway?" He raised an eyebrow. "You must want the money badly."

She picked up one of the photographs delicately between her thumb and forefinger and studied it carefully. She could do this. "What do you propose to pay me for photographs like these?"

"A pound a week if you will pose for me every Sunday afternoon from two until four." His offer came out on a rush of breath.

Fifty pounds a year? Just for taking off her gown and standing still for an afternoon? It was as much as she made as a teacher, working six days a week giving lessons. The sale of naughty photographs must be very lucrative. It boded well for her new career.

Notwithstanding the generous offer, she was sure he could afford to pay her even better and she was not above bargaining. Her father had been a merchant until his bankruptcy and she had learned more than her alphabet at his knee. A good businessman's opening offer was never his final one.

"It is more than most women can earn honestly in a week," he added, mistaking her hesitation for reluctance.

"It is a risk. I am a schoolteacher." She drew her eyebrows together, as if only now were the ramifications of her decision dawning on her. "If it were to become known that I pose for such photographs, I would lose my position and never find another."

"I cannot offer you more."

That was exactly what she wanted to test. "If I am going to take such a risk, if—" She paused, letting her hesitation sink in. "Then I want a half share in the profits as well."

That floored him. "You want what?"

"I want a pound a week and a half share in the profits." It was her body going on display, not his. She would more than earn her fee. "Given I will have a considerable stake in the success of our venture, it will encourage me to work harder for you than I otherwise might have done, naturally."

"I could pick up half a dozen girls off the street who would not ask such outrageous terms," he grumbled. "They would work for a couple of shillings a time and be grateful for it."

"Then why didn't you ask one of them to be your model?" She finally asked him the question that had been burning her for days. "Why did you ask me?"

Eric Twyford looked at the young woman sitting in front of him, her hands folded primly in her lap. She was asking a lot of him—a full half of the profits of his new endeavor. He was tempted to toss her out the door without ceremony for her cheek.

Though, to be fair, her demand was not completely outrageous. He did not stand to lose anything but his time and a small investment if his photographs did not take. Miss Emily Clemens stood to lose her reputation.

English people were funny about such a little thing as a reputation. Personally, he couldn't see the point of having a good reputation and no money—he would much rather it be the other way around. He admired Miss Emily for being willing to risk losing hers for the sake of a good business deal.

It was hard to imagine her as a teacher. Even in her modest grey gown done up to the neck and fastened tightly about her fragile wrists, she looked like a schoolboy's wet dream. If he'd had a teacher who looked like her, he might have paid more attention to his school books.

He knew exactly why he had approached her out of the blue in the park and asked her to model for him. It was more than her looks—he had seen plenty of women who were just as pretty as she was and they had all left him unmoved. What had instantly attracted him to her was a combination of things—the way she moved as if she were made of water, the fullness of her mouth that made a man long to kiss her, the glint of laughter in her eyes even when she looked her most fierce, the swell of her hips under her drab navy gown, and the tendril of hair that escaped her bonnet to curl across the nape of her neck. She was temptation wrapped up in the guise of untouched innocence.

If he were to take on any other model, his profits were not a sure thing. The young woman sitting in front of him was. He was sure he could look all over London for a year and not find the same unconscious blend of innocence and sensuality that had made him react so strongly to her. After years of photographing people, he knew instinctively who would photograph well and who wouldn't. There were plenty of beautiful women around, even here in damp old London, but only a few who could carry their beauty into a photograph. The camera would love her face.

He would not be the only man in London who would react the same way to her—he would stake all he owned on it. With Emily Clemens as his model, he would make more money than he had dreamed of. He was as sure of that as he could be of anything.

No other English girl he had met could hold a candle to her sensuality. Her skin was smooth and fair, her cheeks tinged with the palest pink. Her hair was smooth and straight, and as brown and glossy as a robin's wing. But it was her eyes that captured him, with their innocent gaze full of promise, and of unrequited ambition. They were a deep violet-blue, one of her many fine features, but the one he could never capture on his black-and-white film.

Oh, to be able to capture her likeness in reds and greens and blues. If he could but capture her in glorious, vivid color, he would become wealthy enough to rival even the Vanderbilts. As it was, even in black and white she would make his fortune for him.

To be fair, she deserved to share in his good fortune.

Half of the profits was more than he was prepared to pay, but the success of his plan hinged on her pretty face and well-shaped body, and her willingness to display them to advantage. If she demanded a stake in his success, he would have to yield. "You know why I asked you. Look in the mirror and see for yourself."

Looking somewhat bemused, she raised one shoulder in an elegant shrug. He'd wager that her shoulders were as white and smooth as her face, gently sloped and just begging for the touch of a man's hand. "There is nothing extraordinary about me. With or without my gown."

Surreptitiously he adjusted his trousers under the table. He'd better stop his thoughts going down that track right now, before he took this any further. She was his model, and nothing more. He needed to get his mind off how she would look in her undergarments and concentrate on the money that she would bring him.

Money. That was what was driving him. Wealth. Success. The ability to hold his head up proudly in any company in the land. Though he had been born in the gutters of New York, he would make it to the top. He would make his mother proud of him. All the sacrifices she had made to bring him up, to give him a good education and a decent start in life, would not be wasted.

Sex would be a distraction to his task in hand. Worse, if she were to become any man's mistress, his mistress, she might lose that look of sensual innocence that no man could resist. His fortune was not going to be ruined because his cock stood up in his trousers at the mere thought of touching her bare shoulder. Mixing business and pleasure was a recipe for disaster.

Typically, his cock was not as easily subdued as he could have wished. It continued to bulge in his trousers, refusing to be tamed into submission. No matter. He'd had plenty of untimely cockstands before and lived. Given time, her barely clothed body would be as familiar to him as his own, and would no longer engender any awkward desire in him.

Right now, she represented the lure of the forbidden because, as an innocent and as his model, she was doubly off-limits to him. "A pound a week and twenty percent of the profits," he countered, to get matters moving along before he started to fixate on his distractingly throbbing erection. "After allowing for my expenses for printing and distribution."

"Thirty-five percent after expenses."

"A pound a week and twenty-five percent of the profits. That's my best offer."

"Settled," she said hastily, as if she were afraid he would change his mind if she dithered any longer. "Of course, I shall reserve the right to look over the accounts so I can be sure you are not cheating me."

A common enough practice between business partners, but he baulked at the unspoken inference that she could not trust him. He had never cheated anyone in his life, and wasn't about to start. "I do not want a stranger looking over my affairs."

"There will be no need for that. I shall look at them myself."

That got his attention. "What would you know of accounts?"

"Among other things, in my current post I teach mathematics. And I helped to keep the books for my father when he was alive."

She hid a keen mind behind that facade of gentle innocence, then. Maybe she was the answer to more than one of his problems. He hated bookkeeping with a passion. "If you're as good with accounts as you claim to be, I'll pay you two pounds a week if you will clean up the books as well as model for me."

A frown creased her face, making him want to kiss it off her and smooth the lines from her brow. "What state are they in at the moment?"

He grabbed a box from the corner and tipped an assortment of loose papers onto the card table. "My books." He was sure the papers were all there—he'd gathered them from all over the studio just the week before, promising himself that he would make a start on them when he had a free moment and was in the mood to figure it all out. So far, he hadn't managed to find that free moment when he was in the mood.

"I can see I will have to take on the extra work," she replied tartly, "if I am ever to see a penny of the profits I am owed. How could you possibly tell anything from that . . . that chaos? I should make a start on them this afternoon."

"Modeling first." His cock gave a great leap of agreement. "You can tackle the books later."

She bit her bottom lip in a movement of unconscious sensuality. "You want to start on the photographing right away? This afternoon?"

"There's no time like the present. Come with me." He walked briskly through the shop front, and on into an airy space with a central tableau of a large, stone bench and his imposing wood and brass camera mounted on its sturdy tripod. The roof and most of the walls were made completely of glass, allowing the spring sunlight to stream in, and the floor was tiled with a dark slate. Just outside the windows lay a small patch of garden full of spring flowers and the whole was surrounded by a brick wall for privacy. Though the studio was fully enclosed, the glass made it feel as though it were an extension of the garden. The whole area was a haven of light and calm in the midst of the foggy metropolis that was London.

He watched her reaction with smug pleasure. "My studio." He loved it when people had the same visceral response to it as he did whenever he walked in the door. "You can sit on the bench to start with." From a heap in the corner he picked up a length of red velvet, gave it a perfunctory shake and arranged it on top of the bench. "That will make a good backdrop— sumptuous and textured, but uncluttered."

She eyed it doubtfully, picking at a loose thread with a fingernail. "Are you sure?"

Now that he looked at it with his photographer's eye, it *was* rather tatty. He eyed it thoughtfully before deciding it would have to do. "The worn patches won't show up badly on the film, and you will be lying on the worst of them anyway. We can always add in an extra drape if we need to. Get yourself ready while I set up the camera in the right place."

His camera was a thing of beauty. He traced his fingers over its smooth lines, loving the warmth of the wood juxtaposed with the cold brass. His camera was his mistress, his lover. He knew every inch of it, and loved it better than he loved flesh and blood. His camera never let him down, never was unpredictable or demanding. It asked for nothing but care and respect, and it would repay him by fulfilling his dreams of success.

Behind his camera he felt powerful, as if he was seeing and experiencing life in a whole new way. With his camera in his hand, he would conquer the world.

He and his camera were soon set up and ready to go.

Not so Miss Emily Clemens. She stood in the center of the studio, exactly as he had left her. He turned to her, irritated by her inaction. "You're pretty enough, but no one will pay good money for a photograph of you with all your clothes on," he said acerbically. Time was a-wasting and the light would soon be growing dim. Now that he had found his model, he wanted to get started immediately. He'd spent enough time finding the right young woman. The sight of her in his studio made his fingers itch to train his camera on her.

"What do you want me to do?" she asked, her voice tremulous.

"Take off your gown for starters. Let's see what I have to work with."

"The door."

He looked at her, not understanding.

"It leads onto your shop front."

"Oh, for heaven's sake," he said, striding to the door and turning the key in the lock. "No one ever comes into the shop without an appointment. Sometimes I hardly have a single walk-in customer for days. Still, if it makes you happy . . ." He fought to keep a scowl of impatience off his face. He had to remember that Miss Clemens was new to this game and would need a little coddling at first. There was no use in having a frightened, timorous model who broke down in tears if a stranger stuck his head around the door.

The door once locked, Miss Emily turned her back on him. After discarding her boots and furtively removing her woolen stockings, she started on the row of buttons down the back of her dress.

"Here, let me," he offered, after watching her struggle with the buttons in the middle of her back.

Her body twitched away from the touch of his fingers. "I can do it."

"It will be quicker if I help you."

She stood still and let him unfasten the last of the buttons. Once they were all undone, he pushed the dress off her shoulders. It slid down her body, pooling at her feet.

Her shoulders were as white and smooth as he had imagined them. Of its own volition, one of his hands reached out and brushed the firm, white skin.

She jerked away as if his touch was poison. "Touching me was not part of the agreement we have made." Her voice was cold enough to freeze the Thames. "You can take photographs of me, but that is all."

"Your chemise was crooked," he lied, still feeling the heat of her tingling on his fingers. "I was adjusting it."

She sniffed. "If anything about my attire displeases you, tell me, and I will adjust it myself."

She was touchy, this new model of his, and possessed a sharp tongue. It was just as well that *that* side of her would not be evident in his photographs. "Turn around for me," he said, all business again. "I need to see your lines, the proportions of your limbs, work out which is your best side. People are not precisely symmetrical. I need to discover from which angle the camera likes you best."

Her teeth clenched together to stop them from chattering with fear, Emily turned around like a clockwork doll, allowing him to inspect her on all sides.

"Your undergarments are not the most alluring I have ever seen." His voice sounded as though he had just stepped in something nasty.

"What did you expect? Silk and lace?" She pulled a face. "I am a schoolteacher. My salary barely pays for cotton. I have nothing left over for French lace."

"Cotton won't sell photographs," he muttered to himself.

"I cannot help it."

"Cotton won't sell photographs," he repeated, louder this time. "Do you have any other undergarments? Anything a little more daring?"

She cast her mind over the contents of her wardrobe. All her undergarments, like her day dresses, were plain and serviceable and thoroughly unexciting. Grateful as she was that her sister Caroline's husband had outfitted her and her sisters so generously, she desperately wished for a few pretty things. Pretty, frivolous, impractical things whose main function was to make the wearer feel good about herself. "None much different from the ones I'm wearing."

"Damn and blast. I will have to buy you some more suitable ones. Yet more money down the drain before I earn a single penny."

"Shall I get dressed again then?" Even if it meant that she wouldn't be earning the extra pound for modeling this week, she hardly cared. She would get a week's reprieve before she tumbled headlong into her scandalous new life, and at least she would earn the extra pound for cleaning up the mess of Mr. Twyford's books. That had to be worth something.

Accounting was more her style than modeling in her undergarments, anyway. She didn't know why she'd ever thought she could make a name for herself as a postcard model and attract a wealthy protector. After all, she had always been known as the clever Clemens sister, while her elder sister Caroline had been the pretty one. She may as well put her brain to good use. It was what she was best at doing.

"No, don't." He stopped her with one hand on her arm. "We'll have to improvise. Come sit down and I'll see if I can hide the plainness of your undergarments as well as shabbiness of the draperies. I'll have to be a miracle worker."

Emily sat down, her hands folded primly in her lap, her back straight and her bare knees rubbing together under her shift. This was hopeless. Her career as a postcard girl was going to be over before it had begun, and all because she hadn't the faintest scrap of silk or lace on her pantalettes. No one would buy a picture of her in a plain cotton shift. No one was that desperate. She could see her hopes go up in smoke in front of her eyes.

"Loosen up. You look as if you were on the way to the guillotine."

Mr. Twyford was laughing at her. Openly laughing at her as she sat in front him dressed only in her shift. Her temper started to rise. "If you don't like the way I am sitting," she snapped, "then tell me what I should be doing. I am no mind reader."

"Relax. Feel how beautiful you are. Until you feel your own beauty, you will never make others feel it. Especially not in a photograph."

"I do not feel in the slightest bit beautiful. On the contrary, I feel silly sitting here in my cotton shift. Silly and quite horribly embarrassed." And more vulnerable than she liked to admit, even to herself. If he were to prove untrustworthy, she could not easily escape him and run out onto the street, not half-dressed as she was. The thought that she was trapped in here with him until she got dressed again unnerved her.

"You look beautiful."

"I do?" Her temper waned just a little. She could not stay too angry at a man who called her beautiful, and sounded so sincere when he said it.

"You look beautiful," he repeated. "Young, innocent, and untouched."

"I *am* innocent and untouched."

"And a little frightened. That is the look we need to get rid of—the scared rabbit face. You need to look confident in your own skin."

She stuck out her bottom lip. "I do not look like a frightened rabbit. I am not scared of anything."

"That is better. But not so mulish, either. We don't want you looking like a stubborn donkey."

She had to laugh. Is that the way he saw her? A scared rabbit or a stubborn donkey? Her innocence seemed to be in no danger from him, at any rate. Despite his attempt at comforting lies, he clearly did not find her particularly attractive in her plain undergarments.

The thought made her more stubborn than ever, though she took care to feel it only on the inside rather than show it on her face. She would *make* him think her beautiful. Her future prospects depended on making men think she was irresistible. If nothing else, he would be good to practice on.

Besides, he had no cause for looking down his nose at her. True, she was no raving beauty, but then neither was he. His energy, rather than his looks, made him so attractive.

She would have to use the same tricks as he did unconsciously, and make up for her lack of classical beauty with her other attributes.

Feel her beauty. That was his advice. She closed her eyes and thought back to the time when she had last felt beautiful. It was a long time ago, months ago, when her father had still been alive and she had had plenty of money to spend on lacy under-garments and silk dresses. Cotton and serge were nowhere to be found in her wardrobe then.

A pale pink silk dress had been her particular favorite. She imagined herself dressed in it now, the material swishing around her ankles.

"Open your eyes."

Reluctantly she opened them. The dream was so much easier to keep alive when she could not see the stark reality of plain navy serge in front of her.

As she opened her eyes, he operated the shutter of the camera. "Hold still . . . good. That is much better. What were you thinking of to change so much? Your sweetheart?"

"I was thinking of a pink dress I used to wear, when my father was still alive." The memory of her father made the smile fade from her face. How things had changed since his suicide. He would have been horrified to find her in a photographer's studio taking off her clothes for money.

Or maybe her father would not be so surprised. He had known when he pulled the trigger that his children would be left with nothing. Sometimes she hated him for it.

"Whatever it was, keep on thinking about it. It made you look delicious. But keep your eyes open this time."

With her eyes open, she could not keep the vision of the pink dress in her mind. Instead she focused on the man in front of her. What would he look like if he were the one sitting in front of her in his undergarments and she were behind the camera taking photographs of him? The thought made a secret smile flit over her face. No doubt he would be shocked if he were to know the direction her thoughts were taking.

He operated the shutter again, capturing the look for eternity. "I never knew a woman could have such naughty thoughts about a pink dress. Are you sure you are not thinking about your young man?"

She gave a haughty sniff. "I'm too poor to attract a follower. I don't have one to think about."

If she were to have a follower, though, a man who wanted her for herself and not for the image of expensive exclusivity she proposed to sell to the highest bidder, she would want him to look just like Mr. Twyford. Not fat and contented like most of the men she had once known, but lean and hungry as if he wanted more of everything. More of life itself.

She let her mind wander as she gazed at him.

He had taken off his jacket and rolled up his shirtsleeves. Dark hair covered his golden-brown arms in thick auburn curls. She licked her lips as she looked at him. There was something about him that made her want to sidle up to him and press her body against his.

Sexual attraction—that's all it was. The same need that made tomcats howl in the night as they prowled over the rooftops.

For the first time, she understood what they were howling about.

Two

Emily stared at him as he stepped out from behind the camera to adjust the settings on the front. The fabric of his trousers stretched tight across his buttocks as he squatted down to make a final adjustment on the tripod. Taut and muscular like the rest of him, they made her mouth water.

She didn't usually notice men's buttocks. In her experience they usually weren't worth noticing. Mr. Green, the caretaker at the school, looked as if his bottom would be tough and stringy—worse even than the beef stew the cook served up at mealtimes. The fathers of her pupils who came to collect them at the half-term—she had spied a couple of them from the window when they arrived in their fancy carriages—all had fat, spreading bottoms. She had no wish to see them without a decent covering over them, imagining they would be flabby and saggy and altogether nasty.

Mr. Twyford's bottom was in a different class altogether. It was the sort of bottom that begged to be fondled, that called out to be touched and stroked, to have its lean firmness fully appreciated. It was a pity he was far too poor to be of any interest to her.

He finished adjusting the tripod and turned around.

Emily gulped. His buttocks were not the only bulge in the room that begged to be fondled. The front of his trousers was tented out in a sizeable erection. It caught her eye and she could not look away.

He caught the direction of her gaze and a flush of red mottled his face. With a muffled curse, he turned his back on her. "Don't take it personally." His voice came out strangled. "It's just . . . just something that happens once in a while."

Her mouth twitched as she tried not to smile. Whatever sorry excuse he made for his current condition, it was proof positive he wasn't completely invulnerable to her semi-nakedness. Maybe her cotton shift didn't look so bad after all. Or maybe her naughty thoughts were lending an aura of sultry promise to her appearance. "I won't."

Whatever the reason, it let her know she was doing something right. This was exactly the reaction she wanted to provoke in all the men who would be buying postcards of her. They needed to lust after her, to reach after the tantalizing promise of something more substantial, the promise that would never be fulfilled. To them, she would be an unattainable goddess, a woman to fantasize about in the dead of night when all around them was dark and cold, and she would have the same effect on them as she had on Mr. Twyford.

By now he had scuttled safely behind his camera, affording her only the merest glimpse of hard thigh as he fumbled with the settings. "Try a different position. Recline on one of your elbows, or lie right down on one side and look at me. You look a bit stiff just sitting there."

"Looking stiff isn't always bad," she remarked to no one in particular, as she lay down on the bench, her head propped up against her elbow. "It all depends on your perspective, I suppose." It was naughty of her, she knew, and he would think her a wanton, but the temptation to tease him was irresistible.

To her secret delight, his face flamed red as the sunset again. For a man who made his living by taking risqué photographs of young women in their underwear, he was surprisingly strait-laced and easily embarrassed. His unease perversely made her feel more comfortable in his company. He did not come across as a practiced rake. Not in the least. When he could not hide his tall frame behind his camera, he was as shy of her naked-ness as she was. Her innocence would surely be safe with him.

It would be good, though, if she could make him *want* to seduce her, even if he made no moves to actually do so. Given that she planned to make a living as a rich man's mistress, she needed to be able to make herself irresistible to men. If nothing else, he would provide her with some practice.

He hid his embarrassment behind his camera once again. "Raise your head a little," he instructed her, his voice brusque. "And let your toes peek out from under the hem of your shift."

She arranged herself as he asked, holding herself still with each pose as he took one photograph after another, until the afternoon shadows began to creep over the studio.

Eventually he put his camera aside. "The light's going, and it's getting cold here under all this glass. We'll have to move inside for the final shot and use some background flash."

She rose from the stone bench, shaking her limbs to get the stiffness out of them. Now that the spring sun was gone, the remains of winter could be felt in the chill of the air. Though she had not noticed her physical discomfort while she was posing, now that she was moving again she felt how the coldness of the bench had seeped into her bones. "I hope inside is a little warmer."

He threw a sharp look in her direction. "You're not too cold, I hope?" His look softened considerably as he caught sight of her nipples, which had hardened to pebbles in the cool air.

Self-consciously, she drew her arms to her chest, only too aware of her condition. Blowing on her hands and stomping her bare feet up and down to warm them, she nodded. "I didn't realize how chilly it was getting out here. I'm not in the habit of sitting around in my underwear."

Leaving his camera for the moment, he hurried to unlock and push the workroom door open for her. "Wrap yourself in a blanket and get yourself warm by the gas fire. I cannot have my new model catching a chill."

"Indeed, no. It would be bad for business if I had an ugly red nose and puffy eyes," she agreed wryly, as she hobbled into the more insulated and better-heated part of his studio, making a beeline for the heat and light of the gas fire.

He handed her a thick woolen blanket and she wrapped herself in it gratefully. "Very bad," he agreed, with the hint of a grin.

Wrapped in wool and toasted by the fire, she soon warmed up again. Even her feet started to get some feeling back into them, which was a mixed blessing, since her blisters started to ache all over again as her feet thawed out. She wasn't looking forward to the walk home. By the time she returned to Mrs. Herrington's School for Fashionable Ladies, dinner would be well over. She'd have to spend a few precious pennies on a currant bun from a street stall as she hobbled back.

Mr. Twyford had spent the time hauling his camera gear into the warmer room and setting it up in front of her. "One indoor photograph and then I'll be done with you."

She pulled a face at him, slave driver that he was, and wrapped the blanket tighter around her shoulders. At this rate, her pound a week would be well earned.

He ignored her brief mutiny. "On the armchair, I think. Curl up in it and tuck your feet underneath."

Curled up in the armchair it felt just like she was sitting in her father's armchair in his study, waiting for him to come home.

He looked at her critically through the camera. "It's too dark in here, even for a night shot. I'm going to have to use a flash. And practice a half-smile for me while I get it ready. A little more 'come-hither' and a little less 'little-girl-lost'."

Obediently she tried out a few different smiles, pouting her lips into a kiss and giving him the most inviting "come-hither'" look that she could summon.

There was a bang and a flash of light, immediately followed by a thick, acrid smoke that billowed out through the room. Emily gave a startled squeak and leaped out of the armchair.

Mr. Twyford appeared from behind the cloud of smoke, waving it away from his face with both hands. "Uugh, nasty stuff, that magnesium powder. I won't be able to take another shot until the room clears. That's why I take my photographs in the natural light of the conservatory whenever I can."

"You'll set fire to yourself." The smoke billowing through the room made her eyes water and she coughed. "If you haven't already."

"I have, once or twice. But not recently," he amended hastily, seeing the look on her face. "I'm much better at judging the quantities now and it hardly ever sets anything else alight."

She sniffed. "I hope the photograph was worth it."

His smile spoke of nothing but confidence in his abilities. "One of the best of the session, I can promise you."

Her outer garments were still out in the studio. Tiptoeing out in her bare feet, she gathered them up and brought them inside. "Do you have a private place where I can get dressed?" She knew it was silly to feel shy about dressing in front of the man who had just been taking pictures of her in her underwear, but she could not help feeling that getting dressed was so much more intimate and personal than taking her clothes off.

Thankfully, he seemed to understand. Turning his back on her, he ruffled ostentatiously through a pile of papers on his desk. "I'll set up a screen for you next week."

She pulled her dress on again as quickly as she could, followed by her stockings and boots. When she had done up every last button, she turned around to face Mr. Twyford again. "You can stop rustling about in your papers now. I'm perfectly decent once more."

He turned around. "A pity. I liked you so much better in your shift."

"So, I hope, will all your prospective customers," she replied tartly.

"My sentiments exactly." He took out his wallet, counted out five battered pound notes and passed them over to her.

She looked at the money suspiciously, making no move to tuck it away. "You only owe me one pound." What was he trying to buy from her now?

"One pound for the modeling today. One pound in advance to sort out my books to encourage you to persevere in the task. And three pounds for . . ."

"For?" she prompted him.

"I have no experience in buying women's undergarments," he muttered, his ears an interesting shade of pink. "I have no idea whether they cost three shillings or thirty guineas, but three pounds is all I can give you for them right now. Buy the prettiest things you can. Lace pantalettes, silk stockings, bustiers, whatever it is that you women wear. Think sexy when you choose them. Sexy and skimpy. The less there is of them the better."

"Do you trust me to come back next week, then?"

The thin smile he gave her did not reach his eyes. "I have the pictures I have taken. I'm sure the headmistress of the school you work for would be interested to receive a copy, and to be informed about the bargain we have struck."

He certainly had a point there. She tucked the five pounds away in her reticule, fumbling with the broken strap. The three extra pounds would be enough to buy her a pair of silk stockings and some pretty underthings. How she would enjoy going shopping for some real silk and lace once again, even if it meant she had to model them for Mr. Twyford afterwards. *Especially* if it meant she had to model them for Mr. Twyford afterwards. It would be such good practice.

"And use a few pennies to take an omnibus back to the school where you work."

If she were not careful, her new earnings would be whittled away a few pennies at a time with omnibuses and currant buns and other luxuries. Such things would have to wait until she found a wealthy patron. "I would enjoy the walk," she lied.

"You can't pull the wool over my eyes. I saw the blisters on your feet. Not pretty. Now take my box of papers, take the omnibus home, and I will see you here next Sunday afternoon."

Later that evening, Eric stood in his darkroom, ready to start work. His gaslight, covered as it was with a dark red glass shade, gave a faint glow to the room, barely enough to see by. Knowing the darkroom as he did, that faint source of illumination would be enough. By now, he could develop negatives with his eyes closed.

He drew on a clean pair of gloves to prevent smudging and

carefully placed the first glass plate face up in the developing solution, handling it only by the edges to prevent spoiling the light-sensitive coating that contained the precious image within its depths. Once the plate was covered by the solution, he stood back and watched as Emily Clemens' likeness in negative gradually appeared on the coating of gelatin emulsion. The outlines of her face and body looked faint and ghostlike at first but grew darker and stronger as the solution took effect, until she was there on the glass in front of him in black and white, her pose and expression captured for eternity.

He never wearied of the magic of creating negatives out of thin air, of seeing an image appear where there was none before. It made him feel like a magician—not a cheap one who performed optical illusions and other showy tricks in front of a gullible audience, but a maker of real magic who could command the power of the world at his fingertips.

Her image was clear now, and with a good depth of color. Hastily he dunked the sheet of glass into a tub of clean water to stop the developing process and prevent the picture from becoming too dark. A few swishes in that and he drew it out, still dripping, and placed it carefully in the tub of finishing solution to fix the image. Half an hour later, when the image was firmly fixed on the negative, he pulled it out, gave it a final rinse, and set it out to dry.

One by one, following this same slow, painful process, the photographs he had taken of Emily that afternoon were developed and placed carefully on the drying rack. Taking care not to chip the delicate glass of the plates, he looked critically at them. Though it was difficult to tell the quality of the images while they were still negatives, with the light and dark areas of the photograph reversed, still he was sure there would be some excellent possibilities there.

They had damn well better be good enough to find a buyer. Setting up shop in London had been more expensive than he had expected, and the wealthy customers he needed were slower to materialize than he had hoped. The five pounds he had given Emily was almost the last ready cash he had in the world. He had enough left to buy himself food for the next two or three days, and then all his ready money would be gone and it would be back to hustling tintypes in the park at a penny a piece to get by on. Either that, or starve.

He allowed himself the luxury of a grimace at the thought. He'd gone hungry plenty of times before, and each time the hollowness in his belly hurt worse and the temptation to give in to his despair was stronger. If he didn't find a paying customer for the postcards before the end of the week, his outlook would be very gloomy indeed.

Monday's lessons at Mrs. Herrington's School for Fashionable Ladies were a trial for Emily and her guilty conscience. Sure that her visit to Mr. Twyford's photography shop would be found out and that she would be thrown out on her ear with nothing but the clothes she stood up in, no position, and her reputation irretrievably ruined before she had found the wealthy protector to make it all worth her while, her nerves were horribly on edge. She could not concentrate on her pupils, and finally was reduced to giving them an exercise to copy out by hand to keep them usefully occupied. Even then, her thoughts would not settle. The noise of a door slamming several corridors away was enough to make her jump and look nervously behind her, and when the headmistress passed her in the hallway and gave her a wintry smile, her heart felt as if it would burst out of her chest with terror.

But the slamming of the door was no precursor to anything more dramatic, and the headmistress merely inclined her head and passed her by, her shoes clip-clopping on the bare, wooden floor. No one gave any sign whatsoever that anything was amiss, and Emily finally made it through to the last lesson of the day.

Still, by the time she sank onto her narrow cot, removed her slippers and stockings, and sank her sore feet into a basin of warm, salted water, she was almost regretting the devil's bargain she had made. Never before had her conscience troubled her for anything more serious than a purloined biscuit from her father's kitchen, or a length of ribbon she had borrowed from one of her sisters without asking first.

After the first initial sharp sting of the salt on her blisters, a pain that made her eyes water, the warmth of the water soothed away the ache in her feet and lessened the pangs of her conscience. Sitting there with her feet in the slowly cooling water, she reached over for the box of muddled papers that Mr. Twyford had handed her. Fixing up his books, at least, was a respectable occupation and one for which she need feel no shame. In all good conscience she could not spend the pound he had given her for tidying them up until she had earned it by at least making a start on them.

She patted her pocketbook with glee. It might have been a devil's bargain she had struck, but how delightful it was to have some money to call her own. The two pounds she had earned were burning a hole in her pocket, not to mention the three pounds he had given her for some new underthings. Come Wednesday afternoon, when she and the other teachers were free after an early dinner, she would walk down Oxford Street, open an account at the Bank of England to bank her own two pounds, and then spend every penny of the remainder on something delightfully decadent and frivolous.

In the meantime, she had a heap of papers to organize. With a sigh she started to sort out the jumble in front of her, ordering each paper by date. Once the papers were sorted and all the incomings and outgoings accounted for, she could then draw up a set of accounts for him to follow from now on.

And follow a system he must. She was not to be cheated out of half of her profits in this new enterprise because her business partner was too disorganized to keep track of his business dealings. It might yet prove a necessary source of income if she found herself too long without a wealthy man to take care of her.

Eric did not wake until early the next afternoon. Developing the negatives had taken him most of the night. He'd finally collapsed into bed shortly before dawn, the stack of glass plates taunting him from his workbench. His darkroom was merely a tiny storeroom with heavy curtains pulled over the windows—not an ideal workroom by any means. The drapes kept out the worst of the moon and starlight, but had little effect against the brighter rays of the sun. It meant he had to live a strangely double life, developing his negatives only after darkness fell and he could be sure not to ruin them with an ill-timed shaft of light; and then printing the photographs themselves when the sun was high in the sky and the pictures could be exposed onto the paper to good effect.

He washed and ate hurriedly, and then moved to mix up the batches of chemicals he needed, wanting to start the printing process while it was still light enough to develop the photographs properly.

While he had been preparing the chemicals he needed, a thick yellow fog had rolled in over the city from the river, obscuring everything in its path. He always hated such London fogs with a passion, but today he could almost have strangled its billowing clouds of filth. With a fog like this cutting out every vestige of daylight in its path, he would not be able to start on the negatives before morning came. Another day lost, another day gone before he could hope to see even a modest profit on his undertaking.

Clapping his hat on his head, he stomped out of the door into the sulphurous clouds of fog. He'd print the photographs tomorrow, whatever the weather threw at him. For now it would do no harm to whet the appetites of the booksellers and have them eager to buy his wares on the morrow.

★ ★ ★

Emily kept at the books until nearly midnight, only putting them aside when her weariness meant she could no longer keep her eyes open. Mr. Twyford's affairs were in a mess, a far worse mess than she had expected even given the lax state of his bookkeeping. It was just as well she'd been paid in advance for modeling or she might never have seen a penny of what he owed her. He'd been bleeding money ever since he'd set up shop in London, and selling only a handful of cheap tintype photographs at a penny a piece had meant he could barely keep his head above water.

Even on the first sorting of the papers it had been clear that he had spent far more than he had earned over the last few months. Only when she had started to write the figures up in a ledger had the total amount of the shortfall been so frighteningly obvious. Pounds spent on acquiring his new camera, yet more on his tripod, shillings and shillings on chemicals, and more than she liked to count on other supplies. According to her sums, by now he had next to no money left at all.

Unless he had a few pounds stashed away somewhere that she had no account of, Mr. Twyford was bankrupt. Or if he wasn't now, he very soon would be. He had nothing more to spend. The three pounds in her pocketbook that were earmarked for new underclothes now seemed to her to be an extravagance that he simply could not afford.

As an equal partner in this venture, a venture that looked increasingly likely to be a short-lived disaster, she simply could not justify the expense. She would not repeat her father's mistake, the mistake that bankrupted him and had eventually cost him his life, by spending more than she earned. If they were to have any hope at all of making his photographs of her a success, they could not starve themselves of capital to such an extent.

She was relying on these photographs to attract a patron. If they failed to get her noticed, then she really would be in hot water. She was not naive enough to think she could continue in her teaching post for much longer now that she had started modeling for postcards such as these. The truth of her pictures would come out sooner or later, and then she would have to leave. If the pictures flopped, she would have nothing. No protector and no job, either.

With a heavy heart, she undressed and climbed in between her cold sheets. So much for her plans on a shopping expedition to Oxford Street this coming week. There was no help for it— her business sense and her conscience combined would not let her do anything else. She would have to give the money back.

The following morning Eric had been up since early dawn to finish the contact prints; he paused to look out the window. The day had turned bright, with the sun finally managing to pierce through the sulfurous fog that had lain across the city all night.

A small smile curved his lips as he looked at each of the prints in turn. He was a genius. A goddamned genius. Emily was plainly dressed with no lace or frills, but the end result wasn't too bad even so. Not too bad at all.

He'd been right about the girl's promise. She took a good

photograph. Her natural sensuality shone through in every picture, teasing the viewer with a shy wink and a half promise.

As he'd thought, the last photo he'd taken when she was curled up in the armchair was the pick of the bunch. The look of invitation on her face was unmistakable; it was a look that practically begged the viewer to carry her off to bed and ravish her.

He'd make a photographic biography of her, he decided, and entitle it "The Education of Emily." These photographs would do nicely as opening shots, showing her youth and innocence, and capitalizing on her natural modesty. He could even sell the modest, cotton underclothes as a feature, a promise of more to come as her education progressed.

He tucked the prints carefully into his briefcase, protected between two pieces of plain paper. A number of the booksellers he'd approached the previous day had been cautiously encouraging, depending on whether they liked the finished product, naturally.

These pictures, he was confident, would have them ordering large quantities, and then clamoring at his door for more.

Barely pausing to swallow the coffee he made for himself over the spirit lamp in the corner of his workroom, he grabbed his hat and briefcase and strode out the door, letting it clang shut noisily behind him. He had made his fortune this time. He could feel it in his bones.

Two hours later, he was less sanguine. Bookseller after bookseller had hemmed and hawed over the prints, turning them over with greasy fingers, but although they had leered at the pictures themselves, they had seemed less sure of their ability to sell them to others. The orders he had managed to gather so far had been ludicrously small. A couple of booksellers had asked for five copies of a couple of the pictures "to see how well they sold before they committed themselves to any more," and another had asked for a single copy of each of them for his private collection. Though he had spun them his best story, shared with them his vision of a whole series of postcards based on a single theme, the sensual education of an innocent young girl, none of them had caught on fire at his words. It was hideously disappointing. He'd expected a conflagration, but he'd barely managed to raise a spark.

He ran his hands through his hair with frustration. He'd visited nearly every bookseller on the street and his morning coffee seemed terribly meager and a dreadfully long time ago by now. He jingled the few coins left in his pocket. A plate full of chops and kidneys would fill his stomach nicely, but his lack of success so far wouldn't accommodate such a large appetite. Ducking down a side street, he found a stall selling hot currant buns and handed over a penny for one of them.

Munching it thoughtfully, he headed back to Charing Cross Road, where the majority of bookshops in London were clustered. He would not give up yet. Not until he had spoken to every bookseller in the street, and then to every other bookseller scattered in other areas of London, too, if need be. All he needed was a single businessman with the ability to see the world his way, to see what an opportunity he was offering. Just one outlet for the postcards he would print, and his fortune would be made.

The very next bookseller's place looked the least promising yet. In the plate glass windows stood a series of fashionable engravings, a stack of recent novels, and another of popular sermons. A lady's store, most definitely, and not likely to be interested in the sort of wares he had for sale. It was hardly worth the bother of being turned down.

As he was in the act of turning away to continue on to the next shop, his stomach grumbled. The currant bun had barely taken the edge off his hunger.

He squared his shoulders. He would visit every bookseller in the street. Every bookseller in London, if need be. That was the bargain he had made for himself just now, and it was too soon to be backing out just because he didn't like the look of the place.

A bell over the door jangled as he pushed it open and went inside.

The interior was as dainty and feminine as the exterior. The walls were covered in figured paper and even the counter was upholstered in pink-and-white striped fabric. Behind the counter sat an elderly woman crocheting a skein of fluffy wool, her fingers flicking so fast he could barely see them move. She smiled at him, a kindly expression in her eyes. "Can I help you, sir? Could a new novel take your fancy, or maybe you are after a fashion paper for your lady wife?"

His single-minded determination to sell his photographs was all that kept him from turning tail and running. Instead, he walked up to the upholstered counter and laid his briefcase on the table. "I'm not looking to buy. I have something I would like to show you."

"Some new books?" Her voice, though polite, contained no enthusiasm. "I have to warn you, young man, that I already have a large stable of very reliable suppliers of the sort of books that do well in this store. I really don't think that . . ."

He opened his briefcase and drew out the sheet of contact prints. "Not books, postcards," he interrupted her. "Photographs."

A gleam of interest lit up her eyes and she got to her feet and laid her crochet down behind the counter. "Show me."

Holding his breath, he laid the sheet down on the counter in front of her, half expecting a screech of outrage and to be ordered out of her shop on the instant.

To his surprise, she picked it up and studied it closely, holding the sheet up to her eyes so that she could see it more clearly. "These are very good photographs, young man, if rather tame for that sort of thing. Very well done, indeed."

His tongue was glued to the roof of his mouth with amazement. Of all the reactions he could have received, this was the very last one he would ever have expected. "Thank you."

She was still looking critically at the sheet of contact prints. "I may be interested in ordering some," she said slowly, considering her words carefully. "How many of each do you expect to print?"

He shrugged, as if the question was not firing his soul with renewed hope. "How many would you want?"

She fixed him with her sharp eyes. "I don't imagine I'm the first you've offered these to."

There was no reason to lie. Besides, he had the uncomfortable feeling that she would see through any prevarication he might be foolish enough to make. "No, you're not. I've been up and down most of the street offering my wares."

She sniffed. "And I also don't imagine I'm the first who wants to order some."

He thought of the three paltry orders he had received so far. At least he didn't have to lie in order to pique her interest. "As you yourself remarked, they are very fine photographs," he said with pride. "A number of other booksellers on the street have shown some interest in them, though I haven't committed myself to any large orders as yet." He gave her a winning smile. "I'm still testing the waters."

The expression on her face did not change a jot even with his best attempt to charm her. "I'm willing to order a reasonable quantity of these, Mr.?" Her voice trailed off expectantly.

"Mr. Twyford at your service, ma'am." A reasonable number? How big would that be? A hundred at the very least, he hoped. Even with a huge effort, he could barely keep the excitement out of his voice. That would never do. If she guessed how anxious he was to make the sale, she would lower her offer. "I have a photographic establishment on Moulton Street."

"Well then, Mr. Twyford of Moulton Street," she said, as she laid the sheet down on the counter again. "I am willing to order a reasonable quantity of these. On one condition."

He raised his eyebrows at her. "And that is?" No doubt she wanted to specify the quality of paper or some other such trifle to which he would have to agree if he wanted her custom. Irritating, but not uncommon.

"I want exclusive rights," she demanded to his surprise. "No other sales to anyone in London."

His hopes, so low before he had walked into the shop, were now flying higher than a hot air balloon. She must think they were eminently saleable to place such a condition on him, and, evidently, she was hoping that she could snaffle all the profit to herself. "These are not the only pictures I have. They are merely the first of a series I have entitled "The Education of Emily." I intend to bring out a new batch of pictures every week or two."

She pushed her spectacle up her nose. "So much the better. If these sell as well as I would expect them to, I will gladly place an order for the rest. If the price is right, naturally. How much do you want for them?"

He did a few hurried sums in his head, trying to gauge by her enthusiasm how much she might be willing to pay. "Sixpence a piece for a hundred of them," he offered at last, nearly doubling what he had been intending to ask for them. Six pounds that would be. Even allowing a pound for Emily and another for the books, it was a good profit for a few days' work. "And that's with no sales to anyone else in London." He sighed theatrically. "I wouldn't make the offer to anyone else but you, ma'am. That's most of my market gone, right there. You'll drive me to the brink of ruin with your hard bargaining."

He could almost see the cogs whirring around in her mind as she considered his offer. "Make it thruppence each and I'll order five hundred of them."

Five hundred? He blinked once or twice, but didn't let any

other sign of his surprise show. *That* was an order worth having, and no mistake. "Fourpence each for an exclusive offer," he countered, sliding the sheet away into his briefcase again and snapping it firmly shut. "To be paid for on delivery. No credit."

She hesitated, a small frown creasing her brow, her fingers tapping uncertainly on the upholstered counter.

"Or thruppence if I can sell them anywhere else I like." Not that he'd bother trying to sell to anyone else if she came up with a decent order, but she didn't need to know that.

That decided it. "Fourpence a piece it is," she said, and she reached for her crochet once again. "When can I have them by?"

Briefcase swinging at his side, he tipped his hat to her, barely able to contain his excitement. "You'll have the first batch this afternoon."

On the way back to his shop to set to work, he broke into a happy jig, clasping his briefcase to his heart and twirling it around in the street with feeling. Twenty pounds he'd made this afternoon. If Emily Clemens were here in front of him now, he would dare the worst frosty look she could give him and kiss her soundly. Twenty pounds!

He gave a happy chuckle as he sidestepped over an open drain in the road that was transporting its unmentionable cargo through the city. What did he care if the passersby were looking at him as if he were more than a little mad? Damn their dullness and ignorance. He was a genius and he had just made the biggest sale of his life. The world belonged to him—it was his for the taking.

Three

If it had not been for the completed set of accounts she had labored over and the three pounds she had to give back to their rightful owner, Emily would never have made the long walk back to Mr. Twyford's studio the following Sunday.

Her modeling career, such as it was, was over. Now that she had completed the accounts, she knew that he would never be able to pay her for another week. He simply did not have the money. And there was no way in the world that she would take off her gown again and let him photograph her half-undressed with only the vague promise of payment in the future if her photographs "took." No, she was far too canny to accept a promise of good things to come in the future in lieu of cold, hard cash in her hand right now. He would not be fobbing her off with promises. She would have to find another way of making herself infamous.

She'd agonized over whether she ought to keep the money for the modeling she had done so far, with Mr. Twyford so near bankruptcy, but finally she'd decided she had earned it honestly and so could rightfully keep it. If he chose to waste the last of his money on taking pictures of her in her cotton shift, then he was even a greater fool. She could not be held responsible for all his follies.

He was working intently at his workbench when she arrived, a little out of breath from the heavy bag of papers she had carried all the way from Holbrooke. When she came in, he looked up and his face broke into a smile. "Ah ha, the delightful Miss Clemens." He came toward her and, removing the heavy bag from her grasp and setting it on the table, he took both her hands in his. "How very pleased I am to see you today."

His excessive good humor grated on her nerves. She scowled at him. "I've done your books," she said abruptly. That, if anything, ought to remind him of the dire straits he was in and puncture the bubble of insouciance in which he was floating.

"Excellent, excellent," he said rather distractedly, waving the subject away with an airy hand. "And the new undergarments?" His voice had turned eager and bright once more. "Did you manage to procure some suitable ones for today's photographs?"

Was he being deliberately dense, or was he so careless of his money that he had no concept of the dreadful financial situation he was in? "Mr. Twyford—"

"Please, call me Eric."

"Mr. Twyford," she repeated, more firmly this time. "I have done your books, as I promised, and I did not like what I found in them."

"I'm not surprised," he replied breezily. "I didn't much like the situation I was in last week, either. Barely a penny to my name. I thought I might have to go hustle a few more tintypes to make the price of my dinner."

She heaved an irritated sigh. He wasn't so stupid that he didn't know how bad a hole he was in, then. Just foolhardy in his determination to ignore it. No doubt he was hoping that it would resolve itself of its own accord. "According to my calculations, you have scarcely three shillings left in the world. Less now, as you must have spent at least some of that on food and other essentials since I last saw you."

He grinned at her. "That was last week, my sweet. This week, by contrast, I am as rich as Croesus." He reached into the drawer under his desk and drew out a handful of pound notes, tossing them up into the air delightedly. "That was before your picture postcards brought me in all this."

"You sold some postcards already?" Her head was swimming and she put her hand to it to steady herself. "Of me in nothing but my cotton shift?"

"Five hundred of them, to be exact." He was crowing like a small boy who has won at marbles. "At sixpence a piece."

Fearing that her legs would no longer hold her, Emily sat down rather hurriedly on the upturned box. "Oh." He had already printed and sold her postcards? That meant there were five hundred men in London, maybe more, who had seen her without her gown on. The thought was strangely disturbing. Even more so because, if she was to be honest with herself, it gave her a weird frisson of pleasure to know that five hundred men would pay sixpence apiece for naughty postcards of her. And with her wearing nothing more sexy than an old cotton shift. If they liked her well enough just in cotton, how much better would they like her in silk?

"I hope you're ready to be photographed again, my dear, and in something more enticing this time." He was already moving toward the studio as he spoke. "With a little bit of fast talking I should be able to get my customer to increase her order next week, maybe even to as much as six hundred if the photographs are good enough. As they will be, with me behind the lens, and you in front of it."

Never had she regretted the ill-timed pricking of her conscience more. She should've spent those three pounds on fripperies after all. "I haven't got anything with me." The realization that she had missed out on buying herself some pretty new undergarments was almost enough to make her weep.

Her words stopped him in his tracks. "You mean you walked all the way over here and left your new garments at home? You are a teacher, for goodness sake. You are supposed to be an educated woman. How could you manage to be so stupid?"

"I didn't leave them behind." Her voice was cross. He could at least ask her why she didn't have anything new before jumping to erroneous conclusions. "I didn't buy any."

His scowl would have soured milk in the next country. "Why ever not? Did you spend the money on something else?"

Was he accusing her of stealing? Her temper now thoroughly

roused, she dug into her pocket and slammed the three tatty pound notes he had given her down on the table. "I did your accounts before I had a chance to go shopping and I soon discovered you had no money left. None at all. How could I spend your last few quid on fripperies I don't need when for all I knew you were starving?"

His scowl deepened. "You should have trusted me and done what we agreed for you to do. If I was prepared to go a little hungry for a few days, that was my business. Now we have lost a whole seven days. And we risk losing our best customer, too, when she discovers there will be no new photos to be had this week."

She had tried to do the right thing by him and all he could do was scowl and call her stupid. It wasn't fair. Couldn't he give her some credit for trying? Though, to be fair, she could understand his disappointment. She was eager to get her picture into the hands of another five hundred men this week.

"I could run out now and buy something quickly," she offered, wanting to rectify the situation. There was a seller of intimate apparel just a few streets away; she had passed it on the way here. It was nothing fancy, but surely she could find something there that would do the trick. Something with a scrap of satin and lace was all she needed.

He clapped his hat on his head and grabbed her by the hand. "Good idea. If we hurry, we can be back while there is still enough light to shoot off a dozen photographs. I know your angles better now and which of your looks and poses translate best into film, so the modeling should go more quickly."

Surely he wasn't thinking of going with her. She pulled her hand away from his, digging her heels into the floor. "You cannot go shopping for such things with me." It was the sort of thing her patron might do, but her photographer? Certainly not. "It . . . it isn't proper."

A loud guffaw of laughter burst from him. "My dear Miss Clemens, nothing about your position with me is proper in the least." He took her by the hand again and pulled her outside the door and into the street. "Come on, there is no time for arguing and no point in being prudish about this whole affair. Least of all with me, who has already seen you in your shift. Now, hurry along. We have to make our purchases and be back before the light dims so we don't lose the whole week."

Still she held back, dragging her feet as much as she dared. "I will not dare to hold up my head if you accompany me," she hissed at him out of the corner of her mouth, trying not to attract any unwanted attention from the others going about their business in the crowded street. "Let me go by myself, I beg of you. They will think that I am a gay girl, and that you are buying me gifts." She didn't want to lose her reputation before she had something tangible worth losing it for.

"Nonsense. They will not dare to think anything of the sort. They will think that you are my wife and that I am the most attentive of husbands. I will make sure of it. Now hurry." And he gave her arm a little yank so that she caught up to him with a slight stumble.

"I'm hurrying," she snapped back at him rather crossly. "But really, there is no need for you to come with me. It will be quicker for me to go alone."

He snorted. "I know how women love to shop. I can't wait for you to wander around all afternoon by yourself. Save your breath for walking and we'll get there all the quicker."

She bit her tongue to stop a nasty word from escaping her mouth. He was as rude as any savage. And what was worse, he did not seem to even know when he was being offensive, let alone care.

"Do you know where you are going?" she asked again after a minute, a little breathless from the extremely brisk pace he was setting.

"Oxford Street," he replied shortly, looking up and down the street for a break in the continual traffic so he could dart them across without getting caught under the wheels of a cart. "That's where all the best shops are, I believe."

This time it was her turn to tug on his arm to pull him to a halt. "We shall do nothing of the kind. That's miles out of our road. Come this way." She pulled him into the little side street where she had seen the little shop earlier in the day and headed straight for it.

Though the exterior was plain enough, inside it was crammed full of intimate clothing of all kinds and colors so that Emily hardly knew which way to look. She felt like a child in a sweet store, surrounded by temptation in every shape and color. She wanted to taste a little of everything and not miss out on a single thing.

Mr. Twyford stood just inside the door and looked around him, the tips of his ears turning pink. He gestured around the shelves, loaded with corsets and stockings and all other manner of things. "Go find yourself something pretty, my dear wife," he said, playing at being the benevolent husband and waving her away as the shop assistant approached them purposefully.

Emily gave him a sickly sweet smile. So, he thought he could skip out on her now, did he? She didn't think so. It was time for a little revenge for the abrupt way he had dragged her down here with him. "But Mr. Twyford," she said winningly, clinging tightly to his arm and gazing up into his eyes with her best adoring look. "You must help me choose your gift to me. I shall be quite lost without your exquisite taste to guide me in my choice."

A wave of color crept up his neck and he pulled at his collar as if it were suddenly too tight. "If you insist," he muttered ungraciously, looking less and less like the benevolent husband with every second that passed.

"Oh, but I do," she trilled, enjoying his discomfiture immensely. "Come along, do."

As she looked around the store, her gaze was caught by a shelf of lacy pantalettes. They were just the sort of thing she had wanted to wear when her father was still alive but would never have dared to buy for herself. Luxuriously decadent and just a little bit naughty. She took a pair off the shelf and shook them out to take a proper look. Hmmm, yes, they were just the thing. If cotton drawers could sell five hundred prints, these pantalettes would be sure to sell double that.

The shop assistant appeared behind her. "It is Brussels lace, Madam, and the material is of the finest quality. As soft against your skin as if you were wearing clouds."

She could not resist stroking them. They were nearly as soft as the shop assistant claimed. She held them out to Mr. Twyford. "What do you think of these? Don't they feel nice?"

He reached out one tentative finger and gave them a poke. "Very."

She turned to the shop assistant. "How much are they?"

"Thirty shillings. And cheap at the price. It's not often you get such quality as this. They won't wear out with washing, oh no, not these."

Thirty shillings? Twenty would have been pricey enough but thirty was outrageous. She was about to put them back when Mr. Twyford spoke behind her. "We'll take a pair."

When she whirled around to protest at his extravagance, he winked at her. "Nothing is too good for my new lady wife." To her annoyance he had regained his composure and nothing was left of his former embarrassment except a faint tinge of pink at the base of his neck. "Now, how about a pair of silk stockings to match. And a fine corset. She needs outfitting all over."

"If Madam would like to try on one of our satin corsets," the shop assistant offered, fluttering after them like a small sparrow.

"What an excellent idea," Mr. Twyford exclaimed. "Come, my dear, and try on one of these pretty corsets for me." He held up a scrap of satin barely big enough to cover her breasts. "How I would love to see this on you."

She glared at him, not liking that he was now teasing her. "I think this one would be more appropriate," she said, holding out a plain one made of stiffened whalebone.

"Oh no, that one will never do," the shop assistant twittered, quite horrified at the thought. "A pretty young lady such as Madam should have something to set off her beauty, not a straitjacket like that one. It's made for the somewhat larger matrons who need, uh, *containing*, rather than displaying. Maybe one like this?" she said, picking out a pale pink confection of satin and yet more lace. "Or this?" She held out another one in pale yellow. "This one is very fine."

Mr. Twyford nodded his head in agreement. "Try them both on," he said with a grin. "Along with the pantalettes, of course, to be sure they look well together."

Emily disappeared into the back of the shop with her hands full of garments, glad to escape this new side of Mr. Twyford. He was putting her quite out of countenance.

He had chosen well, though. She didn't know which corset she liked the look of better. They were both so pretty. The yellow one was bright and sunny as a summer's morning, while the dusky pink made her think of early dawn dreams.

She tried the yellow one on first, turning this way and that in front of the mirror to see how it fitted her.

Mr. Twyford poked his head around the curtain.

"Get away with you," she hissed, flapping her hands to get rid of him. "This is no place for you. I am trying on clothes back here. In a *private* room."

He ignored her fussing. "I don't like that one so much. It's too girlish. Not sensual enough. Try the other."

She wasn't going to move with him standing there watching her like a cat watching a sparrow. "Get out."

"Can't a man watch his wife trying on her new clothes?" he asked with mock innocence. "After all, he is the one paying the bills."

"Get out," she repeated, "or I will take all afternoon undressing and the light will be gone before we get back."

His smile broadened. "Now that I would like to see," he said. "It would be well worth missing an afternoon's work to see you undressing all the way."

She put her hands on her hips and glared at him. Really, it was no joke. They might have agreed to become business partners but that did not give him the right to anything else, particularly not to openly watch her try on underclothes in a public shop. He was only her photographer, after all. "Get out or I will quit on the instant and never model for you again."

That had his head away from the curtain as fast as lightning.

Quickly she took off the yellow corset and put on the pink one. It fitted her like a glove, emphasizing the slenderness of her waist and the fullness of her breasts. She hooked it together. Yes, this was definitely the one.

Before she had finished doing up the last hook and eye, Mr. Twyford's head was poking around the edge of the curtain again. "You dressed yet?"

She turned her back on him. "Get away with you." Having

him take photographs of her when she was half-naked was one matter, but having him intrude on her while she was dressing was quite another. It was far more intimate and disturbing, and the hovering presence of the shop assistant in the background only made her more uncomfortable. With such an attentive audience, she couldn't even tell Mr. Twyford exactly what she thought of him.

"I have to make sure that the garment is appropriate and that is suits you. I am an American, you know, and I have to make sure I get my money's worth. Now turn around so I can see it properly."

She gave him a hasty twirl just to get rid of him. "Do you think I would choose something unsuitable?"

"Not at all. I just like looking at you in your undergarments."

Enough was enough. She twitched the curtain out of his fingers and held it in her own while she fixed him with an evil glare. "I am getting dressed now. If you look in here one more time, you will regret it. I am perfectly serious."

He gave her a mock salute. "As you wish, my dear." And he was gone.

Emily dressed herself as quickly as she could. That was the last time she ever cared that he had no money left. Next time she would spend his last three pounds with glee, and hope that he was doubled up with hunger pangs all week. It would serve him right if he was. He deserved to be punished for his insolence.

Once her gown was re-buttoned, she stomped out of the dressing room in a rare temper. Certainly she would never take him shopping with her again. It had been the most mortifying experience of her life.

Her temper was not mollified by the hasty scamper back to the studio, pulled along by Mr. Twyford and his enthusiasm. By the time she collapsed, exhausted, on to the sofa, she was hot, tired, and very out of sorts.

For the first time that afternoon, Mr. Twyford looked at her with sympathy. "You look all done in. Sit there and catch your breath for a minute while I set up the camera." She would have been grateful for his forbearance except for the muttered comment she overheard as he made his way out the back and started fiddling with his camera. "Can't take photos of the girl looking like that. She looks dreadfully cross. No one wants to buy postcards of a wench who looks ready to snap your head off, no matter how pretty she is."

It was true. She *was* cross. The absurdity of it made her laugh. Why should it bother her that he wanted to check out the under-garments in the shop? Letting him look at her was harmless enough. No doubt she would have to get used to far more embarrassing things in the new life she had chosen for herself. For what wealthy benefactor would desire a prudish mistress?

Besides, the clothes had been bought specifically to draw men's attention to her body. She would be wearing her new garments in front of his camera all afternoon, and then the pictures of her wearing next to nothing would be hawked around London for another five hundred gentlemen to leer at. She might as well cheer up and make the most of her afternoon away from the noisy chatter of the girls' school where she worked. The studio was gloriously calm and peaceful in comparison to the stultifying air of the school. She should enjoy the atmosphere while she could.

Rising from the sofa, she went in search of a pitcher and ewer of water, where she washed her face and hands. Feeling much refreshed, she drew out the purchases to inspect them.

Really, they were lovely. As soft and as smooth as ever she used to wear when she was wealthy. The last of her anger dissipated under the influence of the satin and lace.

True to his word, he had set up a screen for her to dress behind. After making sure he was busy in his studio, she undressed to her skin, discarding her woolen gown and her plain cotton undergarments. The pantalettes were the first to be pulled on, frothing out over her legs in a cascade of lacy waves. Then the silk stockings, as cool as ice water against her warm skin. Finally she put on the corset, smoothing it down over her stomach and hips. The pale pink satin made the swell of her breasts look whiter than ever.

Her hair was still up. It did not feel right for her hair to be in such tight control when the rest of her was nearly naked. She took out all the pins and shook it down over her shoulders and back. That was better. Her hair falling over her bare shoulders made her look both younger and more sophisticated at the same time.

Only when she felt comfortable with her appearance in the tiny looking glass set up by the ewer of water did she go in search of Mr. Twyford and his camera.

Four

It had been naughty of him to tease her so in the clothes shop, Eric Twyford admitted to himself as he crouched down and adjusted the leg of his tripod. She had deserved it though, for starting the teasing. Once he had begun to retaliate in kind, she had been so flustered that he simply hadn't been able to resist continuing.

If only she knew how he was suffering for it now.

In the shop he had made the fatal mistake of seeing her as a woman, rather than simply as a model. By poking his head around the curtain he'd only meant to tease her out of her prudery, instead of which he'd ended up teasing himself. God, she was a looker, particularly in that delicious piece of next-to-nothing that he had just bought for her.

The image of her had stayed with him. He was sure it was burned onto his sight. The entire walk home he'd been plagued with an erection that simply wouldn't go away. Not even when he tried to imagine his neighbor, a toothless old crone who must be at least one hundred and three, inside the corset instead of Emily. He could not keep his mind on her saggy, wrinkled skin and bony body, not when he had just seen Emily's smooth, plump perfection.

Even now, his cock was throbbing with an insistence he found difficult to ignore. If Emily had not been in his studio, he would have seen to it himself immediately, but he had no time to waste. Neither did he want to be caught with his hand on himself like any schoolboy, particularly not by Emily. *Her* hand was what he wanted on him, not his own. Her hand and her mouth and that part of her that was made to take a man's parts inside it.

It was a damn shame that she wasn't the gay girl she was so afraid of being taken for. He'd pay a whole pound to have her to himself for the afternoon, without his camera between them. He'd fuck her over and over again until he was as dry as a bone and had no more cum left in him.

The blood was pounding through his cock with the insistence of a river in flood. Damn it, but he had to stop thinking about the girl in this way. Though she removed her clothes for him readily enough, she was not for the taking. She clearly had her sights set on a wealthier man than he was.

She'd laugh in his face if he offered to marry her. Besides, he had no intention of marrying until he had made his fortune, and then he would choose some bright young American girl from a wealthy family who could guarantee him an entry into New York society. A bouncy New York girl with a large dowry and a better pedigree than a duchess—that was the sort of woman he intended to marry.

Even if by some miracle she was willing to spread her legs for him without the benefit of marriage, he could not afford to take a mistress anyway. Women cost too much, and he could not afford the time he would need to spend with her to keep her sweet, nor the distraction from his goal.

He had to stop dreaming about stripping her stark naked, kissing her breasts, and stroking her soft pussy. She was his model. Nothing else.

If he had any sense, he'd be glad that she was such a plague to him. It upped the odds that others would find her attractive, too, and he'd make another twenty pounds this week. A thousand pounds a year he'd make at this rate. It was enough to live like a king.

He grimaced. Make that seven hundred and fifty pounds a year, after Emily had wrung her quarter of the profits out of the business. If she wasn't so damned perfect, he would never have agreed to her demands. He was already regretting that he had given in to her blackmail.

Just then Emily herself walked in through the door of the studio dressed in all her new finery. He felt his mouth grow dry at the sight and his cock leaped painfully to attention all over again. If she wasn't so beautiful he never would have taken her on in the first place. Hell, looking like this, he would've given her half of the profits if she'd stuck to her original demand.

The corset hugged her chest, cinching in her waist and emphasizing the swell of her bosoms as they spilled over the top, barely contained by the lustrous satin. Her pantalettes flared out from her shapely bottom like a waterfall, the profusion of lawn and lace keeping her treasures unfortunately well-hidden. And her legs, encased as they were in shimmering silk stockings, looked as long and lithe as any man would like to have wrapped around his neck as he thrust deep into her hot, wet pussy. . .

"Are you ready?" There was a little half-smile on her lips, as though she knew exactly what she was doing to him and loved every second of it.

He cleared his throat and, dragging his eyes away from her, he turned his attention to the camera once more. "Come and sit on the bench again," he ordered, hiding himself behind the bulk of his camera. It would never do to let Emily see the state of his trousers. She would tease him all afternoon and make his life, not to mention his damned cock, harder than it already was. "I shall be with you in a second."

One final adjustment that the camera didn't need and he felt composed enough to look up again.

Emily settled down on the hard stone bench, looking as comfortable as if she were sitting on a heap of soft cushions. "How do you want me to look this afternoon? Not as demure as last week, I take it? Just a touch of mischief, maybe?"

Any more mischief in her eyes and he was a dead man. "I was planning a series of postcards that one could buy on subscription," he explained, trying not to sound too pompous. "One that showed your gradual inculcation into the fine art of love."

"The Ruin of Emily in pictures?" she suggested in a mocking voice. "How delightful."

"The Education of Emily," he corrected her. "Eventually, if you are agreeable, I will want to photograph you in some rather more immodest poses. But not yet. It's too early for you to show too much daring or too much bare skin."

She nodded, all seriousness now. "I see. Tease them and make them wait. Make them buy the tamer postcards so they get assured a copy of the naughty ones when they eventually appear."

"Exactly. So go easy on the mischief today. You need to look demure and innocent still, though not quite as demure as last week. A little bit curious, a little bit daring, though still too shy to do anything about it."

She struck a few quick poses, getting herself into the mood of the shoot. "Ah, I've got it now," she muttered to herself, as she struck a rather languorous attitude. "Wanting more, but not knowing exactly what and too shy to ask."

Her body, stretched out on the stone bench, was an invitation to sin, but her face was pure innocence. It was a heady combination and it struck the perfect note for the next postcard in the series.

Hurriedly he exposed a photograph, capturing the look for eternity.

Slowly his insistent erection began to subside into a familiar ache. He still wanted her, but not with the same burning and demanding insistence as before. It was much easier for him when he had the camera between them. He could see her as a job again, instead of as the most stunningly sensual woman he had ever known.

The afternoon shadows were growing long before he had finished all twelve exposures he had loaded into his camera. Not one of them a wasted shot, either. He'd lay good money on it.

The sun had just disappeared behind his neighbor's building and he shivered slightly in his shirtsleeves. Emily, he realized with a start, must be feeling the cold far more than he was. He was at least fully clothed, whereas she was quite deliciously undressed.

He dismissed her with a nod before his mind started going down dangerous paths once more. "Go get yourself dressed. We've finished for now."

Getting up from the bench, she stretched herself like a cat. "What do you want me to do with the underclothes?"

"Take them off and parade in front of me quite naked," he suggested with a wink and a leer.

She glared at him. "Ha ha. Very funny."

She thought he was joking? "You did ask," he muttered. What did she expect him to do with them? Set himself up as a seller of ladies' unmentionables? "Keep them. They're yours."

She stopped mid-stretch. "That's not a very sensible financial decision. They are practically brand new. You could resell them for probably three-quarters of what you paid for them today."

"And then have to buy you new ones?" He shook his head. "No, keep them until you tire of them, and we can sell them then. In fact, buy a few more and bring them all with you next week. With a good selection we can mix and match so that it looks like a new outfit every time."

Her face broke out into a smile. "In that case, I shall wear them home. Not the stockings—my thick boots would tear them to shreds, but I shall wear the rest. It will make me feel so wonderfully decadent to wear satin and lace under my drab schoolteacher's gown."

He groaned. That was another image to plague his nights, the thought of Emily wearing such tantalizing underwear under her plain gown.

After watching her depart, he wrapped his thin jacket around his chilled body and headed back inside. He hadn't realized just how cold he had become during the session. Poor Emily must have been freezing, and yet she had not uttered a single word of complaint.

A hot bath would warm him nicely. It would warm him faster if he could share it with Emily, but unfortunately that wasn't in the cards. He'd have to make do on his own.

Finally, after several trips to and from the coal range with buckets of scalding water, his bath was ready.

Before hopping into the hot water, he looked critically down at his body. It wasn't too bad for a man of his age. He was particularly pleased with his firm buttocks, muscles well toned from years of walking. He shuddered at the thought of how some of the red-faced, corpulent men he had encountered recently would look without their clothes. Their poor wives, having to look at their saggy asses.

As a photographer, no, as an artist, he corrected himself, he admired attractive human forms. Women certainly had the edge when it came to beautiful bodies, but that was just his preference. He knew men back in the States who preferred looking at other men's bodies, which was fine for them but definitely not his cup of tea, as they said over here.

Dropping into the steaming water he sighed, thinking of Emily's wonderful shape. Not thin—he hated unhealthily thin women—but not fat either. Though well muscled from her hard time at the workhouse, she had a good layer of padding in the appropriate womanly places. Her breasts, what little he had seen of them, were lovely. Her nipples would be a delicate shade of pink, and would become erect with the slightest lick.

The thought of licking her erect nipples produced his own erection, making his cock stand out of the hot soapy water. His balls ached from his constant state of arousal throughout the afternoon. So too did his cock which had been, in various states of hardness, crushed into his trousers for far too many hours without any attention.

If only Emily were here to take care of things. He closed his eyes, imagining her soft hand rubbing him up and down. Seemingly with a will of its own, his own hand dropped to massage his painfully hard cock, the soap adding a slipperiness that was a poor imitation of what her hand would be like.

Eyes still closed, he rubbed his hand around the engorged head and imagined her in the bath with him. It would be a bit crowded—he would have to dangle his legs out either side of the bath. In this position she would have access to his cock and balls, and even to his ass.

With one hand still stroking his cock, he gently massaged

his very sensitive entrance to his ass with the other. It both tickled and brought pleasure at the same time.

Emily, naked, would be a feast for any artist's eyes. She had a perfect bosom, and a slim waist that was in proportion to her height. Her pussy would not be too covered in hair, despite the current fashion for a thick growth. He himself preferred a lighter covering—it was all the better for tasting the very essence of her womanhood.

The thought of her kneeling over his questing tongue brought him close to the brink.

He moved his attentions to the base of his shaft, away from the sensitive glans near the top. He could just picture her warm, tight pussy deeply engulfing him, riding him with little teasing movements of her hips while he played with her nipples, not too hard and not too soft. His hand returned to full, fast strokes. Then she would rise up, almost removing his slick cock from her cunt before once more burying him to the hilt, repeating the movement over and over, until he was ready to erupt.

With that final image, his orgasm became unstoppable. One last downward stroke and his hips thrust out of the water. With a rush, his cum spurted out in sticky lines across his chest and, so powerful and needed was his release, jetted over his head to the floor below.

Shaking, he collapsed back into the tub, splashing the floor with a wave of water as his breath came in gasps. Goddamn it, but he needed to get Emily out of his mind before she was the death of him.

★ ★ ★

Delicious new underwear really did lift a woman's mood, Emily decided, as, back once more at Mrs. Herrington's School for Fashionable Ladies, she smiled all the way through supper. Each time she moved, she felt the lace of her pantalettes brush her thighs like the caress of a lover's hand, and the satin of her corset hug her tightly across her stomach and breasts. She wished she could wear such undergarments every day. It felt almost as good as it would feel to have Mr. Twyford's hands on her thighs and breasts.

One of the other teachers, a pinch-faced woman with a sallow complexion, eyed her smiles suspiciously over their watery stew and mushy peas. "You are very sunny tonight," she remarked caustically across the table. "Have you found yourself a lover?"

Emily shook her head, refusing to let the other woman's sourness put her out of temper. "Not me. I'm too poor to find a husband, and too proud to want anyone who'd have me on lesser terms." To be sure, six or seven hundred pounds a year to be a rich man's plaything did not, in her eyes, constitute lesser terms than marriage, but now was not the time or place to go into such details. "But how is your beau, the butcher, keeping?" Emily asked somewhat mischievously in her turn. "I haven't seen him around for some weeks." Rumor had it that the butcher, who for some months had been quietly mooning after the pinch-faced teacher, had recently transferred his affections to a stout widow with a thriving stall in the market place that sold meat pies.

The pinch-faced woman's yellow complexion turned an unbecoming shade of orange as she sputtered a few words of denial that a lowly creature such as a butcher had ever dared to cast his eyes on her, or that she would ever welcome his advances even if he did so.

"Ladies, please." The head teacher looked severely at the pair of them through the spectacles balanced precariously on the end of her nose. "Whatever would your charges think if they heard you talking so indelicately? Talking of your lovers at the table? Whatever would the mothers of our darling girls think?" She gave a theatrical shudder. "I really do not want to find out, so can we change the subject, please?" She turned to a mousy woman on her left who was picking up her mushy peas one by one with her knife and fork. "Miss Andrews, do tell me about the homilies in crewel embroidery you have been sewing for the heathens in Africa. They sound so delightful."

As Miss Andrews launched into a monologue about her brother the missionary in Africa, and his delight at receiving her latest gift of three pious sayings stitched into a woolen wall hanging, Emily lost herself in her daydream of riches and independence once again.

Her neighbor at the table, a young woman about her own age by the name of Mary Mittens, leaned toward her. "Miss Snithers is a snoot-faced old cow," she whispered in Emily's ear, under the guise of leaning down to pick up her table napkin, "but you really do look like a cat with a saucer of cream. I can almost see you licking your whiskers as you sit there at the table."

With some effort Emily kept an outright smile off her face. She liked Mary, who taught the girls history and geography, and who was always ready for a bit of pleasant mischief. They both shared a dislike for the prosy Miss Andrews, who taught religion and needlework and talked incessantly of her brother the missionary the rest of the time; and for Miss Snithers, who taught deportment and dancing and was the first to make a snarky comment at the slightest opportunity. "It's not a lover, I can assure you," she whispered back. "Not even the faintest sniff of one."

Mary sighed. "What a disappointment. I was hoping at least one of us had a prospect of escaping the drudgery here by making a fabulous match. And if it's not to be me, I was hoping it might be you. Who knows but that your intended might have a friend with a liking for red-haired women with freckles like me."

Emily thought quickly. She would have to come up with some reason for her good humor, and for possessing the pretty underthings she was wearing. In such a hothouse atmosphere as the school was, such an interesting purchase could not remain secret for long. Someone was sure to see them going out to be laundered, and she would tell someone else in the strictest confidence of course, and before long the entire school would be buzzing about who had bought Miss Clemens a pair of silk stockings, and why.

The last thing she wanted was a buzz of gossip about her newfound wealth. Though she felt guilty about deceiving her best friend at the school, it would be better to tell a lie right away. "I received a present from my sister, Caroline. Quite unexpectedly, too, which made it all the sweeter."

"Her farm is doing well, then?"

"Very. She sent me ten whole pounds to spend as I liked." Ten pounds was a goodly sum that would explain away any little extravagances that might be noticed by her fellow teachers, but it was not so large as to be unbelievable.

Mary's eyes grew as wide as the saucers they were drinking watery tea out of. "Ten whole pounds? Truly?"

Emily nodded, willing Mary to believe her story.

"You lucky thing, to have a sister as generous as that." She made a face as if she smelled something bad. "Mine's as tight as they come, and the husband she married is even worse. They wouldn't send me tuppence if they were as rich as the Queen and I was starving in the gutter. So, what are you going to spend it on?"

"I've already spent some." Her voice dropped even lower. "A pair of silk stockings. Real silk. And a new corset." She made a face at herself. "It was foolish, I know, to squander Caroline's gift on such stuff, but I so love the feeling of silk next to my skin."

"If it puts a smile like that on your face, then it can't be all wasted," Mary observed wryly.

"Miss Mittens, Miss Clemens, please." The headmistress's gaze had swung their way once more. "If you have anything of interest to say, then please share it with the whole table. Whispering at table is not the act of a lady. We must all practice our best behavior, for the mothers and perhaps even a few fathers of our dear charges are going to take afternoon tea with us this very Saturday."

Miss Snithers smirked across the table at the rebuke and Emily felt the familiar irritation rise up in her. What possible relevance did the school, with its petty rules and unspoken codes of conduct, have to the real world, to the world outside its doors? The society within its four walls was a poor mimicry of the social circles in which she had moved before her father's death, a world in which wealth could behave as rudely as it liked and still be fawned upon obsequiously by everyone not quite so well-to-do.

Still less did the school bear any resemblance to the world of the workhouse she had only recently escaped. In places where grinding poverty and desperation surrounded you, there was no respect paid to the niceties of good manners.

Manners, piffle. They were nothing but an excuse for looking down one's nose at others who behaved differently than you.

At times like these, she felt as though she was being suffocated by the rules and strictures at the school. Slowly but surely, the air she needed to breathe was being taken away from her, replaced with a vacuum, a nothingness that could not support life. Slowly but surely, she was dying inside, leaving nothing behind but the desiccated shell of her body.

If she stayed here for too long, she would become as pinch-faced and as joylessly malicious as Miss Snithers. She would rather be dead.

That was why she was willing to risk everything with her venture into modeling. This photographic business with Mr. Twyford had to work. It simply had to.

His postcards would make her famous, and she would have her pick of wealthy lovers. Then she would be free to thumb her nose at the restraints that were slowly suffocating her.

★ ★ ★

As soon as Eric Twyford walked in the door of the bookshop the following week, the owner laid aside her crocheting and greeted him as if he were an old friend. "Mr. Twyford, sir, very pleased to see you I am. Very pleased, indeed. And what have you got to show me today?"

Eric laid out the second set of contact prints of Emily in her new undergarments. They made an impressive array of photographs, if he said so himself. From a dozen exposures, he'd selected the eight best to offer the bookseller. They made a well-formed grouping, showing Emily from almost demure to decidedly full of mischief. Her education in the sensual arts was clearly growing apace.

From the look of satisfaction on the bookseller's face, he had chosen well. "I like them," she said, laying aside her spectacles. "As will my customers, I am sure. The first group were very popular. So popular, indeed, that I am nearly out of them already. If you hadn't come to me this afternoon, I would have been forced to send a runner to your studio tomorrow to restock."

Eric gulped. She had sold nearly five hundred postcards in a week? He'd thought the quantity she'd bought would last her six months or more. He certainly hadn't counted on having to reprint in a hurry.

"I wholesaled most of them," she said, smiling gently at the look of surprise on his face. "Bulk lots to other booksellers not just in London, but all over England and Scotland. Even a few to Wales, and I'm expecting a good order from the Irish sellers as soon as I let them know what I have on offer. They love that sort of thing. The naughtier the better for the good old Irish lads. Postcards of naked women sell like hotcakes over the water."

"You sold my postcards all over England?" He had no idea that she was a distributor as well as a retailer, and clearly a significant one.

"That's how I moved them so fast. So, shall we say another five hundred of the first set? That ought to see me right for another week or two. And you'd better make it a round thousand of the second set. That way I won't have to come running back to you for more in another week."

He swallowed the large lump in his throat. "It will take me a few days to make prints of such a large order. Such short notice will create a few difficulties for me, too. I have other customers waiting for photographs I have promised them." A small white lie, but no matter. He needed all the time she could give him to produce so many.

From under the counter she took a wad of pound notes, counting off a handful for him. "As it *is* a larger order than usual, even for me, I shall give you ten pounds down to encourage you to print them ahead of any other smaller orders you may have, and the rest will be paid on delivery."

He took the money and tucked it away in his pocket. "I'll print yours first," he promised. "My other customers will have to wait. You'll have your postcards as soon as I can get them to you."

It was not sensible to make each postcard an original photograph, he decided as he strode back through the streets to his studio, feeling as though he had just been poleaxed with the suddenness of his success. The work in developing each photograph was too great to turn around and sell it for fourpence, particularly when he had so many of them to do. He'd have to buy a printing machine to help him with the printing so that he could reproduce the photographs much more quickly. The latest order was worth sixty pounds to him. It was more than he usually lived on for a year.

Fifteen hundred postcards. There was no way he could produce that many by himself as quickly as she would want them. Five hundred in a week had kept him busy enough. Even having another pair of hands around the studio would not help all that much, as the quantity was simply too great to do by hand. There was no doubt about it—he needed a machine to help him, a way to automate the printing process so that it did not take so much time, a way to allow him to print a hundred or more identical copies at one time. If he had a printing press, he could concentrate on exposing the photographs and on developing the negatives, on the parts of the process where his knowledge and skill made the most difference.

He knew just the machine he needed, too. He'd seen it at a photography exhibition over in Philadelphia where he had bought his first camera. It was simple enough—a set of copper engraving plates on which to transfer the photographic images, and a small printing press to transfer the ink from the engraved plate to the paper. At the time, owning his own printing press for mass producing his photographs had barely entered his mind, but it was exactly the thing that would help him print as many postcards as he could ever need. God knows where he could get a set of copper engraving plates and a press in London, but there was sure to be a supplier somewhere. He'd just need to find it, and quickly, too.

Damnation, but he supposed he ought to run the notion past Emily before he bought a machine. Not only was she his business partner but, although he was a genius when it came to creating photographs, he had to admit she was better at dealing with accounts then he was. He would talk to her next Sunday without fail. Even if it would take all they had earned that week and more to buy the copper plates, the chemicals needed to engrave the plates, and the printing press he needed, surely she would see the sense in taking advantage of this opportunity to expand their enterprise. He would make her see the sense of it.

Damn it, but he was a genius to see her potential and persuade her to throw her lot in with him. He'd known as soon as he caught sight of her that she would make his fortune for him. He just hadn't expected her to make it so quickly, and with such apparent ease. One big customer, and in two short weeks he was well on the way to becoming a wealthy man.

Shaking his head with disbelief, he shut the door of the studio behind him and strode straight into his darkroom to start the first batch of printing. There was no time to waste—indeed, there would hardly be any time to sleep in the next few days if he was to make up this order in good time. Sixty pounds in a single week. Such orders did not come along every day.

★ ★ ★

Emily stood in the corsetiere's shop looking around at the items on display with an assessing eye. She had not been properly prepared for the first shopping trip with Mr. Twyford, and his teasing had put her terribly out of countenance. She had ended up quickly buying garments that appealed to her, rather than taking any care to choose garments that might appeal to the purchasers of her photographs, to the man who might eventually purchase *her*.

Her newly repaired reticule filled with pound notes clutched tightly in her hand, she stalked around the shop as carefully as a hunter stalking his prey. This time she was ready to spend her money, and spend it carefully on the most sensual items she could find. These new undergarments would make her another small fortune this week to salt away into her now rapidly growing account at the Bank of England. She liked knowing she had a nest egg to tide her over if she ever struck a lean patch in between patrons.

What a good thing it was that she had come to Mr. Twyford. At the rate he was selling her postcards, she would be known all over London in a matter of months. She could almost taste her freedom and independence on her tongue.

She riffled through a stack of lilac corsets, shaking her head as she did so. There was too much of them by far, and the color was too close to half-mourning to be truly attractive. Mysterious, not mournful, was the impression she wanted to convey. The last thing she wanted was to remind men of their elderly maiden aunts who trotted around trussed up tightly in perpetual lavender.

A stack of red and black beribboned chemises were the next to catch her eye. She held one up to the light to examine it more closely before eventually deciding against trying it on. Although attractive enough on the shelf, on closer inspection it proved somewhat all-enveloping. The color was wrong, too. Though the photographs would not capture the color, she would not feel right wearing it. Scarlet was not a color that one would expect a young virgin to wear—it was more the color to suit the inmate of an expensive bordello in St. James, or even a racy young widow on the prowl for her second husband.

Innocence, untouched innocence, was still the image she needed to portray, at least for another few shoots. Then she could get a little more daring, if she chose.

The underthings she had bought last week, though reasonably conservative in their cut, had seemed to please Mr. Twyford perfectly well, judging by the state of his trousers while he was taking the photographs of her. Though she hadn't liked to comment on it at the time, the poor man's private parts seemed to be standing permanently at attention. She wasn't sure if she should take it as a compliment, or whether he had some sort of medical issue that was causing his problem. It wasn't the sort of thing she could discuss with him, she thought, biting back a giggle at the thought of a serious conversation on such a topic. It was just as well it was not her but her younger sister Beatrice who had decided to be a nurse. Such matters would put her quite out of countenance.

On the whole, she preferred to remain ignorant of the exact

nature of his ailment. That way she could reasonably pretend to herself that his stiffness was due solely to her naked beauty. It made her feel better to think that he lusted after her and that his occasionally crass behavior was due to his want of manners rather than his lack of interest in her. For sure, if she couldn't give her photographer a cockstand when she was in front of him in flesh and blood, what hope did she have of attracting anyone else as a black-and-white picture on a postcard?

She riffled through a stack of fine lawn pantalettes rather halfheartedly, not finding anything to take her fancy. Even the photographs of her in her cotton chemise had sold surprisingly quickly. If plain undergarments that showed little skin sold plenty of photographs, then pretty undergarments that showed a lot of naked skin should sell even more. Naked skin, after all, not postcards, was what they were really selling. Naked skin and a fantasy that she was available, that she would look on the purchasers of her likeness with favor and give them a smile and a wink and maybe more. And all for only sixpence.

With that thought uppermost in her mind, she headed over toward the under-bust corsets that covered only the stomach and hips and let one's breasts go naked. One of these, if she dared to wear it in front of Mr. Twyford and his camera, would surely cause his trousers to tent out to even more massive proportions than usual, and sell a thousand photographs in a week.

She picked out a corset in virginal white satin, trimmed with dainty bunches of ribbon. The daring style was not at all the sort of thing a young virgin would wear unless it was for her wedding night, but the white fabric made it seem almost innocent. She held it up against her body and looked thoughtfully into the glass. Yes—the white fabric and the daring style were the perfect contrast. Wicked innocence, and innocent sensuality.

The shop assistant, dressed in a severe gown of matt black satin with strands of jet beads draped haphazardly around her scraggy neck, minced toward her. "Would Madam like to try that on for size?" she offered grandly, as if she were graciously bestowing a favor on an unworthy supplicant.

"Thank you, I will."

Safely hidden behind the curtain, she divested herself of all her workaday clothes and tried on the corset she had selected, looking at herself critically in the looking glass. It fitted her like a second skin, smoothing out her stomach and emphasizing the generous curve of her hips. Her full breasts swelled over the top of the fabric, her dusky nipples standing out in sharp contrast to the white satin fabric. The whole effect looked more wicked and more forbidden than if she had been completely naked. She looked the very picture of innocence exposed.

The thought of showing off her body like this to Mr. Twyford sent a ripple of pleasure coursing through her spine and her nipples tightened into little hard buds of anticipation. He would like it, she was sure of that. The sight of her naked breasts would make his private parts stand to attention like they had the last time. She would summon up her courage and stare at the bulge in his trousers again and lick her lips. His face would turn as flaming red as his hair as he tried his best to ignore what she was doing, and the effect it had on his body.

She loved knowing that she had such power over him, even though he fought it every step of the way. Though he tried to pretend he was only her photographer, and that his interests lay only in making money, she knew that he desired her. How could he not, when she was a fantasy in the flesh, a fantasy that he had helped create, a fantasy that he hawked on the streets for sixpence each?

She was sure that he laid awake at night thinking of her, tossing and turning in his bed and wishing she was there beside him, wishing that he could reach out one hand to stroke her smooth skin. She was sure that he wanted to fondle her breasts and slip his hand in between her legs to touch her private places, to suckle on her breasts as though he were a baby and then slide a finger right inside her to make her squirm with pleasure beneath him.

With a sigh she unhooked the corset and laid it aside. Yes, she would buy it, and then she would flaunt her breasts in front of Mr. Twyford to see if she could get a reaction out of him besides a bulge in his trousers and a clicking of his camera shutter. She would see if she could at least tempt him to kiss her. It was ridiculous to think that she had reached the ripe old age of eighteen without ever having been kissed by a man. Not properly kissed. Not even once. She would make it clear that it was up to Mr. Twyford to remedy the situation as soon as possible. It would be good practice.

After all, her new protector, when she came to choose him, would expect her at least to be well versed in the art of kissing, if not of other, more intimate matters.

She laid the corset down on the counter and, to the shop assistant's evident surprise, drew out more than enough money from her reticule to pay for it.

This corset ought to make Mr. Twyford's eyes pop out of his head. If it didn't, she would swear he was made of iron, more of a machine than a man.

But, to tell the truth, she had no idea whether he laid awake at night and thought about her or not. It simply soothed her to think he did. She could not bear the thought that he was indifferent to her, that he would as soon take a photograph of the Queen in all her royal regalia as one of her dressed in hardly anything at all.

For though it was foolish of her, she certainly laid awake in her own bed at night and imagined him doing all that to her, and more.

Five

The very next day, Emily pulled on her cleanest and whitest pair of gloves. They had a tiny hole in one finger, but any attempt to mend it with her clumsy needle would only make it more obvious than it was now. It was best to leave it as it was.

Her dress was as plain and dowdy as only a schoolteacher's navy wool dress would be, and under it she was wearing her plain cotton chemise and thick woolen petticoats. Not a crinoline or a piece of lace to be seen. Nothing, in fact, to make her look or feel good at all, or to hide the sorry truth that today she was not an attractive young model but a poor schoolteacher in a drab gown.

With a sigh at her dowdy appearance, she straightened her bonnet in the looking glass and set out to face the afternoon's ordeal.

Saturday afternoon tea with the mothers of the pupils. Mothers, and the occasional father. She pulled a face. Whatever malicious person had dreamed up the idea of afternoon tea with the parents every alternate month ought to have been burned at the stake. She suspected it was the current head-mistress, in which case she would pile up the faggots and light the straw herself for the burning.

Teaching the girls was dreadful enough. Though most of them were biddable enough, they were more interested in keeping an eye out for eligible gentlemen than in the finer points of mathematics or bookkeeping. Keeping discipline in her charges was a constant and wearying effort.

She had not counted on the mothers, though, when she had decided to become a schoolteacher to earn her living. This was the seventh Saturday she had had to suffer through an excruciatingly painful afternoon tea with the mothers and sometimes even grandmothers of her pupils. As far as she was concerned, the day couldn't end soon enough.

All the mothers, without exception, thought their little darlings were peerless and without fault. Many of them found fault with her instead—she was too young, too inexperienced, to have sole charge of their daughters. And if she ventured a word of criticism, such as suggesting to the parents of one little Miss Guinevere, who had been a thorn in her side all year, that the young lady in question could perhaps pay more attention to her teacher instead of chattering like a magpie all through her lesson, then woe betide. Guinevere's mother had looked disapprovingly at her and proclaimed that Guinevere was a positive angel when she was at home and as quiet as a mouse, and that the fault must therefore lie with the teacher and not with the pupil. Emily had ended up apologizing to the girl's parents for Guinevere's never-ending chatter.

It was the same with all her other pupils. Sophie wasn't making the progress on the pianoforte that her mother would expect after a year of lessons. It had, of course, nothing to do with the fact that Sophie was bone lazy and refused to practice—it was all Emily's fault. Emily really ought to teach her harder. She was being paid to teach pianoforte, was she not?

Esther's sums never summed, and her handwriting was appalling—ergo Emily must be teaching her all wrong, for she was bright enough, so her mother claimed, when it came to her other lessons. Of this Emily had her doubts, as poor Esther was notoriously hopeless at everything other than dancing, which, it must be admitted, she did divinely.

The whole afternoon was always a torture of apologetic humility. Each time, although she vowed beforehand she would not, she ended up taking the blame for her pupils' laziness or stupidity, and promising she would try to do better in the coming months.

The little round tables were already set out in the best parlor. Emily seated herself at one of them in the farthest corner from the door, her insides clenching with discomfort. It was better than starving in the workhouse, she repeated to herself over and over again, as the mothers, dressed in their widest crinolines and their fanciest feathered hats, slowly trickled in and seated themselves condescendingly with one poor teacher or another. Though her pride was trampled upon here as badly as it ever had been in the workhouse, at least here she had a full belly and she didn't have to share her bathwater with anyone.

From the next table over, Mary Mittens rolled her eyes and then winked at her. Mary, too, hated these Saturday afternoons with a passion and had once confessed to Emily that she feigned a stomachache to avoid them as often as she dared. Emily envied her sense of style.

Now, a tall, dark-haired gentleman with large side-whiskers approached her table. Invitations to the afternoon teas, though ostensibly issued to both parents, were almost invariably attended only by the mothers. Fathers, particularly distinguished-looking men like this one, were rarely to be seen. "You are new to the school, I believe," he said in a booming voice. "You are too young and pretty to have been here long without me noticing you. I swear you can scarcely be long out of the schoolroom yourself."

"I have been here for over a year now," Emily replied cheerfully. Maybe this afternoon would not be as bad as she had feared if a handsome father or two such as this one would take some notice of her, or even flirt with her. She sneaked a peek at him. His bottom was tight and round, and he was handsomely dressed in a black suit with a gold-striped waistcoat to brighten his outfit. All in all, he was definitely worth a second look. She wouldn't mind a protector like him—if he had a mind to afford her. "I teach mathematics and music to the young ladies."

"Lovely, lovely," he said absentmindedly, staring at her

breasts rather than looking at her face. "I do not believe we have met before, though I swear your face is somewhat familiar, Miss . . . ?"

She stifled a giggle. She wasn't aware that he'd actually raised his eyes high enough to look at her face yet. "Miss Clemens."

"Of course. Miss Clemens." He nodded sagely as if she had imparted to him some priceless pearl of wisdom and continued to stare at her chest. "Finella has spoken often of you, and very kindly, too."

She racked her brains. Finella? Which one was Finella? Ah, that was it—she was the mousy one with badly bitten finger-nails and two long pigtails, one of which she continually had in her mouth to chew on it. Not bad with her bookkeeping, if she would pay more attention to her lessons, but her performance on the pianoforte was thumpingly awful. And, she recalled with a sense of unease, the girl had the unsavory reputation of being a dreadful sneak. "How nice," she said weakly.

"Finella is my oldest daughter. I have two others still at home, too young to go to school." He heaved a gusty sigh that shook his side-whiskers and moved his chair a little closer to her. Though he was now crowding her rather uncomfortably into the corner, she merely smiled as he patted her knee in an avuncular fashion. "Poor motherless mites that they are. All they have is their father, a lonely widower, to take care of them now."

"I am sorry to hear it," she replied, rather enjoying his close-ness and the attention he was bestowing on her. What a change he was from Eric, who scarcely seemed to see her except when he was criticizing her pose, and who certainly never wasted any good manners on her.

Her visitor had hardly looked away from her breasts from the moment he saw her. She moved a little closer toward him, pretending not to notice as her breasts just brushed against the side of his arm. The touch sent a tingle of awareness through her.

"I knew you would be," he said triumphantly, clasping his hand to his chest. "I knew as soon as I saw you that you had a good, kind heart. Someone as pretty as a daisy, as indeed you are, Miss Clemens, could not have a black heart. That would be too cruel a trick for Fate to pull. Indeed it would, now."

Though the effusiveness of his compliments bordered on the embarrassing, Mr. Murdoch was the most interesting parent she had encountered yet. He at least treated her as a pretty woman, not as a servant to be humiliated at every opportunity to cast his own importance into relief. "Indeed. You are very kind to say so."

"My two younger girls are, as I have mentioned, too young to go to this excellent school. It is such a shame that they cannot yet avail themselves of the excellent education I have been able to procure for Finella."

"I am glad you are pleased with Finella's progress," she interjected with a smile. He must be a good father as well as a polite gentleman to care so much for the welfare of his daughter that he would actually condescend to visit Mrs. Herrington's establishment and take tea with the teachers. It was only a shame that more of the fathers were not like him.

He carried on as if she hadn't spoken. "They are in need of a governess to restrain the wildness of their natures. In dire need, I might say. If I could tempt you away, Miss Clemens, I would consider myself a fortunate man indeed."

She raised her eyebrows at his unexpected proposal. "I am very happy where I am, Mr. Murdoch." A hasty glance to either side of her gave no sign that either of the teachers seated next to her had heard him. Though he seemed like a pleasant gentleman, it struck her as slightly odd that he would so openly try to woo her away from her present employer while sitting in Mrs. Herrington's best parlor.

"I would make it worth your while, Miss Clemens." He named a sum of money that made her blink at him goggle-eyed. It was certainly a generous offer. Either that or he must be in dire need of a governess if he was prepared to pay such a sum. If she had not recently found out how lucrative a career posing for naughty postcards could be, she would be severely tempted.

As it was, she was simply not interested in being at any man's beck and call as a governess. She would never be able to continue her modeling, or her search for a patron, if she were living in a gentleman's house as little better than a servant. Nor, if she were to be perfectly honest, did the prospect of teaching two junior Finellas enthuse her in the slightest. Finella must unfortunately take after her late mother, for certainly she had none of her father's good looks or charm.

"It is a very generous offer, and I thank you for it, but I am happy where I am now," she repeated, though it pained her to refuse him.

He seemed so genuine and pleasant a man, and she was sure she would have enjoyed being a part of his household. He might even have taken more than a passing fancy to her and set her up as his mistress. Wouldn't that have been a stroke of luck. . .

"I see, though you have the face of an angel, you are determined to have a heart of stone. I would not have thought it of you. Indeed, I would not."

She smiled slyly at him, his continued scrutiny of her making her slightly hot and bothered. "Angels are not always as innocent as they seem. They, too, have been known to fall." That would give him something to think on when he was alone in his bed at night, and encourage him to venture if he were at all serious about making her a less than respectable offer.

His clear appreciation of her bosom had made her all too aware of her body, of her femininity. She was unused to being the object of desire for any man, except for Eric, and then he only desired her because she was half-naked and deliberately flaunted herself in front of him. Here was a handsome and wealthy man who appreciated her with all her clothes on, dowdy schoolteacher clothes that they were. It was enough to turn any girl's head.

He rose to his feet rather ponderously. Though he was well built and shapely enough, he had none of Eric's grace or lightness of foot. Not that she cared so much for such qualities, to be sure. It was what was inside a man that counted the most. That, and having a well-formed backside. She could not abide a man with a flabby rump.

"I have not finished on this matter," he said, bowing to her in farewell. "Indeed I have not. I am hoping you might think over my offer in my absence?" And he gave her a reassuring smile.

As he gathered his hat and walking stick he paused and looked at her, his forehead creased in a frown. "Are you sure we haven't met before, Miss Clemens? The more I think about it, the more familiar your face seems to be, but I simply cannot place you."

Heavens, surely he had not seen her postcard! "I am quite sure," she replied calmly, though inside her nerves were suddenly making her feel quite jumpy. She took a sip of lukewarm tea to hide her agitation. Was Finella's father one of those who had ogled her in her shift? He seemed such a nice, respectable gentleman. Not the type to be buying naughty postcards at all.

Inside, her thoughts were whirling around so fast she could barely keep up with them. There was little enough except her face to link her to the saucy Emily of the postcards. No one would suspect that a respectable schoolteacher would stoop to modeling, and as a teacher at Mrs. Herrington's School for Fashionable Ladies she came into contact with very few men. Would Mr. Murdoch accidentally discover her identity and offer to make her his mistress? He was clearly attracted to her already. She could do worse than a man as handsome as he was.

Mr. Murdoch was still looking at her curiously. "It will come to me. It will come to me," he muttered as he nodded to her and moved away.

Six

The teacup in Emily's hand was shaking as Mr. Murdoch walked away. She put it down before she spilled the dregs of tea in the bottom, clattering it noisily into the saucer. Was she about to reach her goal of becoming a rich man's mistress sooner than she had thought? She felt almost sick with excitement.

The rest of the afternoon passed in the usual interminably awkward manner until at last the remaining parents were ushered out. As the door shut behind the last one, Mary Mittens came over and plonked herself beside Emily with a huge sigh. "Thank heavens that's over for another two months. I can pretend another stomachache for the next one. I won't have pulled that trick for at least six months by then."

Emily slouched back in her chair and kicked her slippers off. "Today was as dreadful as always. Mrs. Scarpers is a nasty old trout, just like her horrid daughter Isabelle will be when she grows up."

Mary looked sympathetic. "She was on at you about Isabelle's dancing?"

Emily nodded. "I told her I only play the pianoforte for the classes—I don't teach them the steps. That's the domain of the dancing teacher, who, I notice, is wisely absent today. Still she went on at me for a good half an hour." She put her head in her hands. The excitement of the afternoon had made her head pound. "I don't see why Mrs. Herrington insists on putting us through this torment every two months. Next time I swear I shall have a sick headache." The way she was feeling today, it would not be a lie, either.

Mary leaned her elbows on the table. "I saw Mr. Murdoch talking to you very earnestly. Don't tell me, he was bemoaning the fact that he is a widower and has three motherless girls at home to care for?"

"How did you guess?" Emily wriggled her toes in her cotton stockings. It was a pity she could not wear her silk stockings at the school, but the headmistress had very strict ideas on the subject of silk stockings, maintaining they were not suitable attire for schoolteachers, who ought, in her opinion, to be dressed with modesty and decorum at all times. Which, translated, meant no silk anywhere on their persons. "He asked me if I would like to give up my position at the school to become a governess for his two younger daughters. Quite a generous offer he made me, too. Surprisingly generous. It was very kind of him."

Mary made a noise of disgust. "He tries that routine on all

the new teachers here, the ones who are young and pretty anyway. You didn't accept, I hope?"

Emily blinked. Mary wasn't usually so forthright with a bad opinion. "The money was tempting, but I don't believe I would enjoy being a governess. One is too dependent on the goodwill of a single family to be quite comfortable. Besides, girls grow up quickly, and where would I be left once they were old enough to be sent off to school?"

"You'd be left in the same situation as the last teacher from here who thought that becoming governess to his two daughters would be a good way to become the second Mrs. Murdoch." Mary gave a disgusted snort. "Fat lot of good it did poor Meg. In less than a year she was turned out without a reference and with a babe in her belly. Mr. Murdoch wouldn't have a thing to do with her after that. He even had the cheek to claim the babe wasn't his, though everyone knew he'd climbed into her bed the week she arrived in his house, and not gotten out of it since. She'd even come back to the school once boasting of her good fortune in snaring him, and of how he'd promised to marry her come the spring." Her brows knitted together in thought. "The Lord knows what's become of her since. I haven't heard anything from her."

Emily shook her head. Mary must be confusing him with someone else. Mr. Murdoch seemed far too polite and affable to be guilty of such a heinous crime. A man who could deliberately ruin a woman and then callously abandon her with nothing to live on was the worst sort of scoundrel. She could not believe it of him. "He seemed like such a lovely man." She wasn't going to admit to Mary that she found him quite attractive, sensual in an understated way. She was getting a little damp in certain places just thinking about him, about what it would feel like to have those long, manicured fingers caressing her body. If Mary's story had any truth in it at all, Meg probably seduced him into her bed and then kicked up a fuss when he refused to marry her.

"I'm telling you, he can be persistent though. He was after me for weeks to be his governess, calling every second day to talk with me. He even got the headmistress to take his side— Lord knows how after what happened to Meg. I had to tell her plain that I wasn't looking to become a whore and that if he pestered me any more, I would find myself another situation. Then she backed off and he left me alone shortly after that."

Mary's story had the ring of jealousy about it, Emily decided. She must be upset that Emily had received the generous offer and not her. She hadn't meant to crow about it, but poor Mary must be feeling a little bitter. She bit her tongue and decided not to say another word about it. Mary was her very best friend at the school and she did not want some ill-founded jealous feelings to come between them.

She would secretly look forward to seeing Mr. Murdoch again. If he was as wealthy as he looked, he was just the sort of protector she would like to start out with.

Still, Mary's story would make her cautious. Her body was not to be won with a few empty promises. She would not so much as allow Mr. Murdoch to kiss her before she was in possession of a pleasant town house and a decent annuity to go along with it.

Eric collapsed into bed on Saturday evening, utterly exhausted. He'd worked every minute of the day and half into the night for the past week and he was so tired he could not think straight any more. He'd barely taken the time to eat, and had even skimped on shaving so that he could develop another few dozen postcards. By Saturday afternoon, he'd printed and delivered the first thousand. Though the bookseller was disappointed he had not finished them all, she did not cancel the rest of the order as he had feared she might, but had promised she would take the rest as soon as he could get them to her.

He could not keep this pace up, not even for the princely sum of sixty pounds a week. Not even for the delicious prospect of seeing Emily in her undergarments every Sunday afternoon. It was killing him.

Somehow or other he'd find the plates and the printing press he needed next week, whatever Emily thought about the idea. She was a smart little thing, for all that she was naturally more cautious than he was. He was sure he could bring her around eventually. But for now all he could do was sleep the clock around and hope that when he woke he felt a little more human than he did now.

It was with an overwhelming sense of relief that Emily escaped the confines of the school and made the long walk to Mr. Twyford's studio the following day. When she was with him, she had nothing to fear and nothing to hide.

She pushed open the door to be greeted by the sight of a red-eyed, unshaven apparition slumped in a chair, looking more dead than alive. He looked up dully as she entered and waved her in. "Forgive me. I really can't summon the energy to move just yet."

"Eric," she cried, forgetting formality as she hurried to his side. "Whatever is the matter with you?"

"I've been working," he said, with a sickly attempt at a grin. "Printing up the fifteen hundred postcards of you I sold last week."

Fifteen hundred? And he'd tried to develop them all himself, by hand? No wonder he looked positively ill with exhaustion. "You can't keep this up," she scolded, hiding her anxiety with a show of crossness. "You'll kill yourself."

"I only just woke up," he confessed. "Was deuced tired last night. Haven't even shaved." He dug into his pocket and tossed her a couple of shillings. "Do me a favor, will you, and go buy me breakfast. I can't seem to move and I haven't eaten since yesterday. Or was it the day before?" Just then his stomach gave an extra loud growl as if to back up his words.

Emily didn't stop to argue. She grabbed the money and fled in search of food.

Half an hour later, with two meat pies, a buttered currant bun and three cups of coffee inside him, he looked much better. He'd even managed to rise out of the chair and was striding around the room, his hands clasped behind his back. "I need a printing press, Em, to do the printing," he said, stopping his pacing and sticking out his bottom lip as if he expected her to quibble over the expense. "I can't do this by myself. It's not sensible even to try. Not fifteen hundred postcards in a single week. It's too much work for one person. It would be too much even if there were two of me."

It was clear he could not keep up this schedule. Though he was at least back on his feet and his stomach had stopped growling with hunger, he still looked like death warmed up. If his mother could see him now, she would surely tuck him back under his blankets and feed him hot possets until he got some color back into his cheeks. "What kind of a press is it that we need? And how much would it cost?"

He named a sum that made her suck in a deep breath. "Ouch." It was more money than she saw in a whole year as a teacher, and would eat away all the profits of their fledgling business for more weeks that she felt comfortable with.

"It would be worth every penny. Without it, the most I can hope to produce by myself is six or seven hundred cards a week. But with such technology at my fingertips, I could print so many thousands. Such a machine would make us rich."

She steepled her hands together. "How does it work?"

"First I would print the photographs on a glass transparency, a dozen at a time for the postcard-sized ones. Then I expose a carbon print under the glass and transfer it to a copper plate. The gelatin on the print sticks to the plate. A quick wash with ferric chloride, which eats away the copper where it doesn't have gelatin covering it, and voila, I have a completely accurate engraved plate of your likeness, ready for printing in the printing press."

Emily's head was spinning as she tried to follow his hurried explanation. What was it with men and their newfangled toys? They were always wanting something newer and shinier to play with, something bigger and better to call their own. Still, in this case he might just be right.

She did a few hasty calculations in her head. If the orders stayed steady at a modest thousand postcards a week, and that was a big if, then the machine would pay for itself in a couple of months. After that, the profits for them both would be significant. Almost enough for her to not need a patron at all.

Even a month was a long time, though, in the game of novelties. Anything could happen in that time. Postcards might suddenly go out of fashion. Or men might simply tire of seeing her and want a fresh face and a new body to gawk at.

Even so, with the press printing out postcards faster than she could imagine, she would surely find a suitable protector before she was no longer a novelty.

There really was no choice in the matter. Not for her. "So, where do we buy one?" she asked brightly.

"There is a man I know of in Cheapside," he said at once. "A photographer. Landscapes, mostly. Mountains and rivers and all that stuff. Not really to my taste, but the public laps it up eagerly enough. He'll know."

They had better buy the printing press before her courage failed her and she reneged on her hasty decision. "We'll visit him this afternoon."

"But the photographs," he protested, as he reached for his coat. Never had she seen a man so torn between two courses of action. "We need to take more photographs while the light holds or I shall have nothing new to offer this week."

"There's no point in having more photographs if there is no way to make enough copies for sale," she said ruthlessly. "Now, go and wash and shave so you look at least halfway respectable. No manufacturer of machinery will talk to you when you look like a raggle-tailed gypsy."

In less time than she would have thought possible he was in the studio again, looking remarkably presentable in a clean shirt and jacket. Quite deliciously edible, in fact. As tasty a man as she could ever hope to find in the whole city of London.

She took his arm, doing her best to ignore the frisson of pleasure that shot through her entire body at his touch. After she had growled at him for adjusting her chemise on the very first day she had modeled for him, he had scrupulously avoided touching her ever since. Even when she was fully clothed he did not so much as brush against her in the passageway. She was beginning to find his politeness irritating.

Mr. Murdoch, for all that he was virtually a stranger to her, had been a deal more forward in his behavior, though he had not offered her anything tangible as yet. What was wrong with Eric that he possessed such self-control around her? More to the point, what was wrong with her? Try as she might, she could not get him to make any serious advances toward her. How would she hook a rich patron when she could not even make a poor photographer dance to her tune?

She was disappointed she would not have the opportunity to model her new corset for him today. His reaction to it alone would surely be worth the purchase price.

Still, there was always next Sunday, and then the Sunday after that, to taunt him with her nearly naked body and practice making a man fall head over heels in love with her. She would tease a kiss out of him sooner or later. A kiss, and maybe more.

Not today, though, she thought with a sigh. This afternoon must be dedicated instead to business.

She held his arm tightly to her, letting the side of her breast brush against his elbow as if by accident, just as she had with Mr. Murdoch. The jolt of pleasure that shot through her as her nipple grazed his elbow was enough to make her suck in her breath sharply and her heart pound like a drum beat in her chest. She wanted so much more.

Wanting more from Eric was a mistake, she told herself firmly. She could not waste herself on a man who could not afford her.

Nonetheless, even looking at printing machines would be a positive pleasure with Eric at her side. "Let's go shopping."

Mr. Murdoch came to visit Emily the following week. Informed by the headmistress only that there was a visitor for her in the parlor, she hurried downstairs, her heart full of joy, expecting one of her sisters to have stopped by. It was probably Caroline come up to town on one of her rare visits from her small estate in Hertfordshire to accompany her husband on one of his business affairs.

The worst thing about being so poor and having to go out teaching was not being able to live with her family. How desperately she missed her sisters, and how happy she was at the prospect of seeing one of them again! For no one else would possibly be paying her a visit—she had completely cut all ties to the life she had once lived, before her father had lost his money and they had been sent to the workhouse. No one but her sisters and her brother even knew where she was, and Teddy was still too young to travel alone to see her.

To her surprise, Mr. Murdoch, in a smart gray suit with a striped orange waistcoat, was sitting on the parlor settee. "Ah, Miss Clemens," he said expansively as she entered. "My two daughters still need a governess, you see. As I promised, I have not given up on you but I have come to ask you to reconsider your decision." He patted the seat next to him. "Come, sit yourself down next to me and we can have a pleasant chat about your new duties."

She sat down next to him as he suggested. "Mr. Murdoch. I was not expecting you." Her disappointment in not seeing Caroline was so acute she could barely summon a smile for him, even though he was just as attractive as ever, and had paid her a very great compliment in coming to visit her. Maybe he had thought more on the broad hint she had given him before they last parted.

"Surprise is a military man's greatest ally, as the great General Wellington always used to say." He gave a smile as if she had paid him a compliment and preened his moustache between his thumb and forefinger. "And make no mistake about it, I am fighting hard to get you to accept a position in my household."

There was only one position she was interested in accepting, and her services would not come cheap. Her eyes were drawn to his moustache and to the fullness of his lips beneath it. What would it feel like to have that mouth on hers, to feel his whiskers tickling her cheek? Would they be rough and scratchy, or would they be soft to the touch? She would quite like to reach out to feel them. "I presume you have come for an update on Finella's progress," she said coyly. "I was going to suggest that perhaps the pianoforte is not her strength and that she take up the harp instead. The harp is a delightful instrument and it has the advantage of being slightly unusual and therefore greatly welcomed at any family gathering or assembly where music is called for. We have a very fine harp tutor among the staff who I am sure will be able to instruct your daughter admirably." She gave him an inviting smile. "If you let me fetch Finella for you, we can discuss her schooling all together."

He was looking intently at her as she babbled away about his daughter. "I am sure we have met before but I have not yet placed you, you know. Depend on it, I will remember sooner or later. I never forget a face."

At his words, she could feel her heartbeat in her throat. Was he about to recognize her at last? Would he offer to make her his mistress now? Suddenly, she did not feel quite ready to receive his offer. "If you will excuse me, I will fetch Finella right away."

"No, no, don't bother," he said, with a winning smile. "I did not come here to talk to you about the girl. I came to talk to you."

"I cannot imagine what you have to say to me, Mr. Murdoch," she said, coyly. "I will have to beg you to excuse me." But still she remained seated, so close to him that their knees were nearly touching.

"Now, now, there's no need to be so shy," he teased. "I mean you no harm. I came to repeat my earlier offer to take you on as a governess to my younger two daughters." He took hold of her hand and pressed it in his own.

Despite her disappointment, she felt a shiver of awareness at his touch. So few men saw past her dowdy clothes and bothered to pay her compliments, let alone take minor liberties with her person. After Eric's annoying reticence even when she paraded in front of him scarcely clothed, she found Mr. Murdoch's forwardness both thrilling and exciting.

Still, she had no intention of becoming a governess, and still less did she intend to become his mistress under the guise of governess. She wanted the freedom to live how she liked, not to hide behind a veneer of respectability, pretending to live within the rules she flouted.

"Maybe you did not think I was serious, Miss Clemens, but I assure you I am. Your headmistress, I am sure, will vouch for my respectability. Not only do my young daughters need a guiding hand, but I am a lonely widower and the sight of your pretty face around the tea table at night would brighten my life no end. Who knows but what you might wheedle a lonely widower into making you a permanent fixture."

She laughed aloud at his last sly suggestion. "Beware of what you offer to poor, young girls. One of us, more foolish than her sisters, may one day think you are in earnest."

"But I am in earnest, Miss Clemens, indeed I am." His eyes under his heavy brows were dark with suppressed emotion. "I can think of nothing more felicitous than reestablishing the family life that I so sorely miss."

Their conversation was not going the way she wanted it to—not at all. If he was going to offer her nothing but a governess's salary and the empty hope of becoming his wife, she was wasting her time with him. "Thank you, but as I said last time you made me the same offer, I am happy here. I do not intend to leave to become a governess." She put a subtle emphasis on the last word. "Now if you do not want to discuss Finella, I must beg you to excuse me." She rose from the sofa with a smile that took all of the sting out of her words, and he immediately followed suit. "Good day, sir."

He raised her hand to his lips with a mournful look. "Goodbye, Miss Clemens."

As soon as he was gone, she marched herself straight upstairs and into the headmistress's private parlor, a cozy room stuffed to the brim with white crocheted antimacassars, framed watercolors, china figurines, and shell-work ornaments. Mrs. Herrington was seated at a small card table shuffling a deck of cards. At Emily's entrance, she brushed them hurriedly out of sight and took up her embroidery frame with shaking fingers.

Emily shot her a look of amusement. Surely playing cards was a harmless enough pastime that it did not need to be hidden out of sight. "If you please, Mrs. Herrington, I would prefer not to receive any further visits from Mr. Murdoch for the time being."

"Mr. Murdoch is a very respectable gentleman," the head-mistress protested, laying aside her pretense at sewing. "And his daughter Finella is a very proper young lady and one of your pupils. I saw nothing amiss in his desire to speak to you this afternoon."

"He was perfectly polite," Emily said hastily, not wishing to give Mrs. Herrington the erroneous impression that he had offended her in any way, or made any untoward advances toward her, "but he is determined to have me as his governess and I am equally determined not to leave here. In such a situation, I find his visits to be rather . . . awkward."

"You will not be leaving us in the near future then?" Mrs. Herrington looked down at her through her pince-nez. "I own I did wonder whether you would be staying with us for very long when I saw him pay such particular attention to you the other day. Though I would be very sorry to lose you, I must say. You can coax even the most determinedly uninterested young lady through her sums."

"You will not be losing me in the near future. Not for an offer such as Mr. Murdoch made to me, at any rate. I do not harbor any desire to become a governess."

That could well be the last she saw of Mr. Murdoch, she thought rather sadly as she left Mrs. Herrington's claustrophobic rooms and climbed the stairs to her own more modest retreat. Forbidding him the house would, she hoped, give him the message that she would not drop into his lap like a ripe plum. If he truly wanted her, he would have to make her a good offer. And if he was not inclined to be generous, well, there were plenty more where he came from. She was not about to sell herself cheaply to the first man who looked at her twice.

As for his hint that he would marry her? She shook her head. Falling for empty promises made by fine gentlemen was such a trite way for a poor young woman to ruin her prospects in life. She was smarter than that. She would barter her respectability on her own terms, in her own time, and for a decent price.

Seven

In the end, several weeks passed before Emily had to model for Eric Twyford again. Once a supplier for the printing press had been located, they needed to find the funds to purchase it. With all the ready money they had earned as a deposit on the postcards, and with Emily schooling Eric behind the scenes as to what to say to bankers to raise their confidence in his business, a bank loan was eventually procured for the remainder. Thanks to Eric's fast talking, he even managed to obtain the funds at a not-too-ruinous rate of interest.

Now that they had the money, the press had to be ordered, inspected, and finally delivered to the studio.

Because Eric's rooms were so small and crowded, there was no space for a working press, not even the small one they had purchased, so they were forced to take over the lease of the vacant shop next door. The new shop had been empty for some months and needed a thorough cleaning before Eric would allow the press to be delivered there. Though he had done most of the work during the week, Emily had spent an entire Sunday afternoon washing windows and wiping window frames until the place was spotless.

Specks of dust in the ink, he told her, as he wielded a mop and bucket with vigor next to her, were a printer's worst nightmare and would ruin a photograph sooner than anything else.

While he tinkered with the press, she took advantage of the additional space they had leased to set up an office area where his files could be kept in proper order. Part of the new shop front she established as a display area, where some of his previous work—some portraits and the odd landscape—was displayed on easels and hung around the walls. She even sorted his developing chemicals and stored them in a separate cupboard well away from the pantry, so he would not accidentally put them in his tea. The only place she did not make her mark was in his bedroom—the door to that room remained closed. She resisted the temptation to even so much as peek inside.

Through it all, she kept a close eye on the books, making sure that Eric did not lose sight of the day-to-day realities in pursuit of his dreams. His vision for the future was so all-encompassing that he found it difficult to focus on such mundane matters as whether or not he had paid his rent for the month, or whether he had bought a sufficient quantity of paper at a good price. He needed someone to help him over all the obstacles in the path that, with his eyes firmly fixed on the horizon, he did not see until he had tripped over them. With her mathematical mind and her experience helping out her father with his books, she was just the person he needed to take care of the details and help make the venture a success.

Though she had not so much as removed her gown for a month, she had certainly earned her pound a week keeping Eric on the straight and narrow when it came to their finances. Incomings and outgoings, interest rates and payment plans—she recorded everything, down to the last farthing, in meticulous detail. Nothing missed her eagle eye. Nobody would ever have cause to complain about her record-keeping—she was determined on that.

Finally, late one Sunday afternoon, just as she was finishing updating the books, Eric was at last satisfied that the press was set up and calibrated correctly. He showed her through the process, pride oozing out of every pore in his body.

It certainly was an improvement on the manual process that Eric had previously used. Instead of having to develop every postcard by hand, dipping the paper in the chemical baths until the picture appeared and then washing it and hanging it up to dry, he could now print a dozen cards at a time. Once the photos were engraved onto the copper plate with the acid— and they were small enough to fit twelve on a single plate—all he needed to do was cover the plate evenly with ink and pass it through the press. With every pass, another dozen photographs were printed and ready to be cut to size.

As Emily watched in awe, he made a dozen prints in just a couple of minutes. They were as ready as they ever would be to begin their mass production of postcards.

She walked back to the school late that evening, knowing that her grace period was over. What they needed now was some more photographs to turn into postcards. It was time for her to put down the cleaning rags and account books and take off her gown once again.

Eric, as usual, was brusque and to the point. "Time to take your gown off again, Em, my girl," he said to her as soon as she walked in the door of his studio the very next Sunday afternoon. "Mrs. Angus at the book shop has run out of patience and is growling at me daily for new stock. It's gotten so that I'm afraid to open the door for fear it's another urchin she's paid a penny to deliver a new growl. Besides, the first of the three installments on the printing press is due in less than a month. We need some more postcards to sell if we are ever to climb out of debt. Lots of new postcards."

Emily knew he was right; she had known all week that it was coming to this, but that knowledge didn't bolster her courage any. This was the moment for which she had been preparing herself ever since her trip to the corsetiere some weeks ago—the moment where she would display more of her body than any man should rightly see. And she was planning to display herself to any scoundrel with sixpence to spend. It was hardly any wonder that his casual words sent a trickle of icy fear down her spine.

The delay caused by the purchase of the printing press had only made her nerves worse. All the bravery she had summoned up at the time she had purchased her new garments had by now evaporated into nothing. The thought of wearing so little made her prickle uncomfortably.

She took a deep breath as she went behind the screen she had set up for herself to make a place where she could dress and undress in private, away from Eric's eyes. Did she really want to flaunt herself nearly naked to Eric, and to half the men in England besides? She could put on the undergarments she had worn last time and Eric would not be any the wiser.

There was nothing to say that she had to wear the new corset, the one that flattened her stomach and lifted her exposed breasts, even though she had bought it in a moment of foolish vanity. She could write it off as an expensive mistake and then forget about it.

It was tucked away in her reticule. She had not dared to wear it under her gown for fear someone at the school would catch her putting it on and wonder about her interesting taste in undergarments. It was hardly the sort of thing that a schoolteacher would wear under her gown. Indeed, it was hardly the sort of thing that a teacher in a respectable girls' school ought even to own. Mrs. Herrington would probably ask her to resign on the mere suspicion that she had purchased such a garment.

She brought it out and dangled it from one finger, looking at it with serious consideration. The sight of it helped to revive her courage. It really was very pretty. Most men would like her in it, she was sure. She would try it on and decide from there whether she wanted to wear it today or not.

Safely behind the screen, she slipped out of her gown, then

took off her bonnet and shook her hair free. Next she divested herself of all her undergarments but her frilly pantalettes. The silk stockings slid over her legs, giving her the same rush of sensual pleasure as they always did. And then the corset.

It showed as much as it covered. More, in fact. Her breasts were bared down to her rib cage.

She squinted at herself in the tiny square of mirror behind the screen. Would Eric think she looked sexy like this? Would it excite and entice him beyond his ability to bear it, like she wanted it to? Would he give her the kiss that she was longing to experience? Or would he be put off by the baring of so much flesh?

There was only one way to find out. If she was going to expose herself, she may as well do it with flair. Slipping out from behind the screen, her hands on her hips, she swept into the studio.

The look of incredulity on Eric's face was worth every ounce of bravery it had taken to display her breasts so openly. "What in God's name are you wearing, Em?" he sputtered as he caught sight of her naked breasts. He took a step backward, tripped over a cushion that had been left lying on the floor, and went sprawling. His elbow gave a nasty crack as it hit the floor and he swore. "Or rather, what are you not wearing?" he asked from his position on the floor, as he rubbed his elbow ruefully.

"You did say that the less there was of my underwear the better," she said, sauntering over to the bench where she usually posed, her firm breasts bobbing slightly as she walked. Her heart was in her throat but she forced herself to sound casual and unconcerned, as if she was so used to being semi-naked that she didn't care what he thought about her. "I took you at your word."

"But . . . but . . ." His voice tailed off into nothing as he simply lay on the floor and stared at her, following her every move with hungry eyes.

She lounged on the bench and arranged herself into a pose for the camera. "What are you waiting for?" she asked, when he made no move to stand up again or to reach for his equipment. "Don't you like it?"

He got to his knees, picked up the cushion that had tripped him and threw it hard into one corner. "Em, what are you trying to do to me?" His voice came out oddly strangled and he twitched his shoulders as if suffering from a sudden twinge.

Glancing down at his trousers, she saw the reason for his discomfort. His cock was a thick rod standing at attention in his trousers. Not even the baggy cut of his pants could hide his state. Clearly he liked her new corset more than was appropriate. Certainly more than was quite seemly.

The sight of his arousal sent the blood rushing to her head, and, judging by the way she was tingling in unmentionable places, to some other parts lower down as well. Though she knew only too well that he was forbidden fruit, his excitement was arousing her just as surely as her naked breasts were doing the same to him.

She licked her lips as she looked at him. How she wished she could have a turn behind the camera and make him pose for her without his clothes on. First of all she would have him remove his shirt, and capture the lines of his back and the brawny muscles of his arm. She'd have him pose as a dockworker on the Thames—they were always standing around with their trousers rolled halfway up their calves and in their shirtsleeves, in a pose that no respectable man would ever imitate.

She'd do one better than that and have him pose for her without his shirt on at all. A wet trickle started to drip from her private parts down her thigh, where it was soaked up by her pantalettes. Thank heavens her pantalettes hid the evidence of her excitement better than a man's trousers ever could hide his. She only hoped she wasn't leaving a telltale damp patch on them.

After a hasty check revealed no awkward patch of wetness, she fell happily back into her daydream. Once she had removed his shirt, she would have him take off his trousers and stand there in his smalls so she could photograph his muscular thighs. That would make all the ladies swoon at the sight.

She wouldn't let him keep his smalls on for very long. Not long at all. After teasing him into taking them off, she'd photograph his buttocks, those hard, taut buttocks that made her mouth water every time he bent down over his camera equipment. How she would like to see them uncovered. Then, when she had looked her fill at his rear end, she would have him turn around to face her and at last she would see that hard ridge of his in all its naked glory.

The thought made her private parts feel damper than ever. She clamped her legs together to stop her juices from running down her leg, but all it did was press her swollen parts tightly together and make her even hotter and wetter.

She looked at the swelling in his trousers again, licking her lips as she thought of reaching out and touching him there, taking him into her hands and stroking him, making him as wild for her as any man could be. Damn it, she wanted him to make love to her.

He caught the line of her gaze and his face turned redder than his hair. "God, Em, I can't help it. You're just making it worse, staring at me like that."

Still she couldn't drag her eyes away until with a strangled curse he turned his back on her and strode into his rooms.

Three minutes later he was back again, the bulge in his pants noticeably reduced and a sheepish expression on his face. He scuttled behind his camera. "I'll be able to keep my mind on my work now," he muttered. "And take some damned photographs without feeling as if I were about to spontaneously combust."

She glared at him, feeling as if he had cheated her on purpose. All her fantasies of him coming back into the studio without his clothes on had turned to naught. He was still fully dressed and, judging by the more relaxed state of his trousers, he had clearly satisfied himself without needing her help. Without even letting her watch him. She, however, was still as hot and bothered as ever.

She wanted to touch herself in front of him to show him what he was missing out on, but she didn't dare. Not where she longed most of all to be touched. She couldn't bring herself to behave so wantonly.

Her nipples were tight and hard with excitement. She brushed the palm of her hand over them, making the sensitive buds tingle. There was nothing so very wanton about touching her own breasts.

Though she was not deliberately posing for the camera, she heard the shutter click. "You're going to have every man in London messing his pants at these postcards if you keep doing that," Eric said crudely.

She turned her haughty gaze toward him. "Isn't that exactly what we want them to do?" She took her breasts in her hands and leaned over as if she were offering them to the unseen viewer. "Mess their pants at sixpence a time?"

The shutter clicked again. "You make it sound so sordid," he complained. "We are creating art here, you and I. Sensual, even erotic, art, but art nonetheless. Worthy to be hung in any gallery in the land."

She spread her fingers so that her nipples peeked out from behind her hands. "Men get excited enough to tent their pants over art?" she asked sniffily, still not over her temper with him. What she was doing could hardly be classed as art. She was not trying to look interesting or artistic. Her goal was much more crass. She was trying to make Eric stand to attention in his trousers again. If she had to be hot and bothered all afternoon, then damn it, so did he. She was supposed to be the temptress here—not the other way around.

"Over art like this they will," he replied, waiting until she had finished speaking and taking another exposure of her pout.

She removed her hands from her breasts and ran them down her sides to her hips. No, that didn't feel quite right. She brought her hands in front of her to cover her mound and moved her arms inward to create more of a cleavage.

"Hold it there. And look shy, as if you were surprised while you were dressing."

She suppressed the flicker of irritation that flared inside her at the bossy tone of his voice, and looked up at him as shyly as if she were a girl of fifteen. However much she hated to be told what to do, irritation wouldn't sell photographs.

Eric clicked the shutter. "That photo," he said with some satisfaction, "will have every man in England messing his pants."

The afternoon's shoot seemed to take forever. Eric shot off his first twelve exposures and then, before she could complain that she was cold and tired and just wanted to go home again and soak in a warm bath, he started to reload his camera with another twelve glass plates. "We're running behind," he said, as he caught sight of the obstinate cast to her face. "Mrs. Angus wants as many new shots as I can give her, and I want to test out the printing press with a decent large run."

"Haven't you taken enough for one afternoon?" She gave a deliberately ungainly stretch. "I have certainly had enough of posing."

"It's still bright outside. We can shoot another twelve exposures before the shadows get too long. Now, put your hands on your hips and give me a saucy look. A look that you might give someone who had just kissed you without your permission, but someone you wanted to kiss you, so you're not seriously angry with him. More like daring him to brave your displeasure and kiss you again."

That was it. She'd had enough of Eric's disregard for her feelings. No man could be that blind. He had to know how excited she was, and how much she wanted him to kiss her. He was tormenting her on purpose. "Maybe *you* can go on all afternoon, but *I* don't want to," she said rudely. "I'm getting dressed now."

He gave an irritable "humph." "What do I pay you a pound a week for but to sit there all afternoon while I take photographs of you? I haven't been able to shoot a single photograph for weeks, and you are carping on about having to sit a little longer than usual for me today? Don't be so ridiculous. Sit back down on the bench and give me a pose."

"Eric Twyford, go to hell," she enunciated clearly. With her hands on her hips as he had demanded of her, she stalked out of the studio and back behind the screen to get dressed.

Stupid corset. It hadn't worked at all the way she had wanted it to. With a grunt of annoyance she unhooked it and threw it on the floor. Buying it had been a big mistake. She would never pose in it again.

Just then, Eric's outraged face appeared from behind the screen. "You can't just walk out on me like that." His voice vibrated with controlled fury. "Get back into the studio so I can finish the session or I will never take another photograph of you again. You will be dismissed."

His threats crystallized her fury. "You forget that I have a quarter-share in this venture," she spat at him. "Without me you have nothing but an expensive machine to reproduce photographs that do not require printing en masse. And I have all your accounts." She gave an evil smile. "Just think of the havoc I could wreak on this business if I chose to. I can't be dismissed as easily as you think."

His face had turned as red as his hair. "Just try me."

"Fine. I will. Now get out of my way so I can get dressed."

"Emily, I'm warning you. I will not brook such insolence."

"*You* will not brook such insolence?" she sputtered. Still dressed in nothing but her pantalettes, she marched out from behind the screen and stood right in front of him, so close that her nipples grazed his chest. "And what about me? Do I have to take orders from you, say 'yes, master' and 'no, master' like an obedient slave? Do I have to suffer your teasing without saying a word? Stand there in my underwear like I am made of stone until my arms ache and not have so much as a cup of tea offered to me to make it more bearable? You will not dismiss me. I have had enough of your ill temper and your unreasonableness. I will leave and not come back."

He took hold of her arms, firmly but not roughly, so she could not move away. "Am I that bad to work for?" His voice had gentled.

His hands were warm on her skin, and the rough linen of his shirt was abrading her already oversensitive nipples until she wanted to scream with frustration. She wanted to rub herself all over him like a cat in heat. "You are worse," she muttered. "I know I should not let it affect me, but I cannot help it. You drive me wild."

"*I* drive *you* wild?" he sputtered in his turn. "Then we are more even than I had thought. Christ, Em, you are the one who is driving me wild. Every day I see you, it takes every ounce of my willpower to not reach out and touch you. And then you come into my studio dressed in less than nothing and expect me to be oblivious?" He drew her in close to him so that her breasts were pressed tightly against his chest and his groin thrust hard into her stomach. He was hard again, delightfully, deliciously hard. "Feel what you do to me, Em. Feel how wild you drive me, every single day."

She writhed against him, standing on tiptoes so she could feel the strength of his hardness between her thighs. She could not help it. She was beyond caring what he thought of her, so long as he took away the insistent ache that had been building up in her body for weeks.

His hard thigh pressed in between her legs, raising her to a fever of desire. She rubbed herself against him, the wool of his trousers tantalizing her until she thought she would melt with agonizing pleasure. Her pantalettes, open between her legs, parted to allow his trousers to touch her directly. She knew she would be leaving a wet patch on him, but she did not care.

She was past caring. His closeness, his maleness, had driven her past the point where she could care about anything but the insistent demands of her body.

"Do you want me to touch you, Em?" His voice was a whisper of sound in her ear. "Because if you do not, you had better move away from me. Now. Before it is too late."

In reply, she only pressed herself more closely against him, slipping her hands inside his shirt so she could feel his skin. His stomach was flat and hard, its muscles taut against her questing fingers. She ran her hands over his stomach and then up over his chest, wanting to feel all of him.

Her wordless invitation worked better than she had expected. With a muffled groan, he gathered her into his arms, his hands on her bottom, pressing her closer to him. "What are you doing to me, Em?"

She drew back slightly, her fingers busy at his buttons. "Taking off your shirt so I can feel your skin next to mine." Something she should have done long ago.

The buttons once undone, he shrugged his shirt off his shoulders and let it fall to the floor. "Kiss me, Emily."

She tilted her head back and touched her lips to his. After weeks of dreaming about what his mouth would feel like on her own, he was finally going to kiss her.

There was no gentleness in his kiss. Only a raw desire that matched her own, a desire that inflamed her beyond reason, beyond conscious thought. Standing in his arms, she felt as though her insides had been turned into a pillar of flame and she was burning up, being utterly consumed by the fire she had become.

His hands moved to her breasts, stroking them with a feather-light touch that made her long for more. She was past wanting gentleness—fiery need was driving her now.

She arched her back, pushing her breasts into his hands. For weeks she had longed for his touch on her and now that it was finally happening she couldn't get enough of it. She wanted more, so much more.

Eric could hardly believe that Emily Clemens, aloof, business-like Emily, was panting in his arms, begging for his kisses as if she were half-starved. His every fantasy had come to life, and in such glorious color that they made a mockery of the poverty of his dreams. Her mouth on his tasted as sweet as honey. Though he tried not to frighten her with his ardor, he could not hold back. He kissed her with all the pent-up passion in his body, stroking her mouth with his tongue, pressing her lips hard with his own, as she moaned with desire and kissed him back.

That was the real miracle—that she was kissing him back, that she seemed to want him. Him, plain, red-haired Eric Twyford from the streets of Philadelphia. Tentatively he reached out to stroke the swell of her naked breasts, still fearful that she would come to her senses and swat him away as if he was some pesky fly. Glorious creatures such as Emily didn't usually give people like him so much as the time of day, but turned their noses up at him and looked the other way as they walked by. He was half convinced that he was in the grip of a dream and that at any moment he would wake up and find himself alone in his bed.

Half-naked and pliant in his arms, she did not seem to be bothered by any of the misgivings that were plaguing him. Neither did she show any sign of wanting to get away from his embrace. Instead she nuzzled closer to him, arching her back to press her breasts more fully into his hands.

Her breasts were full and round, her nipples tight buds of desire. Touching them was almost enough to make him come in his pants. Just seeing them earlier today, when Emily had sauntered into his studio wearing only her pantalettes and a tiny excuse for a corset, had been too much for his self-control. Fearful of embarrassing himself with an involuntary emission, he'd had to excuse himself and hastily remedy his untimely erection out in the back. Now, for the second time this afternoon, he felt himself embarrassingly close to an orgasm.

This time, however, when it happened, he would make sure to bring Emily with him.

Judging by the flush on her chest and her panting breaths, she was not very far away.

Eight

With one hand Eric stroked Emily's back until he was cupping her ass. Tight and round, it was the nicest ass he had touched in a long while. A very long while.

Her pantalettes were conveniently untied at the top, leaving room for his hand to enter. He slid his hand inside them, reaching down to cup her mound, covered in tight, springy curls. With one finger he reached down lower to stroke her clit and the entrance to her cunt. She was wet down there, so wet that her juices were already dribbling down her thigh. His last reservations left him utterly. Her lust for him was real, all right— no woman would be as wet as that if she were only faking.

He didn't think he could get any harder, but he was wrong. Even though he'd taken care of himself just a few hours ago, at the feel and the musky scent of her excitement he was as hard as a rock again. She was wet and would open to him like a flower reaching for the sun. He wanted to push her against the wall and thrust into her without ceremony, hard and fast, pumping into her body until he came.

That would be no way to treat a well-bred young virgin, though, whatever his cock was demanding. He needed to woo her, to introduce her gently to the pleasures of lovemaking so that she came back for more. Ramming her like a horny bull would only put her off.

She made a noise of utter pleasure and ground herself against the palm of his hand as he cupped her. Clearly she wanted more, and he was just the man to give it to her.

With his free hand, he guided her hand to the front of his trousers and ran it up and down the length of his swollen cock. Before he made her come, he wanted to feel her hands on him, stroking him and caressing him as a woman caressed her lover.

She caught on quickly, unbuttoning his trousers and pushing them down over his hips. Free of the confines of his trousers at last, his cock sprang out, ready and eager for action.

She broke off their kiss and looked down at him, her eyes wide with alarm. "Oh my goodness," she stammered.

He stopped her mouth with another kiss and guided her hand to his cock, showing her how to hold him, how to stroke him to give him pleasure.

A rapid learner, within seconds she had brought him to the brink of another orgasm. Just as he thought he wouldn't be able to hold on for another second, he pulled away from her.

"What did I do wrong?" she whispered, her body suddenly tense.

"Nothing at all, Em," he reassured her, every nerve in his body screaming out for the release he had just denied himself. "You did everything so right that I had to stop you or this will all be over a little too soon."

He could feel her body relax at his reassurance. "I thought I had hurt you," she confessed.

"You could never hurt me." It was no more than the truth. He could be flayed alive for her sake, and call it a pleasure.

His self-control once more in place, his stroking of her pussy grew more adventurous. With a gentle push, he inserted the tip of one finger into her tightness and then withdrew it again, slick with her moisture.

She shivered in his arms. "Put your finger inside me again," she whispered into his neck, so softly he could barely hear her. "It felt so good I thought I was going to heaven."

That was not the sort of invitation any man could refuse. Gently he put his finger inside her, slowly stretching the walls of her virgin cunt to accommodate him. Slowly he withdrew it again, and this time put two fingers inside her.

She was tight, too tight to take a man comfortably just yet, but his fingers were a nice, snug fit.

Slowly he thrust them in and out, easing her into the rhythm that he longed to pump into her with his cock.

She wanted none of his slowness and gentleness. Impaling herself on his fingers, she thrust herself up and down on them, hard and fast. Over and over she cried his name, begging him for the release that she needed.

Then her breath caught in her throat and he felt the tremors as her pussy convulsed around him. Wave after wave spread through her body, as she stood there, immobilized in the throes of pleasure.

With his free hand he reached down and pumped his cock, needing only a few strokes to bring himself to the same point of oblivion. He felt the cum rising to the tip of his member, and then, with one last stroke, it erupted in a fountain splattering over Emily's naked breasts.

As her tremors were shuddering to a halt, he wrung the last drops of pleasure from his body.

Emily looked up at his face, her eyes wide. "What did you just do to me?" she murmured in a sultry voice. "I feel as though I have just learned how to soar with the birds."

He nuzzled into her neck. She really was a delight. Far too good for the likes of him—not that he was complaining, mind you. If she chose to slum it with him, who was he to argue? "If I am not mistaken, I just gave you your first taste of pleasure."

"Whatever it was, it felt wonderful." She sighed and nuzzled against him sleepily. "I hope my first protector will be able to make me feel half as good as you can."

Her first protector? The notion made him feel sick to his stomach. Though he had just pleasured her, already her mind was turning to another man. A man who could give her all the good things in life that he would never be able to afford.

"Do you still want to take more photographs of me this afternoon?" she continued. "I'm not sure I could keep my eyes open."

Her rapid return to business gave him a sour taste in his mouth. Was he nothing more to her than something to scratch an itch while she waited for a man with deeper pockets to come along? "I have finished taking photographs for the day," he said curtly. "We have dilly-dallied for so long that there is too little sunlight left for another twelve exposures. Besides," he added, rubbing his cum over her breasts and making her nipples stand up all over again, "you would have to wash first. No man would buy a photograph of you with another man's cum spread all over your breasts."

The heat that spread over her face gave him a grim satisfaction. Beautiful Emily might not belong to him, she might not belong to any man, but he had staked a claim on her that no other man had. He had been the first man to touch her. He only wished he could be the last, too.

Emily walked home late that afternoon, not knowing how she ought to feel about the afternoon's adventure. Her body was still humming with the pleasure of having Eric touch her, but though physically she was as satisfied as it was possible to be, her thoughts were in turmoil over his reaction to what they had shared.

Eric had liked touching her, she was sure of it. Under her clothes she still wore the evidence of his enjoyment, now dried on her body. She had certainly liked having him touch her, and touching him back again. So why had he turned on her afterwards and said things that had made her feel ashamed of what they had just done?

It hadn't so much been what he'd actually said, as the tone in which he'd said it. The harshness in his voice had made her feel somehow dirty, as if she had done wrong by sharing her body with him.

They were both adults, not married or promised to another. Taking a little harmless pleasure from each other did not hurt anyone else.

Innocent she might be, but she wasn't silly enough to think that they had done everything that they could do. Though he had brought her immense pleasure, she was still a virgin. She had given him nothing that meant he needed to feel obligated to her, and she certainly wasn't expecting a proposal just because the two of them got a little carried away in their kiss. Indeed, if he *were* to propose, it would be dreadfully awkward. She wanted a wealthy protector, not a poor husband. She would have to turn him down.

Besides, they shared a perfectly satisfactory business relationship, and she was not about to make any changes to that.

So what was there for him to be so cross about? Why had he suddenly turned so curt and unfriendly, as if he wanted nothing more to do with her now that his immediate need had been satisfied? Was she nothing more to him than an encumbrance to be gotten rid of as soon as she was no longer needed?

No, she did not think so. Eric thought more of her than that, she was sure of it. In these past few weeks they had gone beyond being mere business partners to being good friends. He did not just desire her—he liked her as a friend as well, and he appreciated the help she had given him to set up his premises. So why should a passionate kiss with a woman he liked make him lose his good humor?

She kicked a loose pebble along the cobblestones as she walked, scuffing the toes of her boots. Men were such strange creatures—moodier and more changeable than any woman she had ever known. Eric was the moodiest of all. She did not understand him. Not at all.

The memory of touching Emily, of having her writhe with pleasure in his arms, stayed with Eric all through the week, so he was barely able to concentrate on his work. She had been so sweet and giving, so free with her body, holding back nothing that he'd asked of her, but instead demanding more. A thousand times over he cursed the inconvenient scruples that had refused to allow him to fuck her then and there, hard and fast. She'd been so gone with lust that she would've let him do anything he liked. Her cunt had been so tight that just entering her would have milked the cum out of his cock.

Fucking Emily was not a good idea, he told himself a thousand more times, when he was feeling more rational and less cunt-struck. If he took her as his mistress, he would risk getting her pregnant, and a pregnant woman was no use as a model. Not for the photographs that he sold. His career and his hopes of making his fortune would come to a very quick end if he meddled with his models and ruined them for his camera.

He would have to forget that their little interlude had ever happened at all. Certainly he would have to make sure there would be no repeat of it.

He ought not to have touched her at all, but he hadn't been able to resist her invitation. What man could resist a bare-breasted Emily rubbing herself against him like that?

She had taken him by surprise, that was all. He would be stronger this time and be ready with his excuses if she approached him this Sunday. No longer would his cock rule his head—his head would be firmly in charge from now on.

Even if she begged him just to touch her again with his fingers and bring her pleasure that way, he would have to be strong and refuse her. That way lay danger. If he continued to touch her like that, sooner or later he would weaken and he would take her. He would have to convince himself that he didn't want her.

I do not want to fuck Emily Clemens.

I do not want to fuck Emily Clemens.

I do not want to fuck Emily Clemens.

He shook his head disgustedly as his body responded in its usual fashion. His thoughts were not working the way he intended, but his damned cock was more than ready to get down to business. The more he told himself he did not want to fuck her, the more his mind lingered on images of her naked body, spread-eagled on a bed in front of him, her cunt gaping wetly open, and her eyes begging him to make love to her.

The last thing he needed was a demanding mistress to distract him. His relationship with Emily was volatile enough as it was. Sometimes she was as sweet and soft as a kitten and then she would turn on him with her claws extended and he would have to jump back before he was skewered. They did not need to add sex into the mix to make it even more explosive.

I do not want to fuck Emily Clemens.

He kept on telling himself that all week, and was still telling himself on Sunday afternoon, harder than ever, as he waited for Emily to arrive.

By the time she finally walked in the door, his nerves were so on edge that he could barely look at her. *Forget that you ever touched her*, his head told the rest of him, but the rest of him wasn't listening.

"You certainly made an impression with your last set of photographs," he said, tossing a package at her feet. He'd picked it up from Mrs. Angus earlier in the week and it had sat on his workbench ever since, tormenting him with its contents. "These are for you." He did his best to keep the jealousy he was feeling out of his voice. Emily was a pretty girl, she deserved to have plenty of admirers, he supposed, however much he would prefer to keep her to himself.

She did not belong to him. He did not want her. He ought not to want her.

Emily frowned at his lack of greeting and made no move to pick them up. "What are they? More bills for me to sort?"

"Letters from your admirers, I assume. Mrs. Angus gave them to me when I delivered the last set of your photographs." He'd been tempted to toss them into the Thames on his way back to the studio, but he had dutifully brought them home with him instead. Just because he shouldn't have her, couldn't have her, didn't mean that someone else wouldn't have better luck.

Emily crouched down and gathered them up with interest. "Ooh, how exciting. I've never had a letter from an admirer before." She picked up the topmost letter and ripped it open. "Dearest, most delightful Emily," she read, and then gave a self-conscious giggle. "You are the most beautiful woman I have ever beheld and I worship the very ground you walk upon. I look upon your likeness every day and tell you how much I adore you. How I would like to be able to tell you to your face the depth of my feeling for you. Please will you meet with me? Yours in adoration forever, Simon Cowdell."

He snorted with disgust. Who on earth was so pathetic he must write to a figment of his own fantasies and expect her to reciprocate his silliness? "Don't let it go to your head. He's probably a spotty lad of fourteen who happened upon his father's collection by accident and has some kind of rescue fantasy in his head."

With a toss of her head that told him she suspected his jealousy, she took another one from the pile and began to read it to herself. "Uugh, this one is nasty," she said at once, scrunching it up into a ball and tossing it into the wastepaper basket. "He's a dirty old man who ought to know better than to write such filth to me. I wouldn't care how wealthy he was—I would never become the mistress of a man like him."

He picked it out of the basket and began to read it himself. She was right. The wastepaper basket was exactly where that perverted old man's fancies belonged. Just as well there was no return address or he'd be tempted to go and teach the old fool a well-deserved lesson.

By now she had another letter in her hand. "This man thinks I'm a whore, the spawn of Satan, and the work of the devil and that I'm going to burn in Hell forever for my licentious wickedness." She made a brave face, but he could see that she was upset by the abusive language she was reading. "He needn't be so nasty about it, I'm sure. I'm not hurting anyone by taking off my clothes and letting my breasts be photographed. If he doesn't like my photographs, he shouldn't buy them. There's no sense buying them just so he can offend his sense of morality."

"Toss it out and don't think any more about it," he counseled her. The writer probably wanked himself off over her photographs and then abused her for posing for them. Not that he needed to go into such gory details with her. He grabbed another letter. "Take a look at this one instead. He's offering you five hundred pounds a year to become his mistress."

She grabbed it out of his hand and scanned it in disbelief.. "Five hundred pounds a year? That is a lot of money."

He snatched it back again. "On second thought, I don't think you should look at it." He tore it into several pieces and tossed it into the wastepaper basket. "You may decide that he's offering you more than ever I could, and refuse to pose for any more photographs."

"Don't rip up my letters," she growled at him, reaching into the wastepaper basket and gingerly picking out the pieces with the tips of her fastidious fingers. "I have not yet decided who I will choose for my protector. I cannot afford to reject someone who may be perfectly suitable on a silly whim."

The thought of another man laying his greasy hands on Emily made him twitch. Damn it, but if he were a rich man, he would keep her himself. She'd be worth every penny. "Money is overrated."

"It's not you they are offering it to," she replied tartly.

"They won't be offering you anything at all if we don't get on and give them some more photographs to dream over," he snapped back at her. "Now put them aside. We have work to do this afternoon."

"I have to read them now," she protested. "I cannot take them back to the school with me."

"Reading all that drivel won't bring in the money we need to pay off our printing machine."

Stacking the letters carefully away on a shelf, she made a face at him. "Can't I be in your company for more than ten minutes without you wanting me to take off all my clothes?" she teased.

"No," he replied ruthlessly, refusing to rise to the bait she was dangling so prettily in front of him. "You know that I prefer you as naked as I can get you. As do your other admirers. Get yourself ready. I shall be in the studio."

Waiting for Emily to appear, his mouth started to water at

the thought of what she would be dressed in today. After she had surprised him by baring her breasts for him last week, he had not presumed to give her any advice as to what to wear. Or, more to the point, what not to wear. She was clearly as anxious as he was to make the photographs a success, and was prepared to do more than he would ever dare ask her to do.

Never would he have asked her to display herself as wantonly as she had, but if she was prepared to show herself off nearly naked, he would willingly take the photographs. The photographs of her with naked breasts were selling twice as well as the others. Though Mrs. Angus had ordered two thousand as soon as she saw them, he'd already had to print her up an extra five hundred to keep up with the demand. Thank goodness the new printing press was living up to its reputation. Every man and his dog, it seemed, wanted to see Emily's bare breasts. Not that he could blame them. He'd shell out sixpence any day for a peek.

Just then she walked in to the studio, dressed only in her naughty corset, a pair of pantalettes, silk stockings, and an absurdly high pair of heels which made her legs look twice as long as usual.

"What do you think?" she asked nervously, pirouetting on her heels. "Do you think they will work?"

His mouth was too dry to speak. He could only manage a nod. Emily's body was as breathtaking as ever, and the sight of her nipples, hard as little pebbles, made him ache with desire for her.

How well he could remember his foolish optimism when he had first met her, when he had thought that familiarity with her body would breed contempt. Or if not contempt, at least indifference. He'd been quietly confident that after seeing her unclothed often enough, he would become immune to her attraction and no longer think anything much of it.

How wrong he had been. Even though he had seen her as unclothed as this before, still she had the power to make his cock stand up straight and his balls ache with wanting her. Having touched her once did not take the edge off his desire for her. Knowing how sweet she was only made the wanting worse.

She didn't even have to do anything, not even take off her clothes, and he was wild with desire for her. All she had to do was be herself, to be Emily.

He adjusted his trousers surreptitiously behind the camera. This week he'd made himself ready before she arrived to ensure he did not disgrace himself utterly by coming in his pants just from looking at her and knowing that he could not have her. He'd brought himself to pleasure and wrung himself dry of all his seed before she came, hoping to cool his lusts by his own hand. Though he'd come three times in a row looking at her photograph, still, at the sight of her in the flesh, his cock rose again. Damn it, whatever his head said, he wanted to fuck her. He wanted to peel her stockings slowly down her thighs and strip off her pantalettes. Then he wanted to kiss her mound of Venus and lick her there until she was crying with desire, as mindless for him as he already was for her. Then, when she was begging for him to take her, he would turn her over the edge of the sofa and drive into her from behind, thrusting his cock into her warm, wet cunt over and over again until her pussy convulsed around him and she was crying out in pure delirium. Then, and only then, would he let his seed erupt from his throbbing cock, redoubling her pleasure and flooding her with the proof of his own ecstasy.

The object of his desires was sitting on the bench, her knees together, looking down at her feet. "I wasn't sure about them," she said with a pout as she regarded the embroidered slippers with a wary eye, "but they were so decadent that I could not resist them. I thought they might look very well if I stood like this." Standing up again, she gave him a pose, leaning against the bench and looking back over her shoulder, which only added fuel to his fantasies. That was exactly how she ought to stand as he parted her nether lips with one hand while with the other he guided himself home into her. . .

He shook his head. This was not getting him anywhere. There were a thousand reasons why he should not, could not, take her as his lover. As a postcard model her job was to entice men into wanting to fuck her. She was merely practicing on him. "Hold it right there," he said gruffly, forcing his attention back to his camera. "Hold still. Yes, that's good." And the pose that had driven him almost out of his mind with desire was captured on his glass plate.

The entire session was sheer torture. Each pose that she tried was more provocative than the last. Her breasts cried out to him to be touched, and her nipples peaked into hard little buds of desire that begged to be licked. A look of sultry invitation was engraved on her face so deeply that he could still see it even when he closed his eyes.

Photographs could not be taken with his eyes closed, more was the pity, so he had to force himself to watch her every subtle posture, force himself to watch her every sinuous movement, so that he could capture her for other men to salivate over.

The effort to ignore her blatant invitation, the pursing of her mouth to ask for a kiss, was tremendous. By the time the session was over, his shirt was wringing with sweat. As soon as the twelve exposures were done, he sat heavily on the ground and mopped at his face with a pocket handkerchief. Too much more of this would kill him.

"Are you not feeling well?" Emily's face, as she bent over him, was creased with concern. "You look terribly hot and bothered. Are you coming down with something?"

He swallowed uncomfortably and shook his head. Her breasts were tantalizingly close to his face and the temptation to lean forward and take one of her nipples into his mouth and suck on it was tremendous. The only thing he was coming down with was a heavy dose of lust.

"Are you sure you don't want me to fetch something for you? You look terribly unwell."

He waved her away with one hand. "Go get yourself dressed. I'll be all right in a minute."

To his relief, she did as he bade her and disappeared into the office to get dressed behind the screen.

He sat there, gathering his breath for a few moments. The effort of not touching her had left him feeling like a wrung-out dishrag. Never before had his desire for a woman been so debilitating. With Emily in the same room as he was, he could barely function through the haze of desire that instantly surrounded him.

He bade her farewell as soon as he decently could, almost with a sense of relief. His torment was over for another week. When she was away from him, he was no longer held in thrall to her sensuality, crippled by his need for her. Now that she was gone, he could revert to the sane and practical business-man that he prided himself on being.

That evening Emily sat in the tub of bath water, soaping herself all over as she planned her next move—the move that would get Eric naked between the sheets with her. Damn it, she would sell her body for her freedom, but she would have a bit of fun first. He would be the delicious secret she would keep all to herself.

Despite the way she had posed for him today, he had not so much as touched a single hair of her head. It was as if their passionate interlude of the week before had never happened.

She wouldn't let him forget the passion they had shared, or the desire he had engendered in her. He had felt the same passion for her—she had worn the evidence of it on her body.

Her body was still humming with awareness. She ran the soap over her breasts, innocently at first, and then again, deliberately. Her nipple hardened at her own touch, just as they had under Eric's caresses.

Leaving the soap on the side of the bath, she ran her hands over her breasts and stomach, and then dipped to touch herself between her legs. Bother Eric for leaving her wanting more so badly. She could not resist the temptation to touch herself and take the edge off the hunger that plagued her.

She lay back in the tub idly stroking her pussy as she thought about Eric, about how he had kissed her and touched her where she was touching herself now, and how she had touched him in her turn.

His cock had been strong and thick in her hands. She'd like to have him here with her now so she could touch it again, stroke it, and feel it throb under her ministrations.

He had taken her hand away, fearing that he would finish too soon, and then he had finished himself while she was in the grip of a pleasure so strong that she was well nigh insensible. Next time she would not let him stop her. Next time she would keep stroking him until he erupted in her hands.

The thought of making Eric come brought her to orgasm quickly. A few faster strokes on the secret place between her legs and she arched her head back and swallowed her cries as a little wave of pleasure engulfed her.

She lay back in the bath as her tremors subsided once again. Touching herself produced only a dim copy of the ecstasy she had found in Eric's arms, but until she could seduce him properly, that was all she had.

And seduce Eric she would. She would take him as her first lover and be damned. What did she care for the opinion of the world? It was nothing to her. She wanted Eric in her bed, making love to her as a man made love to a woman, with nothing to come between them.

Even the offers she had received in the post today had left her cold and uninterested. She hadn't even finished going through them to see if there were any real possibilities among them. She didn't want to spread her legs for one of these faceless strangers—not even for five hundred a year. She wanted Eric.

Only when her desire for Eric was out of her system could she turn her mind to the more important task of finding a keeper.

That, unfortunately, posed another problem. She had no idea how to get him into bed with her. He had already seen her half naked and unfortunately he had not been filled with a lust so extreme that he had to ravish her on sight. Despite her best efforts at being seductive this afternoon, he had not been particularly interested. Maybe it was because he was not feeling well, but still, she wasn't at all sure what else she could do to encourage him.

She clapped a hand to her head. Caroline, her sister, would know. What a dunce she was not to have thought of that before. Caroline had been a rich man's mistress, and when he had lost all his wealth, he had made her his wife. Caroline would know everything there was to know about how to attract a man and how to make him want to bed you.

The only trouble with asking Caroline was that she would have to confess to her sister that she was posing half-naked for raunchy photographs. Of course, she would have to confess one day anyway, but she had put off exposing her secret. For one thing, she had a fear of putting the words down on paper in her room at the school where any nosy colleague or servant could chance upon them. She did not trust the post not to let a letter go astray—and she did not want to risk her letter falling into a stranger's hands. Nor had she wanted to talk about her venture prematurely, before she knew whether or not it would be a success.

Now that it looked as though her modeling would be very lucrative, she needed to let Caroline know right away. With her share of the money they had earned so far, even after paying extra on the printing machine, she would be able to pay next term's school fees for both Teddy and Dorothea.

She lay back in the water and closed her eyes with relief. Now that she had a plan, all that remained was for her to put it into action. School was nearly over for the year and the girls would all be leaving soon to return home until lessons began again in the autumn. She, too, would have some free time over the summer, when she wasn't planning lessons for the coming year. It was past time that she paid her elder sister a visit.

The headmistress gave her begrudging assent for Emily to take a few days to visit her sister, even before the end of term had officially arrived. That very Thursday found Emily on the early morning train to Hertfordshire, where her sister now spent most of her time on her small farm.

Though Caroline did not keep a carriage, she sent a pony cart to collect Emily. Sitting atop the cart, her bag at her feet, Emily rattled up the drive to Caroline's pretty farmhouse.

She'd only seen it once before when Caroline, attended by all her family, had married Mr. Savage in the village church. Her schoolteacher's salary did not allow her the luxury of buying train tickets very often, and all Caroline's spare money was taken up with paying for Teddy and Dorothea, her youngest brother and sister, to stay at school. If those two were to have any hope of making it in the world, they needed a decent education. Emily made a face. They needed the sort of education that had allowed her to become a teacher.

At the sound of the pony cart arriving, Caroline flew out of the front door and down the steps. "Emily, how wonderful to see you." She held out her arms to help Emily off the pony cart. "Were you jolted to death in that rattle trap?"

"Not at all," Emily lied, brushing off the back of her gown where she had been sitting on the dusty cart. Her buttocks were numb from the bumping.

Caroline gave a disbelieving snort. "What a fib. I know how awful it is, but we can't afford a carriage. Not unless Dominic's latest scheme bears fruit. Then we might be riding in style once again."

"He has another scheme on the go?"

Caroline tucked Emily's hand into the crook of her arm, took her carpet bag in her other hand. "Of course," she said gaily, as she led the way inside to the parlor. "Dominic would not be Dominic if he did not have a thousand schemes to rebuild his fortunes. And he is doing well, too. We have been able to put some more money into the estate, which was badly needed, and we have even been able to modernize some of the farm equipment, which should increase our yields next harvest time. But enough about me and the farm or I shall go on for hours and bore you to death. Tell me about you. How are you keeping? How is the school? Is Mrs. Herrington as prosy and dull as ever?"

Emily sank down into the soft cushions of the sofa and gratefully accepted the cup of tea that Caroline poured for her. The day was hot and she had been traveling since early in the morning. "Mrs. Herrington is as dull as ever. She does not improve on acquaintance."

"Is she treating you well?"

"Well enough. But Caroline, I do not want to be a teacher forever."

"You can always come and live with me and Dominic. He would not mind at all. We have plenty of room and the farm is doing well enough now to support us all. You know I would love to have you here." She gave a tiny sigh. "I would love to have all of you live here with me, but I know it is not possible. Teddy and Dorothea must stay at school, Beatrice is determined to become a nurse as soon as she may, and poor Louisa must stay in southern Italy where the climate is better for her health."

"We must all make our own way in the world. We cannot rely on you to save us every time we are in need." Emily drained her dainty cup of tea and held it out for a refill. "You still shoulder more of the burden than you ought."

"You are my family. I do not mind."

"I know you do not, but I must do my part. And I have found a way to do it." She hesitated, hoping that Caroline, of all people, would understand her reasons for doing what she had done and not condemn her for it. She could not bear to grieve her sister. "I have become a model."

Caroline clapped her hands together. "How exciting. Tell me more."

"I met a man, a photographer by trade, who asked if he could take pictures of me—"

"I can see why. You are looking very well indeed," Caroline interjected. "Teaching must agree with you more than you let on, you look so plump and pretty."

"He offered me a pound a week."

Caroline's eyes widened. "That's as much as you make as a schoolteacher."

"And another pound a week besides, to do his books."

"Who is this paragon? King Midas, who turned everything he touched into gold?"

"His name is Eric. Eric Twyford. He is an American. And I demanded a pound a week and a quarter of the profits to model for him."

Caroline whistled between her teeth. "I see papa taught you something before he died."

"It is not a respectable position," Emily said slowly. "I pose for him in my underclothes. In very few underclothes. But that is not all. I am going to use the photographs to make a name for myself. I intend to find a protector, Caroline."

"Oh, Emily." Caroline's voice held a world of tears. "If you dislike teaching that much, you should have told me earlier. We would have found something else for you to do if you did not want to live here with us. You need not be forced into doing something you find distasteful."

Emily looked away, not able to bear the pain in Caroline's eyes. She had not wanted to grieve her sister. "The money is good, and I do not mind, Caroline. Truly I do not. I am not in such need that I must rush into a decision. I will wait until I find a man I like well enough to make it worthwhile." She dropped her voice. "Indeed, I hardly know how to confess to you, but I like modeling. I like taking off my gown and putting on the very best silk and lace undergarments and posing for Eric. I like the thought that there are hundreds of men in England who have seen me without my gown on. I like knowing that every man who sees my photograph will desire me and will wish that he could possess me. And most of all, I like seeing confirmation of all that in Eric's face each time he trains his camera on me."

She leaned forward and took Caroline's hands in hers. "The money is good, Caroline. But even if I wasn't getting paid so well, I would still want to do this. I cannot describe it in words, but Eric makes me feel free. He makes me feel like I could do anything I choose to do, be anyone I want to be. He has so much energy that it is a joy simply to be with him."

Caroline looked searchingly at her. "Eric, Mr. Twyford, is more to you than a business partner, I take it?"

"He is only a photographer. He could not afford to keep me even if he wanted to." Emily's voice was almost a cry. "Oh, Caroline, that is one of the reasons why I just had to come and see you. You made Dominic fall in love with you as soon as he met you. He tracked you down in the workhouse, rescued you, rescued all of us, and all for your sake. How did you do it, Caroline? How did you make him fall in love with you? How did you make him want to marry you?" She needed to know her sister's secrets, all of them, to win a worthy protector of her own.

Her sister's face turned pink at the edges. "I hardly know what to tell you."

"I need to know all I can. Tell me everything. Please."

Caroline shook her head. "I fear I have not been a good influence on you. Certainly I should not be encouraging you in such an endeavor."

"You were no older than I am now when you became Dominic's mistress," Emily pointed out, "but still you knew enough to make him fall in love with you."

"I knew little enough then."

"But you know more now, I am sure you do. Please, Caroline, help me."

Caroline paused, her conflicting feelings darkening her eyes. "Are you truly determined on this course?"

"Postcards of me have already been sold all over England. It is too late for me to change my mind now."

Caroline looked at her seriously over the tea table. "I can see you are a hopeless case," she said as she sipped her tea thoughtfully. "I suppose I will have to tell you everything I know so you can be sure that the man you choose will love you quite as desperately as you would wish him to."

The relief she felt almost made her faint. "Thank you, Caroline."

"But you must promise me one thing."

Emily did not even care what it was. She would give her sister everything she owned in exchange for the knowledge she needed. "I promise."

"Promise me you will not be shocked by anything I say, and that you will not think the less of me for what I am going to tell you."

"I promise."

"And that you will never repeat what I have told you to anyone." She fixed Emily with a severe look. "Most particularly our younger sisters."

"I promise."

And with that, Caroline proceeded to tell Emily all that she had learned, and much of what she had done, in her short life as a courtesan.

By the time Emily left Caroline's house three days later, she was imbued with a new sense of confidence and a new determination. With nothing on her side but her pretty face and a sense of adventure, her sister had succeeded in winning the heart of Dominic Savage. Surely she could do the same with whatever man she chose. At any rate, she was going to give it a damn good try. If, after everything Caroline had told her, she couldn't at least get Eric into bed with her, then her name wasn't Emily Clemens.

Nine

Eric peered over his camera at Emily resting at her ease on the sofa, a cape draped carelessly over her shoulders to keep her warm while he composed the first shot. How relaxed she was this week, such a contrast to her first sitting when she had been wound as tight as a clockwork mouse. As she had become more comfortable before the camera's lens her photographic beauty had become even more sensual. She still retained her innocent look, but it was a more confident and daring innocence than before.

He couldn't work out how she managed to look so demure while wearing a corset that displayed all her bosom for his camera. If he had not known her before she started modeling, when she was still timid and afraid of showing more than an inch of ankle below her gown, he would have thought she did not have a single modest bone in her body.

Now he was almost used to the sight of her half-nakedness, her nipples, hard and begging to be kissed, pointing back at his camera. He was even becoming used to his state of semi-permanent hardness whenever she was around. Now he could almost forget about his lust for her for nearly a minute at a time while he was looking through the viewfinder at her pose. Unfortunately, as soon as he looked directly at her again his desire swept over him, redoubled in force, but he was learning to live with that as well. He did not have much choice.

Having framed an image of the first shot in his mind, he was about to instruct her how to move when she interrupted his composing process. "I see from the accounts that the last series of photographs were very popular."

Eric frowned as he looked up at her. "Yes?" he asked curtly. She knew he hated being distracted with idle chatter while he was working. It stifled his creativity, which in turn put him in an ill temper. Surely she knew him well enough to have gathered that by now. She must be deliberately baiting him. For what reason, he could not fathom.

Emily grinned at Eric's evident annoyance. How precious he was about his camera. Speaking to him while he was photographing her was practically a capital offense. "Did Mrs. Angus give any reason why?"

He stood up and brushed his hands against his trousers. "I should think the reason would be obvious, even to a dimwit." He stared pointedly at her breasts. "Both reasons."

"Hmmm." So it *was* the corset she was wearing that had increased the sales so dramatically. She'd guessed as much, but it was reassuring to have Mrs. Angus confirm it for her.

157

So, was this the time to take her photographs to a new level of naughtiness? If exposing her breasts more than doubled her sales, what would showing off her pussy do? Her daring would win her a suitable protector within the month, for sure.

Besides, no man, not even Eric, would be able to resist her if she approached him when she was fully naked and invited him to make love to her.

Eric's voice broke in on her thoughts. "Get rid of the cloak and let's make a start."

With that Emily cast her cloak away from the bench on which she rested and posed for the camera. She knew she looked good. The corset emphasized the smallness of her waist while lifting up her breasts. As always, her nipples immediately went hard when exposed to Eric and to the cool air.

After brushing a fleck of lint from one breast she played briefly with one nipple, sending little waves of pleasure through her body that finished up at her damp pussy. A man liked to see that a woman was not afraid to touch herself for him, Caroline had told her. No man could resist the sight of a woman pleasuring herself in front of him. It drove men wild.

She had always thought her breasts to be one of her best features, not too big and not too small. A handful was best, Caroline had said to her in a playful moment. Luckily, Eric had large hands.

She lay on her side, taking care to provide the camera with an excellent view of her naked bosom. Resting on hip and elbow she cocked her upper leg, her pantalettes reaching just below her knee, showing off her slim ankle.

She held the position while Eric made a few exposures, varying her smile and the tilt of her head each time.

As he took the photographs, Emily decided with certainty that the time was right. She felt a wild excitement at the thought of what she was about to do, the freedom of having decided.

Finally he finished the plates already in his camera and turned his back to her to take them out and swap them for unexposed ones.

With his attention diverted, she quickly untied her pantalettes pushed them down over her hips, and kicked them over onto her cloak. The watery sunlight felt delicious on her dark, wiry hair. Her pussy, she thought, with a barely restrained giggle, had never seen the sunlight before.

She returned to her earlier pose now wearing nothing but the corset. Cocking her upper leg caused her pussy to gape slightly, moist with her juice. She couldn't resist running a finger through her pussy lips and across her sensitive nub. Eric would merely be the first of her many conquests. His hands would be on her there before the day was out, she vowed. His hands, and a whole lot more.

The new plates safely installed in the camera, he turned to resume the photo shoot. It was the moment she had been waiting for.

At the sight of her lying nearly naked on the bench, he gulped and his face went bright purple. His eyes immediately locked onto the dark tuft of hair between her legs and stayed there as if they were glued in place. He took an involuntary step back as if trying to break the spell she had cast over him, and once more he tripped and went sprawling into the pile of cushions.

She couldn't help but laugh out loud at the stunned expression on his face as he fell. Simply showing her pussy had turned him into a clumsy novice with his camera. Not to mention that he must have a wicked bulge in his trousers to make him to move in such an undignified and uncomfortable manner.

She held her pose as he stumbled to his feet and stared again at her. "Em," he said, his voice hoarse and scratchy. He licked his lips and tried again. "Em, do you really mean for me to take a picture of you? Like this?"

Deliberately she rolled onto her front, resting on both elbows to give him a fine profile of her backside. She liked her backside—it was firm and round, just the way it should be. "Do you prefer this view?" she offered. "It's a little more subtle, I suppose, though I wasn't sure that our customers particularly valued subtlety."

He made no move toward his camera. "Em." His face was creased in a worried frown. "Are you sure about this?"

She gave her rump a little wriggle. "What will this do to our sales, do you think? I'm hoping it will make me quite a wealthy woman."

Still he didn't move. "You don't have to pose like this. Your postcards are selling perfectly well as it is. I do not want to do anything that makes you feel uncomfortable."

"What does it matter whether I take off half my clothes or all of them? I do not expect that my patron, when I choose him, will care either way, and it will pay us both well enough."

Finally convinced that she was serious, he began to fumble awkwardly with his camera, all thumbs now where before his actions had been as smooth as her silk stockings.

She watched with amusement as he tried to maintain the air of a professional photographer, but the painful looking bulge in his trousers gave him away. Gave him away in quite a large manner, as well. At least she had the satisfaction of knowing that he had responded to her nakedness as she had hoped he would. She needed him to go one step further though, and touch her as she wanted to be touched. All the lessons that Caroline had taught her would be directed at making him want her so badly that he could no longer resist her.

As she waited for him to direct her to a pose, she wondered if he was ever going to start work. His hard cock seemed to have robbed him of the power of speech.

Taking the initiative, she rolled onto her side, exposing her back and buttocks to the camera, and held still. Finally, she heard the shutter release, and the noise of him beginning to prepare for the next shot.

He eventually got into his usual rhythm of operating the camera while she assumed a number of relatively demure poses that showed off her naked rump but only hinted at the secret at the top of her legs. She had no intention of showing all in the first set—her first immodest pose had been for Eric's benefit, not for the camera. Tease them and keep them coming back for more was Eric's philosophy, and one she agreed with.

Eric stood up and stretched his back out, cramped from

spending so long bent behind the camera. "That's the last plate." Thank God he had finally finished, and without breaking anything. He wasn't sure he could survive taking another dozen exposures of her in her current state of nakedness. The whole afternoon had tested his self-control to its limits. He'd thought after last week that he would be able to resist her, however she tempted him. Now he knew for sure that that was not the case. If she so much as stretched out her little finger toward him, he would be on the ground at her feet, begging her to let him touch her and damn the consequences.

Though his erect cock had subsided somewhat, a fierce ache remained in his balls. He wanted her so badly he could almost taste her on his tongue.

He could not take his eyes off her body as she stretched the small cramps out of her muscles. Despite his best intentions, his eyes were continually drawn to the soft hair at the top of her legs. Dark, but quite wispy, the hair didn't hide any of her pussy at all. Every time she had assumed a new pose he had caught a glimpse of her moist lips, and even once a peek at her tight asshole. It was enough to drive a man to the brink of insanity.

Emily stretched her arms behind her head, thrusting out her pelvis as she did so. Eric's eyes followed her every movement. She felt her nipples contract into hard pebbles under his gaze. "You like looking at me, don't you?"

He started and blushed as he realized she had caught him staring unblinkingly at her mound. "I . . . uh . . . I . . ." he stammered desperately, ducking his head and trying to pretend that he was busily engaged in sorting out his camera gear instead of staring at her like a hungry puppy.

His embarrassment was so endearing. "I don't mind you looking." She liked it. His gaze was as good as a caress on her body, and it made her as hot for him as the touch of his hands on her body would. Her pussy was so wet that any moment now her juices would start dripping down her leg.

She longed to remove his trousers and watch his cock leap free, to stroke the base while licking around the head just as Caroline had told her that a man liked it. Most of all, she needed that hard cock of his buried deep inside her, she needed him to take her now, on the bench where she lay.

"How's this for a pose for next time?" Sitting on the bench she brought her knees up to her chin and spread her feet apart. He could not escape seeing how wet and ready she was for him. Surely he would come and touch her now.

He simply watched her, standing as if all of him were turned to stone. Damn it—she wanted him to do more than watch.

"Or this?" Sliding down onto her back she pulled her knees up and back. She could not make the invitation any clearer without asking him in words to come and make love to her, and she wasn't sure she could quite do that.

Looking up between her legs, she could see he was openly stroking himself through his straining trousers. His mouth opened, but no words came out. Once again his cock had muted his voice.

She gave a pout. "It's not fair, you know, that I am lying here almost naked while you are standing fully clothed way over there. Wouldn't you feel more comfortable over here with me?"

Finally he moved toward her, his eyes still fixed on her pussy. A feeling of triumph almost overwhelmed her as he came within touching distance of her at last. She had hooked him. Now she had to reel him in.

When he stood right in front of her she stroked a finger through her pussy lips then delicately touched it to her tongue. If she had not seen his eyes widen and his cock leap with renewed vigor, she would be horribly embarrassed at touching herself that way. With him looking at her as if she were a delicious morsel he was dying to taste, it was impossible to feel anything but excited beyond all measure.

She again dipped the finger and held it out for him to taste. Hesitatingly at first he touched her proffered finger with the tip of his tongue, then with a soft moan took her finger completely into his mouth and sucked desperately on it.

"Do you like the taste?" she whispered. "Wouldn't you like to taste me directly, to kiss my most sensitive place?"

She lowered her feet to the floor and sat up slightly. He knelt in front of her and she guided his unprotesting head to her pussy.

She gave a little scream as his tongue flicked over her for the first time. Nothing in her life had ever felt better than this. If she'd known how good it was going to be, she'd have taken off her pantalettes the first day she'd met him and begged him to lick her there and then.

His throbbing cock might have temporarily muted his speech, but it had no such inhibiting effect on his tongue. With increased confidence he grabbed her ass and held her steady while his tongue continued licking her pussy.

Her breath started to come in short pants as he teased her with his tongue. She shivered all over with the pleasure of it. He was going to make her come again, just as he had the first time he had put his fingers inside her.

He moved his attentions to her sensitive nub, licking her with the flat of his tongue over and over until she could no longer hold back the tide of feeling that was rushing over her. She gave a cry of pure delight as her body went into spasms of ecstasy that drowned her in pleasure before they slowly receded.

With no control over her limbs she flopped loosely on the bench, breathing in short gasps as she slowly recovered the use of her senses.

When she finally opened her eyes, she caught him grinning at her as he knelt between her legs. "Better?"

A sleepy lassitude had taken hold of her body. "Much better."

He licked his lips hungrily. "You taste good." Then he paused, once again seeming uncertain. "What do you want now?"

Though he'd licked her into oblivion, it wasn't enough for her. She wanted to feel more than his fingers and tongue between her legs. "Take your clothes off," she suggested shyly.

With only a small degree of encouragement, he slowly stood. She unbuttoned his trousers and pulled them down over his hips. Free of all restraint, his cock sprung up, standing as proud and straight as a tree trunk. The purplish head was swollen with desire for her, begging for release.

Unable to resist, she leaned forward and teasingly flicked her tongue over the small slit at the very tip. With each small taste he gave a short involuntary intake of breath, his cock jumping as if it had a life of its own.

Carefully grasping him at the base, she stroked him in short movements while taking as much of him into her mouth as she could. Caroline, her face as red as a boiled lobster, had told her that nothing pleased a man quite so much as having his lover kneeling at his feet and sucking on him while she stroked him.

Caroline evidently knew what she was talking about. She could feel his legs and buttocks straining with pleasure as she swirled her tongue around the ridge of his swollen head.

When he was slick with her saliva, she pulled her mouth away and stroked him with full movements, enjoying his slippery feel. Wet as he was, he would slide inside her with ease. Her pussy tingled at the thought.

Each time she rubbed over his head, he moaned and bucked his hips. It was too much for her. She wanted him to take her properly this time. She let her hand drop.

"For God's sake don't stop now," he ground out between clenched teeth.

"Make love to me, Eric. Make love to me properly."

He looked searchingly at her for a moment, then turned her around to face away from him.

She made a noise of protest. Surely he was not going to pull away from her now?

To her relief he was not pulling away, but positioning her better. "Kneel on the bench."

She knelt as he ordered and raised her rump in the air, thrusting it back at him.

With a gentle hand she felt him pull her cheeks apart. The cold air on her pussy as it gaped open in wet invitation made her gasp.

With one finger he dabbled in her pussy, thrusting in and out of her. "You're wet for me." His voice was full of satisfaction. "You're ready now."

She thrust herself harder down on his finger, not able to resist the feeling of fullness it gave her to have even that little part of him inside her. She had been ready for weeks.

His cock was poised at her entrance for a moment, and then with one slow, deliberate thrust he was fully inside her. It was done. She was no longer a virgin. Emily could summon no sorrow or guilt for what had just occurred, just a savage pleasure that she finally had Eric inside her, where he belonged. She wriggled her ass against him, pushing him as deep as he could go into her. It felt so right, so natural for him to be buried inside her.

He held there for a moment, then started slow full strokes, nearly leaving her before plunging in once more to the hilt.

Just when she thought she could not take it any longer, he paused, buried completely inside her and reached around to tease her sensitive nub. She screamed as his fingers found the right spot and bucked against him wildly. The torment was almost too much to bear. He was driving her almost delirious with need for him.

He moved very slightly, a short grinding movement as he pushed deeply into her, meeting her movement with his own.

His breath started to come in quick gasps as he changed to quick, full-length thrusts that teased her unmercifully, grabbing her ass in both hands to steady himself.

With each thrust his hard cock touched that special place just inside her, the head rubbing in exactly the right place to make her dizzy with need. In just a few moments, she was teetering on the brink of pleasure again. He gave one more thrust and she fell over the edge.

He gave a strangled cry as her pussy convulsed around him, pulsing in strong waves.

Her pleasure proved too much for his self-control. His whole body shuddering, he pulled out from her, splashing his hot cum over her back and ass.

He collapsed on the couch, his body as limp as his now deflated cock, his arms and legs draped every which way.

She looked at him tenderly and traced a finger down his chest. "So, where do we go from here?" Her whole being was overwhelmed with tenderness for him.

Surely he felt it as well as she did, that they had moved on from just being a photographer and his model, moved on from being just business partners. Now that they were lovers it might just change everything. Certainly she could not think of accepting another man into her bed while Eric was still her lover. She would have to make do with the money from the photographs until he tired of her. It would be no great hardship to live simply, not with him at her side. "What shall we do now?"

At her words he leapt up, casting her gentle touch aside. "You're right, I can't dally here all afternoon. I've got photographs to develop and print or Mrs. Angus will have my head. I'd better get on with it." With that he strode naked from the room, only to return a few moments later belting his dressing gown around his waist.

She stared at him, slowly gathering her clothes as he busily moved around the studio preparing to process the shots he had just taken. He seemed to have forgotten her completely as he focused on his work.

Her loving mood evaporated as she watched him clean and dust his damned camera. How could he show such affection for a machine, and utterly ignore her after the intimacy they had just shared? Did he not care that she had just given him her virginity? Did her precious gift mean so little to him? She blinked back the tears of hurt that were threatening to fall.

All he cared about was his blasted photographic equipment. He did not care for her in the least, not as a man ought to care for a woman. What a fool she was to hope that she could change his mind by sharing her body with him. He had taken what she had offered him, what she had almost had to force on him, and then continued on with his work as usual. Nothing but his work could hold his attention for more than a few moments. She had been deluding herself into thinking he was growing fond of her. She meant nothing to him. He did not care for her enough even to want her as his mistress.

Her mood now as dark as the late afternoon sky, she stomped out of the studio, slamming the door behind her.

Eric looked up, startled at the sudden noise. "Em? Where are you going?" After the pleasure they had just shared, he'd thought she would stay around for a while, maybe even take some supper with him; not immediately decamp back to the school with such insulting haste.

Surely she must see that they had a lot to talk about. As soon as he had finished preparing the glass plates for developing, he had been planning to ask her to marry him. He might have come from the gutter, but even he knew that a real man didn't take a well-bred young lady's virginity without immediately offering to make her his wife. She'd probably laugh in his face at his foolishness, but it was the least he could do.

Besides which, he *wanted* to marry her. So much for his plans to marry a New York heiress—he couldn't summon an ounce of regret. He'd rather have Emily than fifty New York girls—if she'd have him, that is. He didn't have much to offer her. She already had a half-share in the business. All he could give her was his heart and his name. It was little enough to offer such a woman.

He shook his head in resignation and returned his attention

to his work, certain he would never understand the ways of women. If she didn't want to marry him, why had she made love with him so eagerly? But if she did want him, why hadn't she waited around for his proposal? Though he adored every inch of her from the top of her head down to the tip of her pretty toes, he couldn't fathom her. Not at all.

Emily sat in her rooms the remainder of the afternoon, hiding her red eyes from the curious stares of her colleagues. After hastily bathing the evidence of their lovemaking from her body, she sat at her desk pretending to herself that she was looking over the notes she had made for tomorrow's lessons, but her thoughts were far from her pupils.

Caroline's advice had worked to a certain extent. She had made Eric unable to resist making love to her. But while the experience had changed her forever, to her desperate disappointment, the same hadn't held true for him.

Eric might desire her, but desire and possibly a vague friendship was all he felt for her. It wasn't enough for her. She wanted love. She needed him to need her. If he did not, then she would find someone who did.

The shadows had grown long when a knock on her door startled her out of her reverie. She opened it to find the kitchen skivvy, Aggie, standing outside, wringing her hands nervously in her apron. "Yes, Aggie?"

"If you please, Miss Clemens, there is a gentleman in the front parlor to see you. Mr. Murdoch."

She was in no mood for flirting. "I do not wish to see him," Emily said firmly. "Please inform him I am unavailable." Inwardly she heaved a sigh. So much for her very first admirer. She had no patience to tease him into an offer tonight, and even less enthusiasm to accept one if he were, by some miracle, to make it.

Aggie remained at the door, her dark eyes large in her skinny white face. "If you please, Miss Clemens, Mr. Murdoch said as he'd thought you might say as much. He asked me to give you this. He said as it might change your mind about wanting to talk to him." She dug into her apron pocket and held out a sealed envelope.

Emily took it and slit open the seal with a sense of resignation. What was Mr. Murdoch up to now?

A picture of herself, one of the pictures with her breasts quite uncovered, stared back at her. On the face of the photograph was written in a large male hand, "I knew I would eventually recall where I had seen your face before".

She felt the blood rush from her head and Aggie's face started to swim in front of her eyes. Grabbing onto the door frame for support, she shut her eyes and willed her dizziness to abate. Now was not a good time to lose her head. She needed all her wits about her to cope with this sudden turn of events. It looked like she would have her protector sooner than she thought.

"Are you taking a turn, Miss?" Aggie asked in a worried voice. "Shall I fetch Mrs. Herrington for you?"

With a great effort Emily opened her eyes again and gave Aggie a reassuring smile. "I'm perfectly fine," she lied. "Mr.

Murdoch is right—I do need to speak with him after all. Would you please tell him I will be down in a moment."

Shutting the door on Aggie, she sat down heavily on the side of her bed and put her head between her knees until she could think clearly once more.

Mr. Murdoch's discovery might yet be the making of her. He had struck her as a kindly man, not as a vindictive one who would try to ruin her out of spite. If he had meant to expose her, he would have gone straight to Mrs. Herrington and had her thrown out of the house on the instant.

No, he clearly wanted something from her. She had no doubt he would want exactly what every man who saw her photographs would want, exactly what she deliberately made them want. Her.

She descended the stairs to meet him, feeling reasonably calm once more. Chances were he had come to offer her what she wanted—the post of his mistress. She only hoped that his offer would be worth accepting. Having to leave the school before the postcard printing was bringing in much money would be a nuisance, but she would not sell herself cheaply to anyone.

She pushed open the door to the front parlor and swept in. Eric might not care for her, but she was still a woman worth loving. She would make her mark on the world yet.

Mr. Murdoch's dark face spread into a calculated smile when he saw her enter. "Ah, Miss Clemens. How lovely to see you. It has been too cruel of you to refuse my visits, but I see my little note had its desired effect."

She nodded briefly. "Mr. Murdoch." Something inside her stomach was turning somersaults. The man in front of her had seen her nearly naked. How was she supposed to make polite conversation under such circumstances?

"Take a seat, do," he urged her, ushering her to the settee next to him.

She took her arm out of his and seated herself opposite him instead. If he expected tears or pleading or any other sign of weakness, he would be sorely disappointed. Her head was too hard for such nonsense.

"Haughty to the end, Miss Clemens?" Amusement colored his eyes gray. "Or may I call you Emily? That is your stage name, isn't it? The name you use for those utterly delicious photographs that you sell all over London." He shook his head in reproof. "Tut, tut, Emily. It is very naughty of you, you know, to take off your clothes like that and pose for such risqué postcards. Whatever would Mrs. Herrington think about your photographs? I cannot think that most fathers of your pupils would be as accommodating as I am prepared to be, if they were to find out your secret. Their wives would not allow it."

"Do you intend to tell Mrs. Herrington?" Her voice was cool and perfectly composed. She was surprised to find how little she cared either way.

"Emily, Emily," he said with a great sigh. "I really would prefer not to, but that depends on you entirely."

She clasped her gloved hands together in her lap and raised her eyebrows for an explanation. "It does?"

"I have certain conditions that would need to be fulfilled to ensure my silence on the matter."

Naturally he would have certain conditions. She sat in silence, waiting for him to offer his terms.

He cleared his throat noisily. "I am a lonely widower, as I am sure you are aware. My wife died some years ago and I have not yet found a partner to share my life with. You are a beautiful woman, Emily, and your photographs are immensely popular among my set. They all, to a man, rave about the beauty of your white breasts, the smoothness of your skin and the look of sultry promise in your eyes. If I were to possess you, to possess the famous Emily who has cut a swathe through all our hearts, I would be the envy of all my acquaintances."

As a businesswoman she didn't want or need all this flowery language—all she wanted was his offer on the table in black and white. "You want me to become your mistress, I gather, in return for your silence?"

To her immense surprise he shook his head. "Oh, no, my dear, I would not insult you with such an offer. I have no intention of taking you as my mistress." He waved one hand in the air. "Morality aside, a mistress is such an ephemeral being, here one day and gone the next. If you were to become my mistress I would have no hold over you—you could leave me any time I did not please you well enough, or when another, wealthier man came along. No indeed, Emily, if you were to become mine, I could not lose you in such a way. Nor do I think that such a life of the demi-monde would suit a respectable lady such as yourself, for in your heart I do believe you are not a whore. I do not want you to become my mistress, I want you to marry me, to belong to me in every way in which a woman can belong to a man." He rose ponderously from the sofa and bent down in front of her on one knee. "Emily, my dearest," he said, taking her hand in his and raising it to his lips. "Will you do me the honor of becoming my wife?"

Marriage? Mr. Murdoch must have lost his head. He was offering marriage to her? She had no money, no family, and thousands of postcards with her naked body on them being hawked around all over England. He could not be serious. She tried to tug her hand away from his clasp. "Don't be ridiculous."

He had a surprisingly tight grip and she could not break free. "I realize you cannot be a virgin, but I am willing to overlook that fact," he said, holding tight to her fingers with one hand, while he placed his free hand on her knee. "Given the certain other benefits that I could expect from our liaison." The hand on her knee started to creep up her thigh, caressing her through her skirts. "You are a beautiful woman, Emily, and I see no shame in confessing that I desire you greatly. I am willing to marry you so I can keep you to myself."

Just then there was a knock at the door. "Cup of tea, miss," came the voice of the kitchen maid through the keyhole.

She glanced uneasily down at Mr. Murdoch. "Uh, come in."

Mr. Murdoch got to his feet hastily and resumed his position on the sofa as the maid brought in a pot of tea and set it on the occasional table in front of Emily.

She welcomed the interruption, and not just because it prevented Mr. Murdoch's hand from creeping back to her thigh. Setting out the cups and pouring the tea gave her a few precious moments to consider her options.

Marriage. He had certainly startled her with the proposition. She had thought only of becoming his mistress. Marriage was so unsettlingly permanent. She wasn't sure she was ready for such an irrevocable step.

In his defense, he was wealthy and handsome, and she liked him well enough. The touch of his hand on her thigh had not been desperately unpleasant. Though he did not set her afire, it would be no hardship to share a bed with him. Certainly it was a mark in his favor that he liked her enough to want to wed her despite rightly suspecting that she was no virgin. A woman appreciated being adored, and she was no exception. Any man who was prone to worship at her feet must have something going for him. Good taste and discernment at the very least.

If she were to wed him, her money worries would be over. She would not have the absolute freedom to live life as she wanted, but neither would she have to cast off all vestiges of respectability. Such a compromise might be workable.

If he were generous, he might agree to dower her sisters, or even to settle enough on them to secure their independence. At the very least she could pay for Teddy's school fees and get him settled into a profession.

But she hardly knew him. She didn't even know if he would prove to be a generous benefactor to her brother and sisters, or whether he would be such a pinchpenny that she would be worse off as his wife than before. Agreeing to marry a man because he was wealthy and did not physically repulse her seemed to be scant enough reason for entering into such a serious contract—a contract that would last for the rest of her life.

Worst of all, he was not Eric. She did not love him. He did not make her weak at the knees at the mere sight of him, turning her legs to jelly and her brain to mush. He did not turn her nipples into pebbles of desire, or make her wet between the legs at the sound of his voice. She did not look at him and long to rip off his clothes and run her hands all over his naked body. She did not want to reach for him and hold him to her chest so she could feel his heartbeat close to hers.

No, she was thinking about it the wrong way. *Best* of all, he was not Eric. He would not make her heart ache for what she could not have, or rip her soul into shreds every time he looked right through her without seeing her. His casual words would not cut through her like a knife, drawing blood with every syllable. He would not blow hot and cold by turns, keeping her confused and insecure. No, he would be quite different.

However lukewarm her feelings were for him now, Mr. Murdoch would love her as a woman needed to be loved. In time, she would grow to love him, she was sure of it.

By now the maid, having poured the tea, had left the room. Emily held her teacup steady in her hand and took a deep breath. "Thank you for the honor you have done me by asking me to become your wife. I would be very pleased to marry you."

A triumphant smile spread across his face. "Delightful, de-lightful. As soon as I recognized your face in that photograph, I knew I had you. I felt sure you would see things my way." He patted the cushions on the sofa next to him. "Come and sit next to me, Miss Emily. Now that you are my affianced wife, you can have no further objection."

His reaction to her acceptance was almost enough to make her wish to retract it. She was not to be "had" like an item of furniture. She was a woman, with her own thoughts and feel-ings, and she had accepted him with her own free will. But, being a woman, she could also change her mind if she chose. "Thank you, but I am perfectly comfortable where I am." She softened her refusal with a smile. After all, she did not want to quarrel with him. Surely he had not meant to sound so calcu-lating—his words had probably just come out wrong.

His dark eyes narrowed at her calm refusal. "Come now, my dear, you lead me to suspect your motives in accepting me. A little obedience to your affianced husband would show your good faith."

"If you insist," she replied calmly, though inside she was gritting her teeth at his authoritarian air. This marriage idea might take some getting used to. She had been independent for too long to take on the yoke of a man easily. Moving over to the settee, she took her place on the other corner, far enough away so as not touch him, but not so far that he could construe it as an insult.

He nodded approvingly as he shifted closer to her so his

thigh was pressing up against hers. "That's better. I like a bid-dable woman who obeys me cheerfully in all matters, be they big or small."

His closeness, which before had pleased her well enough, now only irritated her. She fought to quell her annoyance with him. It wasn't Mr. Murdoch's fault that he was ponderous when she preferred lively, sententious when she preferred laughing, and dark-haired when she preferred auburn. He was not Eric. She must simply get used to that.

"Am I to assume you do not want the world to know that I am the Emily of the photographs?" she asked. "After all, there would be some narrow-minded people who might cut my acquaintance if it were to be widely known. Businessmen, I believe, are not generally known for their liberal ways of thinking."

"You're a smart little puss," he said, patting her hand. "No, to the world you will be Mrs. Murdoch, a matron of impeccable respectability. Only to my particular set, to those of us who revel in the many and manifold delights of the female form, will your identity be revealed. To them I will gloat over my triumph in seizing a prize they all desire, and all of them will envy me."

She raised her eyebrows at his peculiar answer. "To your particular set? What do you mean by that?" His tone had made her feel rather uncomfortable. "Why do they need to know that I am the Emily of the postcards?"

"Think nothing of it, my dear," he said, waving away her questions as if they were utterly inconsequential. "They will not think any the worse of you for being that Emily. I am perfectly confident of that."

"But why do they need to know at all?" she persisted.

He looked at her gravely. "I do not like to have my decisions questioned, Emily. It is best that you know that now so you can avoid doing so in the future."

She raised an eyebrow at him, but he did not smile back. Clearly he was serious. "Indeed," was all she could think of to say.

"I am glad you understand." He slung one arm around her shoulder and pulled her close to him. "Now, Emily dearest, come and tell me how much you are looking forward to being my wife."

She wasn't sure now that she was looking forward to it very much at all, but no doubt he liked his wishes obeyed as much as he liked his decisions not to be questioned. She let him pull her into his arms and put his arms around her, deliberately closing her mind to the memory of Eric's arms around her and his lips nuzzling into her neck. Now she was engaged to Mr. Murdoch, she would have to get used to his touch instead.

If she closed her eyes and held her breath for a moment so she could not smell the slightly acrid smell of Mr. Murdoch in place of Eric's male scent, she could almost imagine it was Eric who held her in his arms.

After a brief and painfully stilted embrace, Mr. Murdoch sighed into her ear. "I had better leave now before the pleasure of your company becomes too great a temptation for me to resist." He set her aside with a pained look on his face, as if it were her fault they were in Mrs. Herrington's parlor where it would be most unwise to do more than snatch a hasty embrace.

"I look forward to your return," she muttered rather unenthusiastically as he disengaged himself. She could feel none of the joy that a newly affianced woman was supposed to feel—there was only a great yawning void where her happiness ought to be.

He got to his feet and clapped on his hat. "We can discuss your financial situation later, once I have decided what would be best to do with the dowry you will bring me."

What was he talking about? "I have no dowry." Did he really think she would still be teaching if she had enough money for a dowry? "My father died some months ago and left me penniless."

His smile did not reach all the way to his eyes. "Your earnings from the postcards will be dowry enough for me. I shall post an announcement in the Times tomorrow and we shall wed as soon as may be. Next Wednesday would suit me very well."

Next week? That was terribly soon. Wasn't it her prerogative as the bride to name the wedding day? She would have chosen a date several months out at least. "As you wish," she murmured, deciding to let it go for now. He was far too used to doing as he pleased. She may as well give in gracefully for now. Once they were married, it would be a different story. He would have to learn that he could not order her around as if she were a child or a servant. She was a woman with a mind of her own, and she would expect to be treated as such. But for now, she merely wanted him gone.

She shut the door on him, sank back down into her chair, and poured herself another cup of tea. A few minutes of peace and a hot cup of tea would help her to come to grips with the absurd turn her life had taken today. She had begun the afternoon by losing her virginity to Eric, the man she had so foolishly fallen in love with, and ended it by becoming engaged to Mr. Murdoch, a man she barely knew.

On second thought, she took a couple of the cakes from the tea tray and munched on them. Though they were rather dry and not very appetizing, she persevered, washing them down with her now lukewarm tea. She was hungry and, annoyingly, Mr. Murdoch's ill-timed visit had caused her to miss her dinner.

Mr. Murdoch slumped in the corner of his carriage, the fervor of desire heavy upon him. The girl had been physically colder than he had expected. It was disappointing to find that he'd have to coax her into more familiarity with him, when he'd expected her to be a forward little whore who would spread her legs for any man who asked her.

He much preferred an eager bedmate, like lusty young Meg had been, before she was stupid enough to let her belly swell with his child and he'd had to turn her out. It was either that or marry the slut, and he had greater ambitions than to marry a penniless governess, however well she pleased him in bed.

It was a pity Emily wasn't more like Meg. Next time he visited her, he'd have better satisfaction than such a chaste embrace had afforded him. Next time he'd get her to unbutton his trousers and slide her hand into his pants. Then she could stroke him until he was hard and throbbing and ready to come into her hand. And at the last moment, he'd pull her on to his lap, shove her skirts out of the way and thrust into her. He was so hungry for her that he'd take her whether she was ready for him or not.

Once she was his wife, he would make sure she was always accommodating to his needs. She would save her favors just for him or she would feel the back of his hand. He would demand that she keep herself ready for him at all times, and for certain of his select group of friends who would appreciate her fine form and whose favors he might need to cultivate.

What a bargaining chip he would have once they were wed— the body of the famous Emily of the postcards, no less. Every man of his circle would be lining up to view her sweet body, the original of the postcards, and he would charge them dearly enough for the privilege. For those who weren't content with a mere view, a taste of her would cost them a small fortune.

She was the lucky break he'd been looking for all his life— the opportunity to make obscene amounts of money without having to break into a sweat for it.

Though the slut was coy on the subject, he knew she ought to have a nest egg put away somewhere. But even if she had nothing now, she would soon make a substantial dowry for

him. Her postcards were eagerly collected, and fetched a pre-
mium price. He would make sure that he was well paid for any
further photographs that were taken of her.

He smiled to himself. He'd visit the girl again in a few days
and have her attend to his needs properly. She hadn't behaved
herself well enough for him to give her the good hard fucking
all women wanted—he'd have her on her knees sucking on him
instead. In time she would learn that sexual pleasure was the
prerogative of a man, and she was there merely to service his
needs and cater to his whims. If he chose to give her some pleasure to heighten his own enjoyment, that was his choice. And if
he chose not to satisfy her, to heighten his desire by leaving her
hungry and wanting more, that was his right as well.

Yes, he would start that lesson next visit. He would make
her take him in her mouth and suck on him until he came down
her throat. He wouldn't even touch her, not so much as fondle
her breasts. That would teach her not to argue with him next
time he gave her an order.

On second thought, he had better treat her with kid gloves
until she was his wife. He could not bear to lose her now she
was so nearly in his grasp. Letting another few days pass before
he took her would not kill him. Once they were safely married,
he would make her pay for his inconvenience in having to wait
for her.

Still, the thought of having Emily's mouth fastened around
his cock had made him unbearably hard. He rapped on the
front panel of the coach. "Take me to Madame Ernestine's," he

ordered the coachman. "And wait for me there while I conduct my business with her." He would wear off his lust on one of her compliant young whores before he returned home.

Eric lugged the heavy parcel back to his studio with a bad grace. The letters to Emily from her admirers were getting more numerous by the week. He would shortly have to hire a hand cart to pick them up from Mrs. Angus and a full-time secretary just to read them, let alone reply to any of them.

Her admirers were rapidly making him a wealthy man, so he ought not complain. Still, he discouraged her from taking too much notice of the foolishness that men wrote to her. If, God forbid, she were to take one of them seriously and accept one of the various offers that were made to her every week without fail, he would be in deep trouble. Whatever her admirers might assume about her availability, they would be wrong. She was his woman now.

Tossing a penny at one of the street vendors, he picked up a copy of the newspaper. He'd worked enough for one day. For weeks he'd done nothing but live and breathe photographs, printing, and postcards. Time to put his slippers on, relax over a pint of porter, and read what was going on in the outside world.

Unwilling to cut short his well-deserved rest and return to the endless process of printing, drying, and cutting postcards, he lingered longer over the paper than usual. That was the only reason that his eye eventually fell on the engagement notices, in which normally he would have no interest.

A name leaped out at him and he blinked and then blinked again, not certain whether he was seeing things. But no, there it was in black and white. Miss Emily Clemens, teacher, of Harrowgate, to Mr. Malcolm Murdoch, businessman, of Russell Square.

The words slammed into his brain with the force of a storm surge breaking against the shore. It was his Emily. It had to be his Emily. The school she taught in was located in Harrowgate. And just how many Emily Clemens could there be teaching in London?

Damn it, how could the woman do this to him? She had taken him to her bed just yesterday, and he would have sworn that she was a virgin. She had lain with him and caressed him and whispered words of love into his ear.

His pint of porter tasted bitter in his mouth. Her words were meaningless, wet sops of nothingness with no substance to them at all. Not even her gift of her body, which he had thought was the most precious gift a woman could give to a man, was worth a fig to her. She had simply tossed it in his direction with as little thought as someone might toss a bone to a hungry dog.

Now she was to be married to someone else? To a businessman of Russell Square, no less. Financially speaking, she had done very well for herself. It would take him a month of Sundays, even at his current pace, to have the slightest hope of competing with such a man.

What hurt most of all was her silence on the subject. In the weeks they had been working together, she had never given so much as a hint that she was involved with another man. And then to let him find out her engagement by accident, through a notice in the newspaper? Not even to have the courtesy of telling him in person that she was to be married? If he had not picked up today's paper by chance, he would never have known what she was planning. Her behavior went beyond rudeness—it verged on the criminal.

He'd thought she was fond of him, loved him even. After she had seduced him in his studio, he had simply assumed they would wed. If he had not been prepared to marry her, he would never have given in to her seduction, whatever temptation she threw in his way. To take a well-bred young woman's virginity with no intention of marrying her was unthinkable.

But what was his love when set against another man's wealth? His porter roiled in his stomach. Emily had made her choice, and she had chosen as so many women before her had chosen.

How foolish and fanciful his dreams seemed to be now. How naive his excitement at making a trifling sixty pounds a week from his photographs. Mr. Murdoch, God rot his bones, must have a solid income of a good five thousand a year to live in such a swell part of town. He would be able to shower her in pearls and diamonds, give her new dresses every week if she had a mind to them, and buy her a fancy carriage to ride around in. Who knows, he could probably even purchase his new wife her own railway carriage so that she did not need to mix with the hoi polloi when she wanted to take a trip into the country.

Which left him where? Stuck in his London studio with an expensive piece of machinery which he had yet to pay for, and no way of making the money he needed to pay for it. With no new postcards to whet the appetite of his customers, demand for the pictures he had already taken of Emily would soon dry up.

He did not expect to see her grace his doors again, not now that she was to become a respectable married woman. With a fiancé who lived in Russell Square, she would have no further need for the pittance he paid her.

In a fit of temper he pulled open the parcel he had lugged all the way from Charing Cross Road. Letters of all shapes and sizes fell out over his floor. He grabbed a handful and flung them into his grate where they caught on the still warm embers and burned away merrily. He kept on flinging letters into the fire until they were all gone and his grate was choked with paper ash.

He glared at the mess he had made. Damn Emily to hell and back again. Even when he burned them, the love letters her admirers wrote to her were more trouble than they were worth.

The news of Emily's engagement traveled around the school faster than a steam train. Her good fortune in landing a wealthy husband was remarked upon by all the teachers, with generosity or with jealousy, depending on their natures.

Miss Andrews promised to make her a cross-stitched homily to frame for her new house as a wedding present, and cross Miss Snithers pasted a false smile on her face and said in a doleful voice that she *hoped* Emily would be very happy.

Even Mrs. Herrington invited her to afternoon tea in her rooms. "I hope you have been happy here, Miss Clemens," she said rather portentously as she handed Emily a cup of tea (brewed a good deal stronger than was usually served in the dining room), and passed her a plate full of fruit cake and meringues.

"Indeed," Emily said noncommittally, rather goggle-eyed at Mrs. Herrington's unaccustomed generosity with the afternoon tea. Teachers were considered unusually lucky if they were served plain biscuits with their cup of tea, and to be offered a piece of seed cake was quite a celebration.

"We hope that you will continue to send Finella to school here. She is a lovely girl and we have enjoyed having her."

Would Mr. Murdoch want her to take over the education of his daughters when they were married? He had not mentioned anything to her. "That will be Mr. Murdoch's decision. But I would certainly be happy to have her stay if that is what he prefers."

Mrs. Herrington nodded graciously and offered her another slice of fruit cake. "I'm very pleased to hear you say so. And when do you think you will leave us to take up your new life?"

Emily frowned as she considered the question. "I will have to consult Mr. Murdoch on the matter." What an annoyance it was not to be in charge of her own destiny anymore, but to have to consult with her future husband and to abide by his decision on such matters.

Mrs. Herrington nodded as if she fully understood that, as an engaged woman, Emily was no longer able to make her own decisions. "You have done very well for yourself." Her nose turned up and she looked rather disapproving for a moment. "Better than many a girl with your pretty face and lack of fortune." Then her face evened out into a smile once again. "I wish you all the best."

Only Mary Mittens was unimpressed with her catch. "What on earth are you doing marrying him?" she asked Emily one evening, as they sat together in Emily's room, sharing a late supper of hot milk and buttered toast. "He does not seem to be the sort of man who will make you happy."

Emily shrugged. "He is wealthy." That had seemed more than enough for everyone else to think she had landed a fine catch.

Mary shook her head in disbelief. "Do you care that much about money that you would make yourself miserable for it? For the rest of your life? Some of the others here would marry a veritable demon if he were rich enough, I know. Miss Snithers would have her butcher in a heartbeat if she could, and he only makes a modest living compared to Mr. Murdoch. I just had not thought you were one of them."

What else good was there to say about her fiancé. She knew so little about him. He was not fat, and his whiskers were not overly scratchy, but that was small reason to marry someone, she knew. He didn't disgust her—that was important to her if she had to share a bed with him. And, best of all, he wanted her enough to marry her, which was more than Eric ever would. Once she was happily married, there would be no cause for her to pine for what she could never have. "He is a respectable man and will treat me kindly."

"As he treated Meg?" Mary's voice had risen an octave in her outrage. "Turning her out of his house without a character and refusing to acknowledge his own child? Those are not the actions of a gentleman."

"It might not have been his." Even to her own ears, the excuse sounded weak.

"Meg vowed it was," Mary said stoutly. "And she was an honest girl before Mr. Murdoch meddled with her. I believe her story."

Once again Emily shrugged, sure that Mary was mistaken. His treatment of the poor girl was, if Mary told the truth about it, inexcusable. Only a scoundrel would behave so badly. She did not think Mr. Murdoch was that much of a scoundrel. After all, he had insisted on marrying her rather than trying to make her his mistress, as she had expected. "He will not be able to turn me out so easily," she said flippantly. "Not when I am his wife. He'll be stuck with me when he tires of me."

"Why did he ask you to marry him?" Mary looked at her curiously. "What hold do you have over him to force his hand like that? You are very pretty, it is true, but you have no dowry."

"Money isn't everything," Emily interjected. Mary's question was more than a little insulting, though she knew her friend did not mean it to be. Wasn't it possible that Mr. Murdoch wanted her for her person alone?

Mary sniffed. "It is to some people. I cannot believe that he asked a woman he has only met once in his life before to marry him out of the blue like that when you have nothing to offer him but yourself. It does not gel with what I know of his character. There must be something more to the story. Something you are not telling me."

Emily could feel her face grow hot at Mary's shrewd guess. "I will marry him soon," she said shortly, wanting her friend to drop the topic before she was tempted to confess her love for another man and her despair that he did not want her back. "There is nothing sinister in Mr. Murdoch asking me to marry him or in my accepting his offer. He wants a wife and a stepmother for his children and thinks I am a suitable candidate. I want an establishment of my own and I am willing to marry him to gain it. It is as simple as that."

Mary shook her head despondently as she finished her warm milk. "You are making a mistake," she warned Emily as she left to return to her own room. "I only hope you see it before it is too late."

The following Sunday saw Eric sitting alone in his studio in his shirt sleeves, nursing a bottle of whiskey and a devil of a hangover. Drowning his sorrows hadn't worked, even though this was the second bottle in which he'd tried to find peace. He still felt as betrayed as he had when he first saw the notice of her impending marriage. Betrayed, deceived, and very angry.

If Emily was in front of him now, he would give her a piece of his mind. He had plucked her from obscurity and given her the opportunity to make herself a fortune, and how had she repaid him? By using him for her pleasure and then tossing him aside as if he were a dirty dish rag—that was how. She had left him with a huge debt to repay, and a broken heart to boot.

He took another swallow of whiskey, wincing as it burned all the way down his throat and settled uneasily in his stomach. He deserved better than to be treated as if he were human garbage.

The bell to his shop front rang, indicating that a customer had walked into his store, but he ignored the clanging. He didn't want any customers today. He didn't want any customers ever again. Thanks to Emily's defection, he had nothing to sell them any more. He was washed up, finished, ruined. He may as well just end it all now.

"Eric Twyford." A scandalized female voice jangled in his sore head. "Are you drinking? At this time in the afternoon?"

He raised his head from his hands and stared, bleary-eyed, at the woman who had just walked into his studio. "Emily? What are you doing here?"

"What do think I am doing here, you imbecile," she snapped at him, cruelly swiping his bottle away from him.

He tried to grab for it, but the drink had made him clumsy and he toppled off his chair, falling to the floor with a crash.

"I had no idea I was going into business with a drunken sot," she complained as she helped him to his feet again. "Would you like to explain yourself?"

He'd bumped his head in the fall, adding to his already splitting headache. The shrill tones of her voice cut through his brain like a hot knife through butter. "Isn't one man enough for you to nag?" he asked, as he stumbled back into a sitting position. "Go and bother your affianced husband and leave me be." Now that she was in front of him, he had no energy left to berate her for her deception. All he wanted was for her to go away and leave him alone in his misery.

That stopped her cold. "What do you know about that?" Her voice was terse.

He gestured to the newspaper. In a fit of masochism, he had propped it against his mantelpiece where he could see the evidence of her perfidy every day. "I can read."

"Why should it bother you that I found a man who was willing to marry me?" she challenged him. "Since you made it abundantly clear that you did not want me. Not that you could afford to keep me anyway."

"Marriage isn't everything." His excuse sounded lame, even to his own ears.

"It means a lot to a woman."

"Piffle." He gave a disgusted snort. "You're only marrying him because he's rich and I'm not. I'm all right for you to have a bit of fun with on the side, but a woman like you wouldn't marry a man like me, even if I was to ask you."

"You never did ask, so how would you know?"

"I'm asking you now," he said stumbling onto his knees. He was quite proud that his voice was hardly slurred at all. "Marry me, Em." He might as well let her put the boot in completely and turn him down out of hand. Call her bluff.

"Get up off the floor. Don't make even more of a fool out of yourself than you have already." Her face looked screwed up as if she were about to burst into tears. "Marriage is not a joke."

"I'm not joking, I shwear." Her doubt made him feel quite affronted. He wasn't humbling himself in front of her and begging her to marry him as a joke. Couldn't the woman tell he was madly in love with her, even after she had deceived him? Didn't she know that he had given up his long-held dream of marrying a New York society princess for her sake, because he did not want to live without her? He had given up his dreams for her, only to have her turn around and accept the hand of a businessman from Russell Square and break his heart. "I'm sherious."

She twitched her skirts away from him. "You are a disgusting drunk."

He thought about that for a moment. "Not usually."

"You are mocking and insulting me."

"I'm not insulting you, you ninny." He sat back on his heels and glared at her. He was the one who was insulted now. When did declaring your undying love for a woman turn into an insult? "I'm asking you to marry me. It's not the same thing at all."

"You're hopeless, Eric. Utterly hopeless." She was shaking her head and looking down at him as if he were a worm. "Even though you have treated me abominably, I had thought I owed you the courtesy to keep on working for you until I was married. We were partners, after all, and the machinery we bought was expensive and still not paid off. But I can see now it will not work. Not if you are going to behave so vilely. You will have to find yourself another model."

He had treated *her* abominably? The injustice of her claim staggered him. She was the one who was mistreating him, not the other way around. "You can't leave me."

"I can, Eric, and I will. Goodbye. I hope you make the success of your life that you deserve."

Before he could stagger to his feet again, she had swept out of the front door and slammed it behind her.

He didn't move. His head hurt. He reached for the bottle of whiskey that Emily had taken away from him, but at the last moment he stopped. She was right—he was a disgusting drunk.

Of course she'd turned him down. What woman would trust the proposal of a man who could not even stand up without falling over? She'd be scared he would forget every promise he made before he sobered up again.

She wasn't married yet—only engaged. There was many a slip between cup and lip, as the saying went. Until she had actually stood in the church and wed her damned Mr. Murdoch from Russell Square, there was still hope.

Not a lot of hope, it was true, but a little was better than none at all.

Ten

Emily's wedding to Mr. Murdoch, held in the parlor of his house in Russell Square, was a quiet affair. Of all her siblings, Caroline and Beatrice were the only ones who could accept the invitation to attend. Mr. Murdoch hadn't particularly wanted any of them there, but she had worn him down in the end. After they were married, her family would be his family, too, she reminded him. Though the thought put a sour look on his face, he relented and allowed her to invite them. But only for the day—not to visit. She wanted to berate him for his meanness, but was too scared that any complaint would result in the invitation being withdrawn altogether. She could not risk that.

She had invited Mary Mittens, too, but Mary had turned down the invitation. She would not watch her friend make such a dreadful mistake, she said with a small shudder.

Mr. Murdoch's three daughters, all as small and sickly looking as Finella, were to make up the rest of the party.

Caroline hugged her exuberantly when she arrived, dusty and travel-worn, having set off before daybreak to get there in time. "Emily, how wonderful to see you," she gushed. "You could have knocked me over with a feather when you wrote me your news, but I am so pleased you have found yourself a happy situation." She looked sideways at Mr. Murdoch's grim, unsmiling face. "I hope you will be as happy as you deserve to be."

Beatrice was not far behind. "A second sister married," she crowed, as she caught Emily into her arms with delight. "And you have made such a fine catch, too." Ignoring Mr. Murdoch, she looked around her at the imposing furniture in the best parlor and sat down on a padded chintz sofa with a sigh of happiness. "It gives me hope that my turn might one day come."

"Of course it will," Caroline replied stoutly, sitting herself next to Emily on the sofa. "You have plenty of time yet."

Mr. Murdoch barely stayed long enough to greet them before he retreated to his study. As soon as the door closed behind him, Caroline looked searchingly into Emily's face. "Are you sure this is what you want? Are you sure this will make you happy"

For weeks now she had been planning to attract a wealthy man to be her patron. Now that she had found one who wanted her enough to marry her, she was not fool enough to turn him away. "Mr. Murdoch will do well enough."

"And Eric?"

She would not cry. Not on her wedding day. "He did not care for me."

Caroline took her into her arms, hugging her tightly. "Emily, I am so sorry. But do not make a hasty decision, I beg of you. You deserve the best."

Beatrice was staring at the meager fire absentmindedly. "Your Mr. Murdoch does not strike me as a kind man. Or an overly generous one either for all his wealth."

Emily flinched at Beatrice's softly spoken comment. It was only too true. Mr. Murdoch had not even offered her a new gown for her wedding, so she was dressed simply in a utilitarian green dress that Caroline's husband had generously outfitted her with more than a year ago, and with no ornaments.

Mr. Murdoch had also omitted the usual bride gift of jewelry for her wedding day. No doubt he thought he was doing her enough of an honor by offering her his name, but the omission still stung her pride.

Before she could reply, Mr. Murdoch was back again with the clergyman who was to marry them.

The clergyman took his place in front of the bay window, open Bible in his hand. Emily stood before him, Mr. Murdoch at her side, as she promised to love, honor, and obey her new husband until death did them part.

There, it was done. They were man and wife.

She had married Mr. Murdoch.

Glad as Emily had been to see two of her sisters again, she felt almost dizzy with relief when they left early in the afternoon for the long journey back home, and Mr. Murdoch's daughters were escorted back to the schoolroom by a harried-looking servant. Her marriage was not a celebration of two lives joining together in Holy Matrimony—it was a calculated gamble on her part that marriage to a wealthy businessman would give her almost as much freedom to do as she pleased as becoming his mistress.

She and her new husband sat together in the parlor, an uneasy silence hovering between them, as he sipped on a large balloon of brandy and she drank a dish of tea. A swallow went down the wrong way and she let out a muffled cough.

Mr. Murdoch looked at her critically as she choked on her tea. "I hope you are not going to prove sickly," he admonished her fretfully. "I can't abide sickly women."

"I am as healthy as an ox," Emily assured him as soon as she got her breath back. "I have scarce been sick a day in my life."

He did not look entirely convinced. "My first wife was a sickly creature. She was always taking one remedy or another for her imagined ills, spending a fortune on physicians. Not that they did her any good. Without a word of warning, she up and died and left me with three young daughters to care for. No, I do not want another sickly wife."

"I doubt she died on purpose to vex you," Emily pointed out.

Mr. Murdoch scowled at her impertinence. "Do not be ridiculous," he said sharply. "I never said she did." With that, he stood up and strode over to the door, brandy glass in his hand.

"Where are you going?" She had been hoping they would

be able to spend some time quietly together on their wedding day. Though they were now man and wife, she hardly knew anything about her new husband.

He turned back to her with a look of irritation on his face. "I am not used to having my actions questioned in my own house. I will see you at dinner."

Emily sat by herself in the parlor until her tea became cold and the afternoon shadows grew long. Mr. Murdoch did not look in on her again.

Dinner that night was a somber affair. Her three step-daughters were, as a special treat, allowed to take their dinner downstairs instead of in the schoolroom with their nurse. Their presence did little to liven the occasion.

"Finella, how pretty you look with your hair done up," Emily started, as they all took their places around the heavy oak table.

Finella threw her a startled look but did not answer.

Mr. Murdoch cleared his throat. "Silence at the dinner table is the rule in this house," he said portentously. "Idle chatter interferes with my digestion."

Emily raised her eyebrows. "But—"

He cut her off before she could say another word. "Do you not understand the meaning of the word silence?" His voice was icy.

"Of course I do. But—"

He set his soup spoon down on the table with a noisy clatter. "Then pray observe it."

With a shrug, Emily picked up her soup spoon and began to eat, but her new husband's manner had completely destroyed her appetite. She picked her way through the elaborate dinner: asparagus soup, a fillet of sole, a roast of beef with cucumber sauce, side dishes of celery and radishes, and, finally, a lemon sherbet. Out of the corner of her eye, she noticed the girls ate even less than she did. No wonder they were so pale and peaky.

It was a relief when she could finally escape into the drawing room, leaving Mr. Murdoch alone with his port and cigars.

On leaving the dining room, the girls immediately retired to the schoolroom. Though Emily waited in the drawing room for over an hour in solitary splendor, Mr. Murdoch did not join her. Finally, impelled by tiredness and a sense of pique, she, too, retired to her bedroom.

The only nightgowns she owned were plain white cotton. She slipped into one, wishing it was silk and lace. Surely Mr. Murdoch would warm up to her in the bedroom, if nowhere else. Sitting at her dressing table, she unpinned her hair and then brushed it out. Then, for want of anything better to do, she slipped into bed.

Sometime later, she was awakened by a heavy tread in the room as someone tripped over the edge of the rug and cursed loudly. She rolled over sleepily. "Mr. Murdoch?"

The mattress sank beneath his weight as he sat heavily on the bed. Without a word of greeting, he got into bed next to her, took her in his arms and fumbled awkwardly at her breasts through the thin cotton of her nightgown.

His breath smelled of port and stale cigar smoke. She turned her head away so she did not have to breathe in the noxious vapors. This was not how she had imagined her wedding night to be.

After pawing drunkenly at her for a few moments, he pulled her nightgown above her waist, positioned himself between her thighs and entered her roughly with a single thrust. She shrank back from the intrusion, but he did not notice. Either that, or he did not care. After thrusting into her a few times, he withdrew, and, with a grunt of pleasure, he spurted his cum all over her belly.

"Good girl," he mumbled approvingly, as he immediately staggered out of her bed and left the room.

Emily was left alone in her bedroom, with her new husband's seed rapidly cooling on her stomach and quiet tears rolling down her cheeks.

Emily's married life quickly settled down into a pattern. Mr. Murdoch was up early in the morning and, after a substantial breakfast, made his way into the City. She lay in late and ate when he had left. It was easier that way. He did not like her company at breakfast.

She entertained herself as best she could during the day, ate a silent meal with him in the evenings, retired to her apartments as soon as was decent, and suffered his brief visits to her at night in an obedient stupor. All in all, life could have been worse. Though she was desperately lonely, she was at least warm and well fed. She would find a purpose and a meaning to her new life in the end, she was sure.

The routine varied only when Sunday arrived. Though Emily lay in later than usual, Mr. Murdoch was still drinking his coffee at the breakfast table when she appeared downstairs.

With rare good humor, he poured her a cup and pushed it over the table toward her. "We have been married a week almost. We must have a wedding portrait taken. One done by the excellent Mr. Twyford. That could make for a most unusual photograph, don't you think?"

Emily sipped halfheartedly at the bitter black brew in front of her. She only liked coffee when it was doctored with plenty of sugar and cream, but she knew better than to turn down what seemed almost to be a peace offering from her new husband. "I quarreled with my photographer a few days ago. He will not be taking any more pictures of me as Emily." She gave a half-laugh, nervous about breaking the news of her complete poverty to him. "I have come to you as a complete pauper, I'm afraid. The only dowry I bring is my five pounds saved in the Bank of England, and a couple of shillings in my purse. I have nothing else to my name."

He regarded her gravely from under his heavy eyebrows. "You quarreled with your photographer?" he asked, to her surprise. She had thought he might be disturbed by her utter lack of dowry, but she hadn't even considered that he might care about her quarrel with Eric. It was a personal matter, after all. "May I ask on what grounds?"

She shrugged uneasily, not wanting to go into the details of their conversation, particularly not on her wedding day. "Does it matter? I have broken off the connection, as I assume you wanted me to do anyway. I do not imagine you would want your wife to continue posing as I have done in the past."

"Emily, Emily, Emily," he said with slow gravity, as if he were talking to an unruly child. "You should not make assumptions about what I would think best and then simply act on them before asking my advice or my permission. I am most displeased with this news. Most displeased indeed."

She shrugged again, not particularly caring what he thought about the matter. "It can't be helped now. He swears he will not speak with me again. And even if he would," she muttered under her breath, "I do not want to speak to him. Ever again."

"Don't mutter, Emily," he snapped. "It is not ladylike."

Her eyes widened. Did even such a small matter as her muttering make him cross?

"You must go and make up the quarrel immediately," he pronounced firmly. "I insist that you visit him this very afternoon to apologize for your behavior."

"But I was not the one at fault," she protested. The idea of apologizing to Eric for his insults was preposterous. "He was blind drunk and he called me evil names and threw me out of his studio."

He waved her concerns away with an impatient gesture. "It does not matter what you think. I have informed you what your course of action must be, and I expect you to be obedient, as a wife ought to be. Which reminds me, you will not invite your sisters here again. I did not like them. Their manners were too common."

She swallowed the protest she was about to make. What sort of man was he that it didn't matter to him that another man had abused her? And he thought to forbid her from seeing her own family? The nasty feeling that had been growing in the pit of her stomach ever since her wedding day suddenly burst into bloom. She *had* been too hasty in marrying him. What did she know of his character? Of his morals? Nothing at all. She had married him based on the fact that his behavior to her, before their wedding, had always been perfectly gentleman-like. Maybe Mary Mittens had been right about his character after all.

Still, she had married him now and she had to make the best of the bargain. "If it would please you, I will go and visit him," she said dutifully, leaving the matter of her sisters until another day. "Though I am not sure he will see me."

"You will have to persuade him into it. I am relying on you to do so. Indeed, I shall come with you myself to ensure that this little contretemps can be patched over."

"Why do you want to visit him?" His attitude toward Eric piqued her curiosity. "Now that I am married I do not want to sit for any more photographs, particularly not if Mr. Twyford were to take them."

"You forget, Emily, that you are my wife and you will do exactly what I tell you to do." The indulgent smile he gave her was quite at odds with the chill in his voice. "If I choose that you pose for more photographs, then pose you will. I will be the king of my own household and will not brook any insubordination from anyone, not from my daughters, not from my servants, and least of all from a wife sworn to obedience. Make no mistake about that."

"But surely you would not want your wife to pose without her clothes on?" She could not imagine many men being happy for their wives to sit for such pictures.

"I should not have to warn you again, Emily, not to assume any knowledge of what my thoughts may be. It is for me to think whatever I choose, and for you to obey. Now off you run and have a lie-down for an hour. I want you in perfect looks when we pay our call on Mr. Twyford later this afternoon."

She had only just obeyed Mr. Murdoch and retreated to the sanctuary of her sitting room when there was a soft knock at her door. Emily opened it to find a black-faced Finella standing outside. "Can I help you?" she asked with surprise. Finella had been markedly quiet and sullen ever since the wedding and had barely spoken two words to anyone. All her overtures of friendship had been soundly rebuffed.

"Are you not going to invite me in, step-mama?" the girl asked with quiet insolence.

Emily stepped aside to allow her to enter. "Of course."

Finella walked in and gave a sniff at the modesty of the surroundings, the faded yellow wallpaper and the old-fashioned furniture, before plonking herself unceremoniously on the best chair. "I don't know what he was doing, marrying you," she said rudely. "You are not the wealthy wife he was wanting."

Somewhat taken aback by the girl's impudence, Emily sat down opposite her. "Sometimes we do not know what we want until we see it there in front of us."

"Pah. It is easy enough to know what Papa wants," Finella sneered. "Our neighbor Sir Pickerton's wife in his bed whenever her husband is away, and one of the upstairs maids the rest of the time. Preferably a buxom and good-looking one, but he'll take whatever he can get even if she's pale and as ugly as a horse, like the one I saw him with last night in the pantry after you had gone to bed. He's not fussy when it comes to fucking maidservants."

"Finella." Emily was truly shocked, not so much by what the girl was revealing about her father, but by the malicious pleasure she took in saying it. "That is no way to speak of your father. A lady should not even *know* such words, let alone say them aloud."

"Father would whip me if he heard me," Finella said nonchalantly. "But then, he is not here, is he? And if you tell him, I will deny it, and then he will whip you instead for lying, as he whipped my mother."

"He whipped your mother?" Her lunch roiled in her stomach. If it were true, she had just wed a man who had beaten his first wife. And meddled with maidservants to boot.

"Often enough that she died of it." The fierce bitterness in her eyes undercut the casual tone of Finella's voice. Though clearly trained in the school of hard knocks, she was still too young to hide her feelings successfully. "I saw him myself when I heard her cry out in her room and I bent down and looked through the keyhole." She gave a smile that lit her savage features. "It's amazing what I have learned by looking through keyholes. All about Mrs. Pickerton and the upstairs maids, for instance."

Emily swallowed the wave of nausea that threatened to overcome her. Mary Mittens had been right about Mr. Murdoch's character after all. What reason would poor Finella have to lie to her? And about her own father, too. "A young lady should not peep through keyholes. And most especially she should not repeat what she has seen if she has ever succumbed to the temptation to peek." A wave of pity for the young girl swept over her, but she was too wise to show it. Nothing would wound the girl's pride so much as a show of pity from the woman she had come intending to hurt. "Why are you telling me this?"

"Because you are young and pretty enough and he does not deserve to marry you." Unshed tears made the girl's eyes shine brightly. "He should stick to nasty old crows like Mrs. Pickerton—she is old and has a pinched face and an evil temper when she thinks he is not looking. He does not deserve anything better than her. Aunt Mavis agrees with me. She is mother's sister, and she doesn't like papa either. She says he is a ratbag and a scoundrel."

Poor Mrs. Pickerton did not sound as though she had won Finella's affections either. "You do not want me as your step-mama?"

"Not if you will make my father happy. I hate him," she burst out passionately. "I wish I could live with Aunt Mavis instead of with him. He does not deserve to be happy. He deserves to be miserable, as miserable as he made my mother."

Emily sighed. "We all deserve to be happy, if we can be without hurting anyone else."

Finella sat in silence for a moment, biting the skin around her thumb thoughtfully. "He is not rich, you know," she mumbled in between nibbles.

Emily blinked, thrown off-course by the sudden change in topic. "I beg your pardon?"

"He has no money anymore. I found that out by listening at keyholes, too," she added defiantly. "He made some bad investments and was looking out for a wealthy woman to marry. I heard him say it was a damned shame that old Pickerton was taking such a confounded long time to die because his widow would be ripe for the picking."

"You should not be telling such tales about your father."

The girl stuck out her bottom lip. "I'm only telling the truth."

Emily had a nasty suspicion that Finella *was* telling the truth. "You should not tell tales even if it is the truth. I do not think your father would care for the entire town to know of his financial embarrassment."

The girl shrugged. "I do not care about him. So are you happy you married him now?"

Emily smiled sadly. "What is done is done," she said, evading the question. The less the girl suspected how badly her words had rattled her, the better.

"Are you going to tell Father what I have said?" Though the girl strove to hide it, her bravado was close to crumbling. A real note of fear at the prospect of being told on had entered her voice.

"A lady does not repeat what has been told to her in confidence," Emily stated firmly. She would not have the girl whipped on her account. "I presume that everything you told me about your father was told to me in confidence?"

Finella nodded.

Emily smiled at her. "Then I shall respect your confidence and I shall not breathe a word of our conversation to him."

Finella stood up to leave, a cautious hope replacing her earlier fear. "You really shouldn't have married him," she said earnestly, pausing at the door. "He's not a nice man and he will not be kind to you. I don't like him at all, even though he is my father."

Her heart broke for the poor child. "Thank you for your honesty. Not many young women would be brave enough to come and tell me what you have told me."

Finella's pale face glowed under the compliment. Emily suspected that she received few enough of them. "Good day, stepmama." This time there was no insolence in her voice, but a wistful hope as she tiptoed toward her own room.

"Good day," Emily called down the hallway, receiving a little wave from the girl as an acknowledgment.

She stepped back into her room, shut the door, and put her head in her hands, wondering just how much of what Finella had told her was true. Had she really married such a monster? A man who beat his first wife to death and slept with his neighbor's wife? A man who seduced a parlor maid in the pantry the week after his wedding?

Of course, much of it might be make-believe. The child was crying out for attention, for the love and tenderness she had never received at home. Still, she would not be asking her husband about the truth of the allegations. She had no doubt but that he would harshly punish anyone, including his own daughter, who crossed his temper. The poor thing did not deserve a father who beat her. No child did.

Eric was cutting the prints with a guillotine when the shop door opened. "Be with you in a moment," he called, as he set aside the completed postcards and strode into the shop front.

Though she had her back to him, he knew her the instant he saw her. "Em?"

Slowly she turned around to face him. Her eyes were dark hollows in the paleness of her face. "Mr. Twyford."

He rushed over and took her by the hands. "Em, have you been ill? You look so pale?"

She drew her hands away with a slight shake of her head, a mute entreaty in her eyes.

It was only then that he noticed a tall, bushy-browed gentleman in a fine, dark suit standing just inside the door, flicking a piece of lint off his sleeve with a fastidious sniff. He looked at Eric and gave a toothy smile. "Mr. Twyford, I presume?"

"The very same," Eric replied, forcing a smile. The man's patronizing air grated on his nerves, but he kept his countenance.

The stranger held out his hand in greeting. "My name is Murdoch, Murdoch of Russell Square."

Eric scowled as he shook Mr. Murdoch's hand. So this was the pill that had asked Em to marry him? The suit he had been admiring just before now seemed to him to be flashy and over-dressed, a way of arrogantly displaying how much money he had. What the devil was Mr. Murdoch coming to visit him for?

"I see you recognize my name."

"You're Em's man, I guess," he said with forced casualness. What the hell did she think she was doing, bringing her new man in to gloat over his broken heart. It was cruel of her. He had never thought her cruel before. "I saw the notice in the paper."

Mr. Murdoch's eyebrows raised at his deliberate familiarity. "Mrs. Murdoch and I were married last week."

They were married already? Irrevocably married? "Con-gratulations." The word stuck in his throat but he forced it out nonetheless. "I hope you will be very happy." He could not bear to look at Em. He heartily wished them both to the devil.

"Thank you, thank you. Now, I would be obliged if you would take a portrait of the pair of us. A wedding portrait on our wedding day." He turned to look at Emily. "Mrs. Murdoch, may I suggest you make yourself more comfortable? I want this to be a portrait worth looking at." The last was said with a knowing leer that made Eric want to smash his face to pieces.

Emily did not move at his unsubtle suggestion. "No." Her voice was calm, but firm.

"I beg your pardon, Mrs. Murdoch?" Mr. Murdoch's brows lowered and he gazed stonily at his wife as he did not believe her refusal. "Did you not, just a few days ago, promise to obey me?"

"If I am to have a wedding portrait, it will be with my clothes on," she hissed at him under her breath, though loudly enough for Eric to catch her words. "I have not come prepared to model in my undergarments. I will not do so."

With Mr. Murdoch still scowling at his wife's disobedience, Eric led them to his studio and sat them side by side on the stone bench. "Look happy," he said perfunctorily, but he may as well have held his breath. They both glared at him as if he were their executioner.

He ran off a single exposure. No point in wasting more film on the two of them. "That will be ten pounds unframed or twenty framed," he said, more than doubling his prices out of pure spite. "You may come back in a week to collect it."

Mr. Murdoch gave a delicate cough as he handed over the money. "You will have guessed by our presence here that I am well aware of my wife's other career."

"You needn't worry about that," Eric broke in wearily, instantly guessing where the man's conversation was going. "Em came to visit me the other day and said she couldn't pose for me anymore on account of her getting married soon. I won't be taking any more photographs of her. Not unless you want another wedding portrait."

Mr. Murdoch did not look overly pleased at the news. "That is exactly what I was afraid of." He paced up and down, his hands clasped behind his back for a moment. "Mrs. Murdoch informed me that you two had quarreled, and I insisted that we visit you immediately to apologize for her behavior and to make any amends we could." He turned to Em with a false smile plastered over his face. "You cannot afford to quarrel with your photographer. Indeed, you cannot."

Emily turned away from him with a scowl. "I do not see why I should not," she muttered under her breath as she moved away.

Eric's mouth had dropped open in shock at Mr. Murdoch's words. "You want me to keep on taking photographs of Emily? Even though she is your wife?"

"I have no intention of letting such a profitable line of business out of my hands," Mr. Murdoch said sharply. Beside him, Emily sucked in a harsh breath of surprise. "Of course, the contract you have with her will have to be re-negotiated so that, as her husband, I receive a fair share of the profits. And I will insist on having some input into the shoots as well. Your photographs, fine as they may be, do not go far enough for my taste. Or for the taste of many gentlemen of my acquaintance, who prefer their pleasures rather more . . . uh . . . *sophisticated* than is currently provided for by the English market."

Eric was getting a bad feeling about this. Emily was staring speechlessly at her new husband as if his words had shocked and sickened her as much as they had him.

A very bad feeling, indeed. "What exactly are you suggesting?"

Mr. Murdoch's toothy smile reappeared. "We need to get more inventive with your poses, my dear," he said to Emily, though it was really Eric to whom his words were directed. He ignored the look of disgust on his wife's face. "Nothing of your loveliness should be hidden. Nothing at all, if you get my meaning." He chucked her under the chin, as one would do to reassure a small child. "And your behavior is too modest—you could be far more daring. I have some props in mind for you to use—chains and whips, interesting items you could play with in a sultry manner, that sort of thing. I think such cards would sell very well. Very well indeed."

Eric swallowed the lump in his throat. Was the man serious? It revolted him to think that he might be.

"Then, when we have thoroughly examined all facets of Emily alone," Mr. Murdoch continued, now addressing Eric directly, "I would like to introduce another woman into the picture and have her and Emily engaged with each other in various delicious poses. A month or two later, we can bring in a man, too. Or even better, two men, and photograph them while they are intimately engaged with the girl. *Very* intimately. Such pictures, my dear fellow, would more than make up for the investment losses I have recently sustained." He heaved a sigh. "Such a damned promising venture the railways looked to be, too. Still, my wife is a far better investment. She will make me rich, and with almost no capital outlay required."

Emily gave a choking cough, but did not say a word.

This was the sort of man that Em had married? A man who'd watch his wife be fucked by strangers and then sell the images on the street? A man who had married her not because he loved her but because he could make money out of her?

And what of her? Had she agreed to this . . . this perverted idea of her affianced husband? "And what does Em think about this?" He could not look at her. If he saw any signs of agreement in her face, he would be sick all over Mr. Murdoch's shiny boots.

Mr. Murdoch was still lost in his dream of riches. "The photographs themselves will not be the only source of funds. I will have men around the country paying huge sums of money to become a part of one of the famous Emily's pictures. As Emily's husband, I will naturally retain one hundred percent of any such fees, but I will allow you a generous commission on the sale of any photographs you may take."

Sexy photographs of Emily's almost naked body, yes, but to photograph two people—or more—actually engaged in the act of coition? With his Emily? That was going way too far. He stole a look at her and took heart from the haunted expression on her face. "Have you agreed to this proposal, Em?" he asked softly. "Is this really what you want to do?"

Mutely, she shook her head. She looked, he thought, too shocked to speak.

"My *wife*," Mr. Murdoch interrupted, with a heavy emphasis, "will not be required either to think or to agree. She will be required only to obey the commands of her lawful wedded husband. In other words, she will do as she is told or she will face the consequences."

Eric clenched his hands into fists at his sides. This bounder had married Em to force her into what amounted to no more than prostitution? It was a filthy idea, dreamed up by a filthy and depraved man. "I don't take pictures like you are suggesting," he said stiffly, battling the urge to ram the man's teeth down his throat with his knuckles. "You had best find yourself another photographer."

The satisfied smirk on Mr. Murdoch's face faded a little. "You are a professional, aren't you? There would, of course, be a generous commission involved."

Eric walked to the door and held it open. "If you will excuse me, Mr. Murdoch, I have work to do." He wanted the man out of his sight before he did him permanent damage.

Mr. Murdoch's face turned slightly gray around the edges at this abrupt dismissal. "But we will be needing—"

Eric cut him off before he could utter another word. "Good day, Mr. Murdoch," he said, taking the older gentleman by the elbow and steering him out onto the street. He had to shove him slightly to get him over the threshold. "Don't bother coming back."

Emily shot him a desperate look as she left in his wake. "I cannot stay now," she muttered. "Please, wait for me later."

He watched the pair of them enter a handsome carriage that had been waiting for them at the corner of the street. His back was ramrod straight, while hers was bent over as if she were in pain.

He couldn't let Em stay with such a scoundrel, even if she had married him. Not even if she swore black and blue that she was crazy in love with him. Before he let her waste her life on such scum, he would hogtie her, throw her in the hold of a ship, and take her off to the Americas with him.

Not until early evening could Emily escape the house unde-tected. Mr. Murdoch, furious at her refusal to undress for him in Eric's studio, had berated her all the way home in the car-riage, and ended his lecture with a couple of hard slaps to her face. On the pretext of bathing them in cold water so they would not bruise, she had retired to her room as soon as they arrived back at Russell Square.

She had eaten a solitary supper on her own. Thankfully, he had not requested her presence at the dinner table. The sight of him, her husband, at the other end of the table would be enough to turn her stomach.

Then, while Mr. Murdoch was safely getting sozzled over his port in the dining room as usual, she had scurried down the stairs and out into the street.

Once safely around the corner and away from any danger of prying eyes, instead of hurrying with her eyes firmly fixed on the cobblestones at her feet, she dawdled her way to Eric's studio, her mind furiously planning her next move as she walked along.

Crowds of people, tempted outside by the last of the sun, lined the streets. A chimney sweep skipped by, and she twitched her skirt out of the way of his broom before it could be stained by the soot that clung to him like a badge of office. A handsome young soldier strode past her, his uniform crisp and clean, and a brace of medals on his chest resplendent in the sun. Hers were not the only eyes that followed his progress—a couple of girls walking arm-in-arm in front of her giggled as they stood still to watch him go by.

Everything today had led her to one inescapable conclusion. She could not stay with the monster she had married. His plans for her, the grandiose ideas he had shared with such satisfaction, had made her feel physically ill. On hearing his plans for the first time she had been so shocked she had not been able to think straight, but had merely followed him back to his house like the obedient wife he took her for.

No, she could not stay in his house with him. Not for another minute.

She was counting on Eric to put her up for the night. In return she would continue modeling for him despite their quarrel. For the sake of his own self-interest, if nothing else, he should be willing to help her. In the morning, she would make her way to Caroline's house in Hertfordshire. That would be her refuge.

As she stopped at a crossing, a street sweeper darted in front of her to sweep the roadway for her. She tossed him a couple of farthings, which he caught with a practiced hand, flipped up into the air with a grin, and then tucked away in a pocket in his trousers.

She had accepted Mr. Murdoch's proposal in foolish haste. His daughter's behavior ought to have alerted her that something was wrong. Poor Finella clearly lived in fear of her father's notice ever lighting upon her. It was hardly a wonder that the girl had bitten her nails with nerves and sneaked around the school on her tiptoes, accustomed as she was to living with a father who had such exacting expectations of female obedience.

A pale woman, her thin frame drowned in a gown three sizes too large for her and her gaunt face shadowed by a huge bonnet, was stopped at a street stall. As Emily passed her, she looked nervously this way and that before digging a coin out of her pocket and purchasing an apple, which she bit into with greedy relish. The purple stains of a faded bruise marked one of her cheeks, and her sleeves were pulled right down over her wrists, half covering her hands.

Would she be reduced to a state like that in a few years, Emily wondered uneasily, if she were to stay with this marriage? Afraid even to buy an apple without her husband's express permission?

"Emily."

Lost in her thoughts, she gave a start at the sound of her name. "Eric?"

Spruced up in his best suit, his hair tamed as much as it could ever be, and his chin clearly freshly shaved, he looked good enough to eat. Only a stray smudge of ink on the very tip of his nose betrayed his occupation. Her heart did a little flip at the sight of him. She longed to rush into his arms in the middle of the street, but she held herself back.

He took her arm and tucked it into the crook of his own. "I thought you might come this way. I have been waiting for you."

The touch of his hand on hers made her ache with longing but she could not bear to pull away.

In silent communion, they had set their faces toward Eric's studio. As soon as they were over the threshold, he locked the door behind them. "Can I make you a cup of tea?" Though he looked searchingly at the reddened palm prints on her cheeks, he did not ask her about them. She was grateful for his tact.

She nodded, her mouth too dry to speak, simply watching him as he pottered around the back room, filling the kettle with water and boiling it over the spirit flame before placing two heaped spoonfuls of tea into the pot and filling it with the boiling water. He poured her a cup and added a splash of milk from a crock keeping cool in the pantry shelf.

He handed her the cup and watched her take a sip.

The mouthful of tea had wet her throat enough to speak. "Thank you. It is very good."

Giving her a grave smile, he poured his own tea and took a seat opposite her. "Mr. Murdoch surprised me today. I would venture to guess he surprised you, too."

She started at the sound of his voice and spilled a drop of hot tea on her lap. "He did. So did his daughter. She told me how badly he beat his first wife." She touched her hand to her still-aching cheek. "At first I did not know whether to believe her."

He ran his hands through his hair, ruffling his neatly combed locks. "You don't belong with him, Em."

The air in the room felt cold and she could not suppress a shiver. He took a shawl and folded it around her shoulders, and she nestled gratefully into the warmth. "I have married him now. I am bound to him. I cannot undo what I have done."

"You can't stay with him." The words were an order, not an entreaty. "I will not let you."

"No." She gave a small, sad smile. "I cannot live with him. I am going away to my sister's house in the morning."

"You will stay with me until then?"

She nodded gratefully. It was what she had hoped for when she ran to him. "It will be too dangerous for me to visit town to model for you for a few months, but you can bring your camera into the country. Caroline would not mind."

They were both silent for a moment or two. Then Eric spoke, his voice hesitant. "There is a possible way out for you that I can see. A way you can be free of him."

Her heart leaped into her throat. The only true escape for her would be Mr. Murdoch's death. Surely that was not what Eric was hinting at. "What do you mean?"

"He thought to gain your obedience through his discovery of your secret life as a model. But what if he had a secret of his own, one that he did not want the world to know? If you possessed a similar secret about him, you could demand that he divorce you or have the marriage annulled as the price of your silence."

"Divorce him?" The idea had not even occurred to her. Mr. Murdoch would never agree to it. She was worth too much to him. The most she could expect was to leave his house and live in hiding—his wife, but yet not his wife.

He gave a twisted smile. "As a divorced woman, you could never hope to move in exalted society, but then it would be no worse than being a postcard girl, surely?"

She shrugged. "He may have twenty such secrets for all I know, but they do me no good because I do not know a single one of them."

"If there is one," he said with confidence, "we can find it out."

"How?" Even in the midst of her despair, his optimism was infecting her with a desperate hope.

"I am a photographer. I take pictures, scientific records of the truth." He shot her a grin. "What's more, the gullible public thinks that photographic images are in all cases accurate representations of reality."

She gave him a puzzled frown. "Aren't they?"

"Sometimes, yes, they are. But there are a multitude of ways in which photographs can be distorted, altered, to show a representation of reality, not reality itself. If we cannot find a secret out about him, we can create one in my darkroom. That will do just as well, particularly if it has a basis in fact."

"You would help me do this? You would make your camera lie for me?"

"Your postcards have made me more money than I have ever seen in my life before. It would be a shabby thing if I did not return the favor as far as I can. Tell me again, exactly what did the daughter tell you?"

Thus prompted, Emily related to him everything Finella had told her about Mr. Murdoch's lack of wealth, his mistreatment of his first wife, and his liking for maidservants and for the wife of his neighbor, Pickerton.

"Pickerton, Pickerton." Eric's face creased in a frown. "Where have I heard that name before?"

"They are a neighbor of Murdoch's in Russell Square," Emily added. "And Mr. Murdoch had apparently thought of marrying his widow if he died. Perhaps the threat of a scandal with Mr. Murdoch and Mrs. Pickerton might be enough to frighten him into agreeing to a divorce. What do you think?"

Eric strode up and down the studio, deep in thought. "Of course. I have it." He snapped his fingers in the air with triumph. "Pickerton, if he is the one I am thinking of, is in the Lower House. A Tory, I believe, and rather an embarrassment to his party. Rumor has it that he's involved with some rather nasty types—organized criminal gangs from East London. Extortion, blackmail— you name it and he's been accused of it. He's too canny to be easily caught, though. The mud never sticks to him, and he throws enough money around that he gets reelected every time."

Emily gulped. "*That* Pickerton?" Even she had heard of the aging criminal mastermind who had attained a veneer of respectability in his later years, even marrying the spinster daughter of an impoverished Earl and joining whatever society would welcome him and his tainted millions. She must be the Mrs. Pickerton that Finella had mentioned. "Mr. Murdoch is a braver man than I thought to be having an affair with the wife of a man like that." He'd surely pay a heavy price to keep that little tidbit of gossip out of public view. However much he might want to keep her in his clutches to pay his bills, keeping his throat uncut has to be worth more to him.

"He's playing with fire, that's for sure. Pickerton is getting on in years now, but his mind is still supposed to be as sharp as ever. He'd gut any man he caught with his wife."

"I doubt a simple threat would convince Mr. Murdoch—we would need solid photographic evidence. But how would we ever catch them in the act?"

Eric grinned. "It isn't necessary. I'll need a clear photo of his face, and another of hers. Once we have those, nothing could be easier. I can craft a photograph in my darkroom that would have the protagonists themselves swear that I had caught them in *flagrante delicto*."

"The wedding portrait," she suggested with a glimmer of humor in her turn. The irony of using their wedding portrait to obtain a divorce pleased her. "That would serve him right, the filthy swine, treating me as if I were nothing but a common harlot bought for his pleasure. But what of her?"

"Tomorrow morning I will pay a visit to Russell Square. An itinerant photographer will not make any eyebrows rise. I shall knock on every door in the street and offer cut price portraits of the eminent inhabitants. I may even get some real commissions out of it." He grinned. "I wouldn't turn down the extra work, especially now that I have the printing press running so smoothly."

She squared her shoulders. "I will come with you."

"It is too dangerous for you to come. What if Mr. Murdoch should see you?"

"He will be out scouring the countryside for me, not looking for me right under his nose. Besides, I will wear a bonnet to cover my hair. He will not recognize me unless he comes close enough to see my face, and I will keep a watch for him."

"You can act as my assistant, then."

"But if Mrs. Pickerton doesn't bite?" she asked worriedly. "Or if her servants turn us away without letting us in? What then?"

"You underestimate my abilities to charm servant girls into opening the door to me." He winked at her. "But if my legendary charm fails, then we take a very long afternoon tea in the park with our camera trained casually on her door. She will have to come out eventually and then, bam, we have our photograph."

It was possible, she thought as a yawn crept up on her. It might just be possible to salvage a life for herself, even after the disastrous mistake she had made. Maybe everything was not lost after all.

Eric was watching her with hawk eyes. "You're tired," he said accusingly.

Now that she thought about it, she could hardly keep upright for weariness. "Exhausted," she admitted. She had not slept well the night before with nerves, and the day's events had taken a terrible toll on her.

Without another word, he picked her up as if she weighed no more than a feather and carried her into his bedroom. He threw back the crazy patchwork quilt that covered his bed, laid her on the sheets, and started to unlace her boots. "You can sleep here tonight."

"But what about you?"

He shrugged. "I will take the sofa in the parlor."

Taking his hand, she held it tightly in her own. "Please don't leave me," she said with a shiver. "I am afraid."

The last thing she knew before she sank into a deep, dreamless sleep was the feel of Eric's arms around her and his whispered promise that he would never leave her.

Eleven

The next morning saw Emily, neatly dressed as befitted a photographer's assistant, in a dark brown skirt and a modest cream shirt with ruffles down the front and an enormous bonnet covering her head and reaching around the sides of her face. She and Eric walked along Russell Square, knocking on the door of each house of the square in turn, offering portrait sittings at bargain prices.

Though Emily kept a sharp eye out for any sign of Mr. Murdoch, there was no hint of his presence. He had probably dashed off to Hertfordshire at daybreak to look for his runaway wife at her sister's house. She would make sure to write to Caroline and put her mind at ease this very afternoon.

By the time they reached the door of their target, Mrs. Pickerton, they already had in hand three commissions for portraits to be taken in the following week. "That's not bad going," Eric murmured to her as they walked up the steps to ring the doorbell at number fifty-three. "It's amazing what a difference it makes having a pretty assistant beside me. Instant credibility. None of them would've looked twice at me if I'd turned up on my own. I tried a similar tack when I first arrived in London and the servants chased me away as if I were a beggar."

"So I'm useful for something other than taking off my clothes?" Emily inquired acerbically. Picking a fight with Eric was easier than worrying about whether Mrs. Pickerton would receive them or not. All was not lost if she would have nothing to do with them, but it would certainly be easier if she would agree to pose for a portrait.

A burly footman answered the door at their knock. He listened impassively as they spun their tale and replied only that he would see if his mistress was at home.

"What if she won't see us?" Emily whispered as they stood on the doorstep waiting for the footman to return.

"Then we retire to the park and wait for her to appear."

"But what if she doesn't have any engagements this afternoon? She might not come out of her house for a week. We can't stay in the park until then."

"Would you rather stay married to Mr. Murdoch and have him turn you into little better than a common prostitute?"

"I'd rather stab him in his lying, cheating heart," she hissed.

"I don't fancy a vacation in Botany Bay, thank you all the same. I'd much rather sit in the park and canoodle with you as if we were lovers until Mrs. Pickerton appears."

Emily glared at him. If making love with each other didn't qualify them to be lovers, she didn't know what would.

Just then footsteps could be heard on the other side of the door. Eric nudged her in the side with his elbow. "Don't scowl so, or he won't let us in for fear that you'll curdle all the milk in the dairy."

Emily just had time to poke him back hard in the ribs with her own elbow before the door opened inward and the footman reappeared, his face as impassive as ever. "Mrs. Pickerton will see you now," he said. "Follow me."

He led them upstairs to a pretty boudoir and ushered them inside. Mrs. Pickerton, wearing only a flimsy wrap, was sitting on a stool in front of her dressing table, fixing her hair in the looking glass. As they entered, she turned, a haughty look on her face. "You are the photographers, I presume?"

After Finella's description of the woman, Emily had expected to find an aging and ugly harridan, but Mrs. Pickerton was nothing of the sort. Though a few crow's feet around her eyes bore testimony to the fact that she was no longer in her first blush of youth, and the odd fleck of gray could be seen in her dark hair, she was still a very handsome woman. Emily could well believe that she had a temper, though. Her face, handsome as it was, bore a narrow, pinched look, as if the owner of it had spent a good deal of her life looking at the world and finding it wanting.

Eric took off his hat and bowed politely. "Indeed, Ma'am, I am Mr. Twyford at your service, photographer to high society and to all the fashionable ladies in town. Usually I have ladies knocking on my door all day and night clamoring for me to take their photographs, but for today, for you only, Ma'am, I will take a portrait of you and have it framed in solid wood for only ten pounds. You couldn't get a better photographer to do so much for you, even at double the price."

"I have been meaning to get my portrait done as a gift to my husband," she said rather languidly, "but sitting to be painted is such a bore. I thought you might be rather faster."

"Indeed, Ma'am, photography is perfectly suited to busy society ladies such as yourself, who do not want to sit and twiddle their thumbs for hours while a painter painstakingly tries to capture the essence of their beauty with his brush and paints. Photography, Ma'am, is instant. I click open the shutter, you hold still just for a moment, and presto, the photograph is ready for me to take back to my studio and develop. There is nothing more to it."

She examined her nails in an idle fashion. "I suppose I have a half hour to spare before I must dress for dinner. Can you be finished before then?"

"Certainly, Ma'am." Eric was all smiles and charm. "It won't take more than a moment to set up my tripod and then I can take your likeness right away. Is there any particular pose you would like me to capture you in? A favorite gown? Or," he suggested slyly, "something a little more daring for your husband? A love-token for his eyes only?"

She stared at him, her gray eyes cold. "An intimate photograph. Is that what you are suggesting?"

"Of course, Madam is the best judge of her husband's tastes and whether he would appreciate such a gesture."

A smile flickered briefly over her face. "I suppose I could pose for you without my gown. Mr. Pickerton might be amused at the novelty."

Eric bowed. "A photographer is much like an artist, Ma'am. I will take a photograph of you in whatever pose you might prefer. And I guarantee confidentiality to all my clients. No details of this sitting will ever pass my lips."

Mrs. Pickerton rose from the stool and moved over to the four-poster bed that stood in the corner. "I have a fancy to have a photograph of me as the mistress of a king, lounging on my bed in the manner of a courtesan," she said, stroking the velvet coverlet absentmindedly with one hand. "That would please Mr. Pickerton. He thinks of himself as a sort of king. A king of the underworld. Can you do that for me?"

"Of course, Ma'am. And may I congratulate you on the novelty of your idea. You will make an inspiring photograph." He turned to Emily and snapped his fingers at her with a wink. "Help Madam arrange herself appropriately while I set up the tripod."

Not until Mrs. Pickerton threw off her wrap and stood before them stark naked did Emily really believe that she wanted to pose for a nude photograph. Her face flamed and she didn't know where to look.

Padding naked across to her dresser, quite unconcerned about Emily's or Eric's presence, Mrs. Pickerton rummaged through a jewelry box. "Clasp this around my neck," she ordered Emily, handing her a choker of diamonds that looked as if it would have cost as much as twenty printing presses. Emily hooked it together as Mrs. Pickerton added a pair of matching earrings.

She looked at herself in the glass and nodded coolly. "That will do very well."

Padding back over to the bed, she lay down on her side, propping herself up on one elbow. "Fix the curtains," she said imperiously to Emily. "I want them open, but not all the way."

Emily hurried to drape the curtains prettily, and then to arrange a pile of pillows artistically around Mrs. Pickerton's head. "A length of gauze?" she suggested, holding up a transparent scarf she had spied on a chair. "That hides the angles and makes everything look softer."

Mrs. Pickerton gave her a cold look. "No gauze," she snapped.

"Indeed, no," Eric agreed with another wink for Emily when Mrs. Pickerton was not looking. "We need clarity and vision for this photograph. The sultan's favorite wife in the seraglio is the vision we are aiming for. Seductive, luxurious, and just a bit decadent."

Mrs. Pickerton's frown unbent slightly.

"Now, smile at the camera," he encouraged her. "Look at it as if it were your husband and you wanted to entice him into bed with you."

Emily thought rather that Mrs. Pickerton looked like a black widow spider might look, enticing a juicy fly into her web, but Eric seemed satisfied enough. He took one exposure, and then another. "Now, sit up against the pillows and put your arms behind your head. Excellent. Now, prop one arm behind your head and let the other fall into your lap."

In just the half hour allotted to them, Eric took the last exposure. "Thank you for your patience, Ma'am. I will choose the best exposure and have the portrait ready for you in less than a week."

Throwing her wrap over her shoulders and knotting the sash about her waist, she fixed him with a hard stare. "I don't give charity. I won't pay you for it if I don't like it."

"Madam, your husband is sure to adore it. You have my personal guarantee on that. If it does not make him fall even more deeply in love with you, I will not charge you a single penny." With that, he clapped his hat on his head and strode out of the door, camera in hand. Emily hastily collected the remainder of the gear and scurried after him.

Not until they were safely back in the studio with their precious plates did Emily allow herself to relax. "You did it," she chortled, grasping his hands in hers and dancing him around the studio in her delight. "You got a photo of her, and an even better one than we could have hoped for. I never dreamed she would throw off all her clothes like that and ask for such a portrait. But what luck. What fabulous luck."

Eric grinned as he whirled her around the floor. "The perils of being a photographer. Women constantly taking off their clothes and throwing themselves at you. Still, she was better-looking than I expected."

The joy evaporated out of her all of a sudden and she pulled away from his grasp. "Her breasts were starting to sag." He was supposed to be helping her out of the mess she was in, not taking advantage of the situation to ogle another woman's naked body.

"I never noticed."

She gritted her teeth. "And her waist had thickened."

"I wasn't looking at her waist."

"You are a disgusting old lecher. She's almost old enough to be your mother."

"Does it bother you that I have to look at other naked women?"

"Of course," she snapped at him, and then stopped. "Not," she added rather lamely. There was no reason that she should mind him looking at other women, except for the fact that she did mind. A lot.

He had promised her nothing, offered her nothing beyond a helping hand and a moment's pleasure. She was fooling herself if she thought he cared about her. "Why should it bother me? You are free to do as you please. I was merely pointing out that she wasn't particularly worth looking at. Or worth photographing either, if I didn't need her likeness to get me out of a terrible pickle."

"You wouldn't be jealous, now, would you?" He leaned toward her and nudged her with his elbow. "Jealous that you caught me looking at another woman?"

"I wouldn't dream of wasting my energy on such a useless emotion," she said with a sniff.

"You are jealous," he crowed. "Even though she was twice your age and not a tenth as pretty."

"That's not what you said before."

"Come now, Em. Let's not quarrel. Though we have a perfect photograph of her, we still have a lot of work to do to get the picture we need."

"What do you need me for?" she asked, still rather crossly. "You have a picture of her and you have a picture of him. Can you not just glue them together, or whatever it is you have to do?"

"*She* is naked. *He* is fully clothed. We will need another photograph yet before I can manufacture a realistic picture of the two of them embracing. A photograph of a man's body. A naked man's body, and one as close to his build as we can get so I do not need to blur out his edges too obviously."

Emily gulped. She hadn't thought of that. "Who will you photograph for that?"

"*I* won't photograph anyone. You will photograph me."

Her eyes boggled out of her head. "You are going to strip so I can take your picture?" How would she ever keep her hands off him if he was standing naked in front of her? "No, I can't do that." She would embarrass herself for sure.

"Do you have anyone else in mind who would allow you to take naked pictures of him?" he inquired rather grumpily. "And then manipulate them so that you can blackmail your husband into divorcing you?"

"No one," she admitted. The only man she could think of was her sister Caroline's husband. He might come to her rescue if she begged him to, but she would very much rather not ask. Besides, he was miles away in Hertfordshire.

"Then I will have to do. Come, I will set up the shot and show you how to use the camera. It's so simple a child could do it. All you will need to do is click the shutter."

It wasn't the thought of learning how to operate a camera that had Emily's nerve ends tingling and her chest feeling tight with anticipation. Eric was going to take his clothes off and pose for her, naked, as she had posed for him so many times. She would be the power behind the camera, with the ability to capture his likeness however she wanted to. The lenses would be trained on his body, on his hard thighs and his well-muscled chest. Her fantasy of gazing at him through the eye of the camera would be coming true. Though part of her was terrified at the prospect, her fingers itched to be clicking the shutter. "Show me how, then."

He led her into the conservatory and showed her how to operate the camera until she was comfortable that she had grasped the basics.

Once she was ready, he looked around the glass-walled room thoughtfully. "We shall need a background that is as uncluttered as possible," he muttered. "That way I will have to do less manipulation of the final image." He strode back into the studio and came back with an armful of blankets. He spread one out over the tiled floor and then began to drape another over the windows behind. "Come give me a hand to cover the windows."

"I thought you needed plenty of light for photography," she said, as she draped the blankets as best she could over the windows, tucking them in behind the sash to hold them up.

"With blankets on the windows you can take pictures of me

standing up or lying down," he said as he worked beside her. "Either way it will look as if I am reclining on a bed. The pictures will be easy to work with. Mr. Murdoch will be utterly convinced the photos are real."

Emily's insides suddenly clenched. This had to work. It just had to. She could not stay married to Mr. Murdoch, not for all the wealth of India. The thought of him touching her again, even just brushing her hand with his lips, made her shudder with disgust. She would rather become a nun and have no man touch her again than be forced to endure it.

Eric called her mind back to the present. "That's as uncluttered as I can make the background," he said, as he smoothed out a fold in the draperies. "Now, let me focus the lenses on the blanket on the floor for you."

He fiddled with his camera for a moment and then stepped aside. "It's all yours."

This was the moment she had been waiting for. She peered through the viewfinder, the focus tight and sharp. "I'm ready. Go lie on the blankets for me."

Uncharacteristically, he did not race off immediately to get stuck into the task at hand. "Are you sure you know how to use the camera?"

Hadn't he just spent the last few minutes explaining the inner workings to her in more detail than she wanted to know? She shooed him away. "Of course I do."

Still he lingered, fussing around her like a mother hen with her chicks. "Are you sure you can work the shutter?"

With malicious amusement she realized what was bothering him. She had felt the same way the first time she had posed for him. "Surely you are not nervous about stripping naked in front of me?" She shook her head and tut-tutted at him. "I have stripped for you for weeks without making half the fuss you are."

"I'm a man," he said sulkily. "You're a woman. Women's bodies are made to be looked at."

"And women like to look at naked men just as much as men like to look at naked women, I'm sure," she replied equably. "You just don't like it so much when the shoe is on the other foot, do you? Making a woman strip for your camera is perfectly all right, but taking off your own clothes is something different, huh?"

The scowl he gave her would have frightened small children into fits. "I am not an ogre and I do not take advantage of women. I never made you do anything you didn't want to do. I asked and you accepted, when you could just as easily have refused."

"And I am not making you do this. I didn't even ask. You offered. But if you want to back out now . . ." She let her voice trail off into a deliberately insulting silence to provoke him into standing his ground.

It worked just as she had intended it to. "I have no intention of backing out," he growled at her. He sat down on the stone bench and removed his boots, kicking them off into a corner. "I keep the promises I make."

She watched from behind the camera as he shrugged off his jacket and then his shirt. If only she dared to step out and run her hands over his bare chest, to feel the softness of his skin under her hands. But she didn't dare. No, it was safer to stay where she was and admire him from afar.

Her resolution to stay a safe distance away was put to the test when he stepped out of his trousers and stood in front of her dressed only in his smalls.

The air in the conservatory suddenly seemed to grow hot and close—she wanted to run over to the windows and open them to breathe in some fresh air, but she was glued to the spot. Her eyes refused to leave his body.

Why was it that a temptation she knew to be out of her reach, a temptation that she knew would be bad for her if she gave in to it, only seemed to become more attractive the more unobtainable it was?

She swallowed as she stared at him. Judging by the state of his smalls, he would not mind if she came closer to him. He was hugely aroused, the hard ridge of his cock jutting out clearly through the fine linen.

His face colored as he saw where she was looking. "Stop staring at me," he grumbled, adjusting himself more comfortably inside the linen. "You're only making it worse."

And indeed, she was making it worse. As she looked at him, the ridge grew longer and thicker until it could no longer be contained by his smalls but jutted out over the top.

"Damn it, I may as well get this over and done with," he muttered, as he drew the linen down over his hips until he stood before her, proudly and gloriously naked.

She couldn't help licking her lips at the sight. He was on display for her. Every bit of him. She wanted to kiss every inch of his body, to run her tongue over him to taste the salt of his skin.

Her nipples, hard with desire, tingled against her shirt and she could feel the moisture start to well up inside her pussy. Just looking at him, proud and erect, made her almost weep with longing.

She could not touch him, though. She could not even let him know how much she wanted to touch him. "Stand up by the window." She was proud that her voice did not shake as she gave him instructions. "Let me take one of you from the back to start with."

Obediently he moved over to the window that was covered with the blanket and struck a pose that would look from behind as if he were embracing someone.

His erection was no longer jutting up in front of her to distract her, but his ass was another, almost worse, distraction. Tight and round, it was just made for grasping. Her palms could almost feel the weight of his buttocks.

Her pussy felt as if it were on fire and she fought the desire to reach down and touch herself just to take away some of the burning. She didn't want the touch of her own fingers on herself. What she really wanted was the feel of Eric's body against hers, the touch of his hands clasping her to him, and the hardness of him as he thrust into her, slowly and deeply, as if their lovemaking would last forever.

Irritated with her foolish fancies, she lined up the pictures and released the shutter with a huff. She was only fooling herself if she thought he wanted her for more than a minute. All he cared for was his damned camera and his damned photographs. He did not care that she was a living, breathing woman who wanted him with all her heart.

Her escapade with Mr. Murdoch had taught her that much. Even if Mr. Murdoch had turned out to be noble and honorable and all the things that he was not, still she would not be happy to be married to him while Eric Twyford stood tantalizingly just out of her reach. She did not want just any man. She wanted Eric, who stood in front of her as naked as the day he was born.

He shifted his pose slightly and she released the shutter again.

She wanted Eric—that much was clear to her. The only question was, what was she going to do about it?

Could she take the little that he had to give her and be satisfied with that? Or would it kill her to walk away from him when he had tired of her? For he would eventually tire of having her warm his bed. He had showed her plainly enough that she meant nothing to him beyond a convenient outlet for his natural lusts.

He was posing for her now not because of any softer feelings he held for her, but to safeguard his interest in his investment, both in her and in his printing machine. If she were to remain married to Mr. Murdoch, Mr. Murdoch would clearly try to cut Eric out of the major share of profits in their venture. As his wife, she would have little, if any, voice in the matter. She had already discovered, to her cost, that he did not like to be crossed in any way.

Eric's ass was getting just too tempting to resist. No woman could see such delectable goods and not eventually want to taste them. "Turn around and let me take a shot of you full on."

After a moment's hesitation, she saw him square his shoulders and then he turned to face her.

If anything, his erection had grown further while she had taken the first photographs. Splendid, that was the word for him. Simply splendid.

Mr. Murdoch did not have such a magnificent appendage. She had to suppress a giggle at the thought that they might be found out because Eric was so much more of a man than the one he was trying to impersonate.

Eric's face turned as black as thunder at the sound of her laughter. "I don't see what's so damned funny."

"You hardly look like a man about to embrace his beloved," she chastised him. "Come now, show a little tenderness. In the mood you're in, a woman would be afraid to get too close to you for fear of having her head bitten right off."

How good it felt to be the one in charge, the one giving the orders and expecting obedience. She decided that she rather liked being a photographer, almost as much as she liked modeling for the camera.

Annoyingly, though, he simply looked blacker. "I can look any way I damn well please. You won't see my face when I'm finished with the picture."

She looked through the viewfinder, but even with his face out of the picture, something still did not look right. "Your body posture is all wrong. Relax a little. Look more as if you are about to have a romp in the hay and less like you are ready to fight for your life."

He gestured at himself. "Isn't this good enough?"

"It's a start. A good start," she hastily amended as he opened his mouth, a look of outrage on his face. "But it's not enough. A woman needs more than a big member waving in front of her to want to embrace a man. She needs to see some softness in him, some vulnerability, some hint that she means more to him than a quick affair. Your body looks too hard, too masculine. No one would believe that you are on your way to an assignation. Not even when you look like that."

"How I am supposed to look less hard?" he grumbled. "There's no chance of that when you're looking at me as if you want to eat me."

She felt her face go hot at his crudeness, but she ignored the provocation. "Think of the last woman you were ever in love with, the last woman you ever pined hopelessly for."

He took her suggestion, she could see it immediately. No longer was he confronting her with barely tamed aggression, but his posture had changed subtly to a strength that was calculated to defend rather than to attack. "Better, much better," she said, releasing the shutter to capture his image. If only he would look at her like that, all her dreams would come true. "Close your eyes and think of her. Imagine the color of her hair, the taste of her skin, the softness of her breasts."

Who was he thinking of, and what had been so special about her? She wished she knew how the mystery woman had won Eric's heart. Certainly thinking about her had softened his stance, taken the rigidity out of him. Well, most of it anyway.

As he relaxed he became even more desirable, and the wetness in her pussy was becoming unbearable. Seeing him stand naked in front of her like that was just too much for her self-control. He'd made love with her once, presumably he'd do it a second time if she approached him the right way.

"Can you hear her? Think of her smell as she just stepped from a hot soak in the bath." She looked through the viewfinder and took the photo. The expression on his face spoke more than his cock, which was just starting to lose its hardness as he stood there, eyes closed.

It was too much for her. She walked over to him, thoughts of taking any more photographs forgotten as she looked at his face, the face of the man she loved.

"Were her hands soft as she touched you?" With a delicate fingertip she traced a line over the head of his cock and down the shaft. As her finger tickled the sensitive underside it gave a jump, as if it had a mind of its own. She repeated the motion several times, and again the spasm on each stroke, each time he got a little harder until once more he stood fully erect.

Reaching down to a pile of props, she picked up a silk scarf and placed it over his eyes. Knotting the scarf behind his head she whispered in his ear. "Think of her, of her touch."

He trembled slightly with his sight gone, but stood his ground. She slowly pushed him down to the bench where he lay somewhat awkwardly with his legs hanging over the end. Awkward or not, she couldn't help but admire him. He was everything she had ever wanted in a man, and for this afternoon he would belong to her. Only to her.

As quickly as she could she removed what few clothes she wore. Leaning over him once more she dragged her hard nipples over his smooth chest, then brought one to his mouth where he licked and sucked her to even more hardness.

"Can you see her now? Were her breasts small and firm, or large and voluptuous? Can you remember her nipples, their shape, their taste?"

Sliding down she licked with the tip with her tongue.

"Did she lick you here, and take you in her mouth?"

He moaned as she slowly engulfed him as much as she could. Holding the base she bobbed her head slowly, enjoying the smooth texture, savoring the ridge around the head. With his hands guiding her she moved around so that her pussy was directly over his nose and mouth. She pulled back from his cock, now slick with her saliva.

"Ahh, so you would like to taste me too? Do you recall her tangy taste?" With her wet cunt only inches from his mouth she inserted two fingers and rubbed that sensitive spot just inside. She brought her slick fingers to his mouth and allowed him to lick them clean.

"Did she have much hair on her pussy? I have only a light mat. Would you like to taste me?" She lowered herself onto his questing tongue, then raised, teasing, forcing him to lift his head to maintain contact.

Bending over to once more suck on him she allowed him to lick her in return. Let him try to think of someone else now, she thought with some satisfaction. Certainly he seemed to be completely engrossed in her, not holding back at all. He might well be thinking of his last love, but it didn't show in the way he greedily licked at her.

With his expert tongue causing her own breath to come in short pants, she lifted her head from him but continued long stokes with her hand. Each time she reached the base he thrust his hips up, trying to get more pleasure from her massage. Whether he was thinking of her or someone else she no longer cared, she just wanted him as deep in her as she could manage.

Wriggling down, she stood at the edge of the bench, legs on either side of his so that she was poised over his cock, she lowered herself till he was buried deep. Supporting herself on his legs, she started long strokes with her body.

Her arousal intensified as he grabbed her ass and quickened the pace, then to her pleasurable gasp of surprise he easily slid a finger, wet with her juices, into her ass.

All too soon she felt him strain with his impending orgasm.

His body quivered with waves of pleasure, causing her own sensations to build to an almost unbearable peak.

Suddenly, with an animalistic grunt, he bucked his hips hard and she felt his hot cum spurting inside her, her pussy contracting around him with her own orgasm as she cried out in pure pleasure.

Her breathing recovering, she slowly straightened her legs, allowing him to slip from her. He lay there, still half on– half off the bench, still blindfolded, while their combined juices oozed from her onto him. He continued to lie there as she walked over to the camera and took a few pictures in his supine position, now limp and wet from their lovemaking.

He didn't move as the camera shutter made its distinctive sound, nor did he speak. What was he thinking, who was he thinking of? Was he thinking of another woman still, or had she driven all thoughts of his first love from his mind? He was so hard to read, this American.

With a small sigh she left him to his thoughts, heading for the bathroom to wash up. Eric had his picture, she had had her fun, and now it was time to face reality once again.

It took Eric all day and half the night, triple exposing the negatives, to get Mrs. Pickerton, Mr. Murdoch's face, and his own naked body on the one picture. All the time he was aware of Emily's presence beside him, silent and watchful, her every hope riding on his mastery of his trade.

Finally, he achieved the look he was aiming for—a sharp

focus on the faces so they could be clearly identified, but a soft blur on the bodies, particularly on his own, to ensure that the fake could not be detected. He had even managed the placement of the bodies so it looked as though they were embracing in a very intimate manner. If he didn't absolutely know the picture was a fake, he'd swear it was genuine.

He was a genius and he had created a masterpiece. A real triumph. What a shame that the technical brilliance he had used to create the illusion in front of him would have to remain forever concealed.

He hung the picture up to dry on the line he had extended from one wall to the other and dried his hands on his printing smock. Really, people were so enormously gullible that they deserved to be taken in. They took photographs as faithful representations of the truth, little knowing that a photograph could show as distorted a picture of reality as ever a painting or a poem could. Photography was an art, not a science, but few people had the faintest conception of the deceptive uses to which it could be put.

He could almost summon up a spark of pity for Mr. Murdoch. The poor fellow was about to have his hopes of keeping Emily destroyed by nothing more than a bare-faced lie. A magnificent, technically brilliant lie, but a lie nonetheless.

When he showed Emily the final picture he had made, all dried and ready for display, she was flatteringly astounded at his skill. "It looks so real," she murmured, tracing over the lines with the tip of her finger. "Remarkably real."

"You think it will pass muster?" he asked proudly.

"Thank you." Her eyes were filled with tears, tears that he longed to kiss away. "Thank you for helping me."

It was on the tip of his tongue to confess his love for her and beg her to marry him as soon as she was free, but he kept silent. He did not want her to agree to marry him for fear that he would not go through with the plan. Proposing to her now would make him no better than Mr. Murdoch.

Though his was a hopeless case, he wanted her to love him for himself. If she could not do that, he would learn to live without her somehow.

He offered her his arm. "Shall we take a cab to Russell Square, then and confront your husband?"

She swallowed hard. "Yes, we had better."

Their drive to the Square was conducted in silence, broken only by the clip-clop of the horse's hooves, the swish of the cabbie's whip, and his shouted insults to the others on the busy roads. The noise of the street filtered through to them despite the closed windows, but inside the cab neither of them spoke.

As they drove along, Emily snuck her hand into his. Her fingers were ice cold and he covered them with his own to warm them. "Everything will be fine," he whispered into her ear.

She gave him a wan smile and clasped his hand tightly with her own, not letting it go until the cab deposited them outside Mr. Murdoch's residence on Russell Square.

The footman looked down his nose at them and showed

them into the smaller parlor while he ascertained whether his master was at home.

After some minutes, Mr. Murdoch descended the stairs and greeted them coolly, though his eyes were sparkling with suppressed fury. "Mrs. Murdoch, I see you have chosen to grace my house with your presence once again," he said, his voice dripping venom. "And Mr. Twyford, this is an unexpected pleasure. What brings you to my house?"

Eric kept his hands firmly in his greatcoat. "Business," he said shortly.

Mr. Murdoch raised his eyebrows. "Indeed. In that case, Mr. Twyford, please follow me. Mrs. Murdoch, you may retire to your room. I will deal with you later."

Emily quietly ignored his order, instead following him as he led the way into a small, low-ceilinged room. Seating himself behind the desk, he steepled his hands together and looked at the pair of them. "Well?"

Eric did not take a seat. Neither did Emily. They would not be there long enough.

Beside him, Emily cleared her throat. "I do not want to be married to you," she said firmly. "I want a divorce. Or an annulment. Take your pick."

Mr. Murdoch looked from her to Eric and back again. "Are you feeling quite well?" he asked, his voice tight and controlled. "Or has the heat been getting to you? Maybe you ought to take a seat before we discuss this any further."

Emily clasped her hands behind her back. "I am perfectly

well, thank you. And I am also perfectly serious. There is nothing to discuss. I am requesting that you divorce me."

Mr. Murdoch's face went red with anger at her directness. "You are out of your wits," he said, his voice vibrating with barely controlled fury. "I shall do no such thing. You ought to be whipped for even thinking of such an abomination. And then whipped again for your disobedience."

In the silence that followed Mr. Murdoch's threat, Eric took the photograph out of his breast pocket and laid it on the desk in front of him. "I would not be so quick to threaten Emily. Not when she has a particularly interesting photograph of you and your lady friend to share with the world."

Mr. Murdoch had picked the photograph up and was holding it between his thumb and forefinger as if it were about to explode. His face had turned a pasty shade of white and his fingers were trembling.

"What do you think?" Eric asked, rubbing salt in his wound. "Your neighbor, Mr. Pickerton would be very interested to see this photograph, don't you agree? You claim a proprietary right over Em by virtue of her being your wife. Doesn't Pickerton, too, have a right to know what his wife is doing while he is away from home?"

"How much do you want for it?" Mr. Murdoch's voice was a croak of fear and his fingers twitched with a desperate desire to rip the incriminating picture to shreds.

Eric shook his head. "It's not for sale. Not for money."

Before anyone could stop him, Mr. Murdoch tore it across

with a vicious movement and continued to tear the pieces until they were nothing more than confetti. "You are more the fool," he sneered as he tore frantically at the paper. "I would have paid as much as twenty pounds for it. But now it's worth nothing."

Eric calmly drew another copy of the photograph from his breast pocket and tossed it casually onto the desk in front of Mr. Murdoch. "I fear you have misunderstood the essential nature of photography. As long as I have the negative, I can print as many copies as I choose. You have destroyed nothing."

Mr. Murdoch's eyes glittered with rage as he picked up the second photograph and examined it. "Do you have the negative with you? I demand to see it before I hand over a single penny."

"It is not for sale, as I said before. And I am not that much of a fool to walk into the lion's den unarmed. I have the negative stowed safely where you will never find it. It would make an interesting companion piece to the Emily photos. Sales would no doubt be brisk."

A vein in Mr. Murdoch's temple was throbbing. "I presume you had some purpose in coming to threaten me. What do you want from me, if not money?"

Eric let a cool smile drift over his face and he took his time before he answered. "Emily does not want to remain married to you, but as a woman it is more difficult for her to obtain a divorce. Give her her freedom, and we will keep your secret. But if you refuse, this photograph will find its way in short order to Mr. Pickerton. I am sure your imagination could conjure up what his likely reaction might be." His smile widened. "No doubt Emily would be perfectly happy to suddenly find herself a wealthy widow."

Mr. Murdoch gave a ghastly smile. "You're bluffing me. The old fool will be dead within a month and then you will have nothing to bargain with. Emily will have to come back to me then."

"Maybe he will be dead in a month, though I believe you have been rather optimistically predicting his imminent demise for some time now. But his sons by his first wife won't be. I doubt they'd find these photographs amusing. They are not well known for their sense of humor."

Mr. Murdoch drummed his fingers on the desk. "I will give you a thousand pounds for the negative and all copies you have made of it," he said eventually. "To be paid for by a draft on my bankers." He picked up his pen and twirled it between his fingers. "I will write it out for you here and now, if you do not believe me."

Emily could not stifle a gasp. Such a sum was a small fortune for a working man like Eric. "It is not for sale," she snapped.

Mr. Murdoch fixed his gaze firmly on Eric, ignoring her interruption. "Is the foolish whim of a girl worth more than a thousand pounds to you? You're a businessman. You understand the value of cold, hard cash."

Eric did not answer right away and Emily felt her toes grow cold. Eric could not accept Mr. Murdoch's offer or she would die.

Mr. Murdoch pressed home his advantage. "Women are fickle creatures. Witness her behavior to me. She will leave you too, you know, and you will have thrown away my generous offer for nothing."

Eric reached for Emily's hand and clasped it tightly in his. "It is not for sale. Not even for a thousand pounds."

Emily heaved a sigh of relief and clung to Eric's hand with a fierce grip. He had turned down a princely sum for her sake.

Reading their body language, the last breath of bravado seeped out of Mr. Murdoch and he sank to his desk, deflated. His dark face looked withered and aged in his defeat. "Well, Emily, if that is truly your wish, I suppose I have no choice but to sue for divorce. On the grounds of adultery, naturally."

She nodded, relief flooding her face. Whatever price she had to pay to escape him, she would pay it willingly. "Name whoever you please as the guilty party. I will not contest it."

"I only wanted to wed you for the money you would bring me," he added spitefully. "If I weren't badly in need of the funds, I would never have dreamed of marrying such a cheap slut as you have shown yourself to be. You have no birth, no breeding, and little enough beauty—with your clothes on, that is."

She drew in a sharp breath at the sudden vicious attack. "Good day, Mr. Murdoch. I trust you understand we shall not be seeing each other again."

"It is just as well you will not be living in my house," he spat venomously at her back as she walked out of the door. "I would not have my daughters corrupted by the likes of you."

She stopped just outside the door. Her conscience would not allow her to leave his daughters in such a house, not if she had the faintest chance of being able to help them. "Thank you for reminding me," she said coolly, turning to face him for the last time. "You will also immediately send Finella and her sisters on a visit to their Aunt Mavis. A very long visit. Ten years or so should be sufficient."

"You b . . . bitch," he spluttered, his outrage almost robbing him of the power of speech. "Who are you to tell me what to do with my own daughters?"

Eric leaned over the desk and stared coldly at Mr. Murdoch. "Another word to Em, and Mr. Pickerton will receive a copy of the photo in the morning with my compliments. I suggest you organize the visit posthaste." And he turned on his heel and followed Emily outside.

The Hansom cab was still waiting for them just down the street as he had asked it to do. He gave the direction to the driver and joined Emily inside. "He may be your husband, but as of now you're free of him. Married or not, with a threat like that hanging over his head, he will not dare to approach you again."

"Thank you for your help," she replied woodenly, her eyes fixed on her boots.

He stared at her in surprise. What was the matter with her that she appeared so despondent over her escape? Did she regret saying goodbye to the wealth she would command as his wife? Was the thought of the scandal that her divorce would doubtless cause making her regret her decision? Or had she been in love with Mr. Murdoch after all and was upset over the illumination of his character? "Are you not pleased to have gotten the promise of a divorce?"

The carriage went over a bump, jolting her body into his. She righted herself with a sigh. "Until the divorce comes through, if it ever does, I am still married to a scoundrel." She shook her head sadly. "No respectable man will ever want me, not even as his mistress."

The bleakness in her eyes made him want to weep. "Any man would be pleased to have you by his side," he retorted. "You've got a good head on your shoulders, and a warm heart to go with it. You'd make a damn fine wife."

She sniffed. "A man wants more than a sensible wife. He wants a woman he can be proud of, a woman he can introduce into society, not a scandalous divorcee."

"Well, you're plenty pretty enough, too," he admitted, "which should make up for your sharp tongue and bad reputation as far as most men are concerned."

That raised a smile. "You are not helping," she said sternly. "I am trying to resign myself to a single life and you are accusing me of being a nag."

"A very pretty nag," he amended, taking her hand in his. "That makes all the difference."

"Does it make all the difference to you, too?"

He gazed at her face, every tiny imperfection of which had grown so dear to him. Even when she was old and gray and had no beauty left to speak of, he would still love her. "I'm a special case."

Her shoulders slumped visibly and she drew her hand out of his, leaving him feeling quite bereft. "I see." Her voice was small and she sounded tired and dispirited.

He could not help it. He had to know what she felt about him now, even if she rejected him out of hand. "Do you not like me at all then?" he asked wistfully. "Is my love so distasteful to you? Because if it is, I will understand. I am not a practiced lover and I have so little to offer you. I know you only gave yourself to me the other day out of gratitude for my help, but I was not strong enough to refuse your gift. I wanted to touch you so badly, but I will not mention my feelings again if they distress you."

"You love me?" She looked as if he had just poleaxed her instead of declaring his affection.

"Of course I do," he retorted, almost offended that she could doubt it. "Haven't I made it clear enough to you already? I love you so damn much that I would even walk away from you if you asked me to. I couldn't love you any more than that."

She was still looking at him as if he had three heads, but at least the look of woe had disappeared from her face. "You have never said a word to me of love."

"I made love to you twice, no, three times. If that is not a declaration of love, what is? I even asked you to marry me once."

Her nose wrinkled at the memory. "You were drunk at the time."

"A man has to screw up his courage somehow. I was steeling myself for rejection. And you rejected me, just as I expected." The sting of that had not ever left him. "You went from my bed into the arms of another man."

"You didn't really want to marry me. You only made love

to me because I deliberately seduced you. I did it on purpose, you know. I wanted to make you fall in love with me just for practice. It was cruel of me, I know, but I ended up hurting only myself."

He could not suppress a grin at that. She had tormented him into making love to her, teasing him until he could not hold out any longer. "True. It was all your fault. If you hadn't taken off all your clothes and practically begged me to ravish you, you would still be a virgin."

His agreement didn't improve her temper any. "You see what I mean? I do not want you to feel sorry for me."

"Don't be a ninny. Look, I'm a genius when it comes to photography—"

"Modest, too," she interjected grumpily.

"—but I'm not so good with words," he continued, ignoring her interruption. "I always say the wrong thing at the wrong time, even when I don't mean to. But believe me, Em, I love you. I want to marry you, if you will have me when you're free. We could go into partnership for real—you can run the finances and I will take the photographs. We won't have much to start with, but that will soon change. Your photographs are stunning and the public loves them."

A horrid thought crossed his mind as he spoke. Would she think that he was another Mr. Murdoch, out to exploit her for every penny? "But do not feel that you have to keep posing for me if you do not want to," he added hurriedly. "We will manage perfectly well without that. Portraits and landscapes are very popular. And I could always find another model to pose for the Emily photographs if you would prefer not to continue."

"You would really marry me? A scandalous divorcee whom you will never be able to introduce to your clients?"

"Who gives a fig about what the customers think. I adore you. I was frantic when I thought you preferred another man. That was when I knew I could not live without you."

"Do you think I will allow you to take photographs of any other woman without her clothes on once we are married?" She shook her head. "No, sir. There will be no more Mrs. Pickertons for you."

"Does that mean you accept?" He felt as though he was swimming in happiness. "You want to become my partner and make beautiful photographs with me?"

"I love you, Eric, with all my heart. I have always loved you, almost from the moment I first met you. I will gladly live with you as your mistress for as long as you want me to." She smiled shyly. "Maybe one day I will even live with you as your wife."

Just then the carriage stopped outside the door to Eric's studio. He sprung out of the carriage and took her in his arms. Without a thought for the gawping onlookers in the street, he whirled her around until his head spun with the sheer joy of being alive. "You have made me the happiest man in the world today, Em. Together we shall be unbeatable, we shall have the most successful photography business in all of England. Royal Academy of Arts and Millionaire's Row, here we come. With you by my side, I can conquer the world."

Epilogue

Five years later

Emily sat in the church with tearful happiness in her eyes, as Finella Murdoch walked down the aisle on Eric's arm. Finella's eyes were shining with joy and love as she approached the altar. With a look of deep affection, Eric handed her over to the young man standing waiting for her, and stepped back.

Finella and her young man spoke their vows in clear voices, vowing to love, honor, and cherish each other as long as they both did live. Emily wiped a tear from her eyes as Finella's new husband took his young wife in his arms and they shared their first kiss as a married couple.

The wedding breakfast was held in Emily and Eric's new house in Mayfair. Mrs. Pickerton had been so pleased with her portrait that she had not only paid Eric the sum of ten pounds for it, but had tipped him handsomely and recommended him to a number of ladies of her acquaintance. In a few short months, he had become the premier society photographer, much prized for his polite manners and the way in which he kept his own counsel, no matter what kind of photograph he was requested to take. And Emily had continued to run the business part of his affairs with great aplomb.

Their runaway success had recently enabled them to purchase a new house in the best part of London—just in time for Finella's wedding to a young shipbuilder from Bristol, whom she had met while living with her Aunt Mavis.

The reception was a quiet affair. Finella's younger sisters, looking plump and pretty and almost grown-up, were wreathed in smiles, as was their Aunt Mavis, with whom they had lived ever since Mr. Murdoch had first sent them away. A scattering of friends and Finella's parents-in-law made up the rest of the party.

Finella came up to hug Emily. "Thank you, step-mama, for everything you have done for me."

Emily gave a humpf. "Step-mama, indeed. You make me sound like an elderly matron when I am barely half a dozen years older than you are."

"You will always be my step-mama. You never did get around to divorcing my father," Finella added mischievously. "Indeed, you have me to thank for being able to marry your Eric at last. If Father had not been so furious that I had become engaged without his permission to a penniless shipbuilder, he never would have fallen into a blind rage and accidentally walked out in front of a carriage."

Emily twirled the gold ring on her finger. After three months, she had become accustomed to its weight on her hand. It was the outward symbol of the love that she and Eric had continued to share, the love that would outlast the end of their days. She could not be sorry that Mr. Murdoch's accident had made her happiness complete. "Which reminds me," she said, "I have not given you your wedding present yet."

"You have put on a wonderful wedding breakfast for us," Finella said. "James and I have much to thank you for already."

"I was still officially your father's wife when he passed away," Emily continued. "And half of his estate came to me as his grieving widow."

Finella gave an unladylike snort. "I dare say you grieved even less than I did. And I would dance on his grave, if the mud would not ruin my pretty new shoes."

"Eric and I do not want his money, nor need it. It rightfully belongs to you and your sisters." She took a bank draft out of her reticule and pressed it into Finella's hands. "Here is your share of it."

Finella's eyes widened as she stared at the paper in her hand. "That much? But I thought . . ."

"His investments must have done better recently." Emily patted Finella on the hand. "Now, off you go to find your new husband. He will be missing you already."

Eric came to stand by his wife, and wrapped a loving arm around her waist. "She did not suspect anything was amiss?"

Emily shook her head. "She was surprised, but believed my explanation that her father's affairs had gone better lately. Our addition to her inheritance will give them a large enough stake for James to buy a share in his cousin's shipbuilding business."

Eric nuzzled into her neck, sending shivers of pleasure skittering down her spine. "You are a good woman, wife of mine."

Emily leaned back into her husband's embrace. After five years of being together, his touch still set her on fire. "And you, my love, are the very best of husbands."

LEDA SWANN is the writing duet of Cathy and Brent. They write out of their home overlooking the sea in peaceful New Zealand. When not writing they have busy lives working in the technology industry, bringing up four children, and enjoying an adventurous outdoor life that ranges from the mountains to the sea.

LEDA SWANN